MATCHING POINTS

DRIFTWOOD COVE SERIES

NANCY J. FARRIER

River Ink
PRESS

Cover design by Ken Raney

River Ink Logo by Ardra Tsuei

Published by River Ink Press, Winkelman, AZ 85192

Scripture quotations from the New King James Version of the Bible.

LOC #2020912809

ISBN: 978-0-9990547-7-2 (E-book)

ISBN: 978-0-9990547-8-9 (Paperback)

Created with Vellum

To my extended family: Aunts, Uncles, Cousins and more.

Growing up as part of a huge family (Dad had ten siblings, Mom had six siblings) I learned the meaning of having a close support system. From our holiday dinners to summer reunions to the birthday get-togethers (because someone always had a birthday) we learned to laugh and to disagree but mostly to love. But the one thing that stands out is how my family was there if you had a need.

Always. Without fail.

Love you, Rhines and Hildebrandts. You are the best.

1

Asia Jessup stepped into the shade of a large ginkgo tree, whose fan-shaped leaves rippled in the coastal breeze, and lowered her backpack to the ground. The trembling in her knees echoed through her. Oh, to just sink onto the grass, to avoid what she'd come here to do. She rolled her shoulders, wincing at the burn of tired muscles. California. Hard to believe she was back. Sweat beaded on her forehead. She leaned back against the tree trunk. If only she could escape.

Far from here.

Across the street, her destination looked cool and inviting. The small shopping area appeared well attended. An antique shop. A beading store. A yarn shop with a cute baby garment on the sign. A barbecue restaurant, I-BBQ, at the back of the area.

That must be the source of the tantalizing aromas.

At the front of the mall was Cinda's place, A Time to Sew quilt shop. Old watering cans and milk cans overflowed with bright flowers. A wooden bench, probably rife with splinters if one were to sit there, held an array of succulents. Eye-catching quilts adorned the windows. Cinda's teenage bent toward decorating and color had certainly stayed with her as an adult. She'd created a spot of beauty.

The last place Asia belonged.

What am I doing here? She hadn't had a bath in two days, and the stench of prison clung to her. But that was only right. No matter how many showers she took, she couldn't wash away the filth of what she'd done.

Or what she'd endured.

She fingered the bit of money in her pocket, two crumpled ones and a few coins adding up to all her worldly wealth. She huffed a short laugh. This place was where she'd spent a couple of idyllic summers staying with her *cousins*. But now...they wouldn't want her here.

So why did you spend all you had to come here?

She closed her eyes. Because her only hope lay here in Driftwood Cove.

An ache grew in Asia's chest. Mom... She died, and no one told Asia. More her own fault than anyone else's. She *told* her mom not to contact her, to keep away from the shame of where Asia ended up.

Mom's life choices hadn't been good, and Asia suspected when it all happened that her mom didn't have long to live. No way she'd make Mom's last days harder.

The small box in her backpack became a boulder, weighing her down. All she had left from her mom. Her childhood. Pain twisted through her, the freshness of loss not yet dimmed by time.

Loss...and guilt.

What kind of daughter felt relief at not having to deal with a mother's addictions anymore?

She squeezed her eyes shut to stop the burn of tears.

A breeze lifted the tendrils of hair that escaped her braid. She breathed in the salt-laden freshness, a scent she'd almost forgotten. A profusion of bright flowers grew along the street, their fragrance adding to the sweet memories. How she'd loved it here. Could almost hear the laughter she'd shared with Cinda...and the weighted moments with Ian. *Leave it to me to fall for the bad boy in town.*

Tingles shivered through her. At least she wouldn't see him. He'd be long gone by now.

Hopefully, he hadn't ended up like her.

"Please don't let Cinda hate me." Asia's hand tightened on the strap of her backpack. Loose threads brushed against the back of her hand. Her meager belongings weighed next to nothing. Her breath stuttered in her chest.

Who would want her with her past?

With the secrets she came to reveal?

With the burden she carried?

Who would care enough?

She froze. *Run. Turn and run.* Her inner voice drowned the sounds of traffic and the squabble of birds fighting for position on the overhead lines. She wanted to run, but she couldn't. She had no place to go.

Nowhere to call home.

No one.

You have Me.

The words whispered through her, chasing away the negative thoughts.

"Okay. You've come this far." Asia firmed her wobbly knees. She and Cinda had been so close, even exchanging emails after their two summers together. But would Cinda welcome her now?

"Only one way to find out." Asia checked the traffic and forced her leaden feet to step off the curb. Her stomach rumbled as the scent of barbecue grew stronger. She hadn't eaten since yesterday morning when she splurged and bought a granola bar and a cup of coffee. She had no idea when she would be able to eat again. If Cinda didn't welcome her, maybe she could find a homeless shelter that served meals.

The flowers outside the shop were as lovely close up as they were from across the street. Asia leaned down to stick her nose in the center of a pansy, and one of those childhood memories came to life when the delicate petals hugged her nostrils in a feathery brush. She hadn't done that in years. Not since her last summer here when she'd helped plant flowers around the Bryants' home.

Several varieties of red, yellow, white, and purple blooms were scattered in pots in seeming disarray, but Cinda had studied flower arrangement. The succulents on the bench were familiar, but Asia didn't know their names. When she lived in Tucson, she learned to prefer the less prickly succulents to the thorny cactus that dotted the landscape.

"You're stalling." She reached up to pull a few strands of her hair free from the backpack strap. Her stomach growled again, and she tried to shut out the delicious smells that wafted around her.

She stared at the door. *All you have to do is reach out and turn the handle. Maybe Cinda isn't even here.* Her arm stayed glued to her side, her feet stuck to the sidewalk, and her brain couldn't register why she'd come. In the distance a door slammed. A car honked. A splat of bird poo landed a few inches from her shoe.

Asia snorted. "Thank you, bird, for that comment. And for missing me."

Two shorts steps brought her within reach of the doorknob. The cool metal contrasted with the warm day. The hairs on the back of her neck lifted. She'd almost rather be back in the horrible place she'd come from than to face this uncertainty.

"Here, I'll get that for you."

The warm baritone startled her. The arm reaching past her made Asia shoot backwards. Right into the man who belonged to the arm... and the voice.

She stifled a shriek. Jumped forward to crash against the doorjamb. She couldn't escape. Tall planters lined both sides of the walk. He blocked the exit. Her pulse hammered. Her breath panted in gasps. Asia curled her fingers into claws and whirled around, her backpack scraping the building.

"Hey." He jerked his arm back and raised his hands, eyes wide. "Take it easy. I didn't mean to scare you."

Her back ached. Wavy lines fluttered across her vision. She needed to get out of here.

Now.

"Asia? Asia Jessup?" The familiarity of his voice steadied her. He took her hand. She trembled and fought to return to reality.

"Asia, is it really you?"

She blinked. He sharpened into focus. Blue eyes. Sandy blond hair. The smile that quirked up at the corners. Dimples.

Ian.

What was he doing here? He should have moved on. Fulfilled the dreams he'd shared with her.

Or went the other way and ended up like her. In prison.

"Ian. I thought..." She swallowed. Tried to gather her thoughts. "What are you doing here?"

He grinned. Straight white teeth. Crinkles at the corners of his eyes. That unruly lock of hair still fell across his forehead. The one she'd loved to twist around her finger. Asia closed her eyes and forced the longing away.

She wasn't that girl anymore. That girl died long ago.

"What are you doing here?" Ian rubbed his thumb across the back of her hand. Butterflies took flight along her traitorous nerve endings.

"Cinda will be thrilled. She mentioned you just the other day and wondered how you were." His denim eyes sparkled.

"I thought you were leaving this town." Asia wanted to bite back the words. "I mean, you always wanted to go away to school and live somewhere else."

"I thought so too." Ian chuckled.

The sound brought a memory of them snuggled together talking, laughing, and... well, she wouldn't go there.

She. Would. Not.

"Turns out by the time I had my history degree I realized I wanted to come back here. I didn't want to teach, but that turned out to be the best use for my diploma. So I did my second favorite thing." He nodded his head to one side.

Was she supposed to know what he meant? Second favorite thing? What had he liked besides history?

"That's my place." Ian motioned with his chin. The breeze ruffled his hair, making the blond glint in the sun.

She turned. "You have a yarn shop?" The thought of Ian trying to work a pair of knitting needles almost made her smile.

He threw back his head and laughed. "If I tried to knit a sweater, I'd end up so tangled in yarn, you'd have to make me into a giant cat toy." He squeezed her hand.

She tugged free.

"That's my place. I-BBQ. Best barbecue this side of Texas." He winked.

She couldn't resist. "You've tried all the barbecue places between here and there?"

"I've tried a number of them. Plus, I got a scholarship and went to Texas A&M. My third year I roomed with a kindred spirit, and we learned how to make barbecue to sell at the games. Tailgate time. Extra money is like manna to a college student." He brushed the lock of hair off his forehead. She curled her fingers tight against her jeans.

"Turns out our secret ingredient caught some attention. People liked the taste. We made it through college with some extra cash. My roommate and I parted ways, and I came back here to open a restaurant." Ian stuffed his fingers in his pockets. He studied her. Oh, how well she knew that all-perceiving gaze.

She wanted to shove the past three years behind an impenetrable barrier. At least he didn't know her as well as he used to. In fact...

He didn't know her at all anymore.

~

Was she really here? Yes, and still as beautiful as he remembered. Maybe even more so.

She'd always said her looks came from her mother's heritage. Where was Asia's mother from? Taiwan or China? He didn't remember.

Asia had never known her father and had been reluctant to talk about him or about her home situation. But she'd told him enough.

Her dark hair, a shade too light to be called black, gleamed in the sun. And those eyes, moss-green with hints of brown, looked right through him. Though they seemed even more guarded now than when she'd been a teenager. And something was missing...

His heart twisted. Every time he'd looked into her eyes, he'd always seen how much she cared for him. Now...there was nothing. He should have tried harder to find her after the last summer they'd had together.

The summer she saved his life.

"What brings you back to town?" Ian stuffed his fingers farther into his pockets to keep from reaching for her. "Does Cinda know you're here?"

Her gaze turned wary. She shook her head. "No. I thought I'd, um, surprise her. If she's in town." She rubbed her palms on her jeans. "Is her dad still here?"

"Her dad's here." His smile faltered, but he forced it back. Her dad's story was Cinda's to tell. "So is Glenna. Their mom passed the summer after you were here the last time. We, Cinda and I, thought that was why you didn't come back."

No response. Well, this was awkward. "We thought Cinda's mom might be the reason you came. I guess we didn't understand whose side of the family you were from."

Asia shifted away from the door. "I didn't either."

"Hey, you want to go for a cup of coffee or something? I could show you my place. Give you a mean barbecue sandwich. On the house." He winked again and gave her the heart-melting grin she'd loved. "I have an in with the owner."

"I'm here to see Cinda." She fumbled behind her for the doorknob. "I should go on in."

"She's teaching a class right now." Ian motioned to the cars lined up in a row behind him. "You would just have to wait for--" He checked his watch. "--thirty minutes. Plus the time it takes to get the ladies lined up with material for their next project."

Asia studied the flowers in the pot next to her. She'd never been impulsive, but now she seemed to take forever to make up her mind. Ian waited. Just like he did all the time back then. Her stomach rumbled loud enough to be taken for thunder. A dark flush crept up her cheeks, and he chuckled.

At least part of her was intrigued by his offer. "Come on." He took a step toward the restaurant. Her head dropped forward for a moment, the movement almost unnoticeable.

He noticed.

They sauntered down the sidewalk, side by side. Nostalgia swept over him, and he fought the urge to take her hand. His fingers twitched with the remembered feel of her small palm next to his.

He opened the door for her, and they stepped into his domain. The smell of barbecue intensified. Meat sizzled in the open pit. A hum of voices wove through the air as lunch goers chatted. A few called out a greeting to him.

Asia shrank back, her backpack brushing his chest. Ian placed his hands on her shoulders and felt fine tremors running through her. What had happened to the saucy, I-can-do-anything girl he'd fallen for all those years ago?

They'd been drawn together by their wounded pasts—he, the rebellious bad boy, and she, the wounded healer. Looked like they'd both changed.

"I have a table in the back that will be more private." Ian leaned close so she could hear him over the cacophony. He could feel the stares of a number of townsfolk. He'd be fielding questions about her for sure. He doubted any of them would remember her. Most of the friends they'd known had moved away.

He slipped his hand to cup her elbow and led her around the dining area. Giving a subtle motion with his head, he caught Meg's attention. Best waitress he'd ever had. She'd have menus and a table ready in no time. She would also see that they were afforded privacy. That would be good. It would let him catch up with the girl he'd never forgotten.

And the woman she'd become.

Once they were seated, the paper bag Asia picked up off the table rattled in her hands. She set the menu down and put her hands underneath, out of sight.

"Choose anything you like. The bag printed with the food choices is for your leftovers and so you'll have the menu anytime you want to place another order." Ian watched her concentration. That hadn't changed about her. She'd always focused on whatever task came her way, giving her whole attention until she accomplished what needed to be done.

"Ready?" Meg stopped by the table, her tablet and pencil in hand. "I can give you a few more minutes if you need, but our menu is pretty short." She winked at Asia, her brown eyes twinkling. "I've been trying to get the boss to add some items, but he's resistant to change."

"I remember that." Asia's lips trembled on a smile. "What would you recommend?"

Meg studied her. "You don't look like you could eat a whole rack of ribs." She narrowed her eyes and pursed her lips. "Our most popular is the barbecue pork sandwich and chips, but if you want a little less fat, the barbecue chicken sandwich is good too." Her pencil hovered over the paper. "I would recommend the chips. They're made from scratch as you order them. That's something the boss did right." She patted her ample hips. "My downfall."

"Sounds good then. I'll take the chicken sandwich and chips." Asia handed her menu to Meg.

"Oh, no, honey. You keep that. There's a couple plastic bags in there and, trust me, you'll need them for leftovers." She jotted down Ian's order and hurried away.

"You seem to be doing a good business." Asia spoke as she stared down at the menu.

"I do all right." He ignored the empty tables. So much for the noon rush. "I'd like to find a way to increase business but haven't hit on it yet."

"Maybe your waitress has the right idea. You could offer some different items. Do you have lunch specials?" Asia glanced up at him, her green eyes almost black in the low lighting.

"I've toyed with the idea but haven't come up with anything. I'm making some money, so I didn't take it further. I have thought of adding in a night of music. Maybe we can talk about it sometime."

Ian held his breath. He wanted to hear that she would still be here tomorrow. Next week.

Next month.

Next year.

"I don't know much about running a restaurant." Asia shrugged. "Mom and I didn't eat out much."

She shifted in the seat, her gaze darting toward the door. What was going on? Was she afraid? He fought the urge to scoop her into his arms and protect her. "Enough about me. I want to know where you went when you disappeared. I know you lived down in LA somewhere, but then you weren't around at all."

"My mom moved to southern Arizona. I used to email Cinda, but I stopped."

Were those tears in her eyes? She blinked and ducked her head, her fingers toying with the utensils.

He couldn't resist. He reached over and put his hand on hers. "I know things were bad with your mom. Did it get any better?" She shook her head. Clearly this was painful for her. At one time they were close enough to share horrors and talk it through. Asia had saved him with her willingness to listen when everyone else wrote him off as worthless. Now, though...

He needed to give her time and be open to listening when she needed to talk. One thing he knew, though, as sure as if she'd said so...

She needed someone.

"Oh, my." Asia's mouth fell open as Meg slid an oblong plate in front of her. Meat covered the bottom half of the bun. Beside the top were vegetables and pickles. To the side, a mound of still sizzling chips threatened to topple over everything. Asia's eyes had grown so round, Ian wanted to throw back his head and laugh.

"How am I supposed to eat all of this? You've given me enough food for a week." Asia sent Meg an imploring look.

"Oh, honey, this is the usual. Stick around here, and you'll have plenty of meat on those bones of yours. The big mystery is why the boss is still so fit instead of having a paunch like most men would." Meg slid Ian's plate in front of him and fast walked back the way she'd come.

"Now you understand the doggie bag menu." Ian flipped out his napkin and drew in a deep breath to savor the scent of the pork he'd ordered. He'd never get tired of the sweet and tangy taste of barbecue.

With one delicate finger, Asia touched the tower of chips. She broke off a piece and put the sliver in her mouth. Her eyes closed. She hummed. Her lips tilted up. "Those have to be the best I've ever had." Her face relaxed for the first time since he'd seen her this morning. Now he could see the girl he'd known years ago.

He shifted in his seat. Watched Asia put together her sandwich. What should he talk about? He didn't want to see the frightened-deer gleam in her eyes again.

"How is your mother? Is she still in Arizona?"

Asia paused in the act of picking up the piece of sandwich she'd cut in half. Her cheeks darkened, and her chicken slithered from the bun to her plate. She ducked her head, but not before he saw, once again, the sheen of tears in her eyes.

2

THE BURN behind her eyelids fought against the twisting in her stomach. Ian's simple questions brought back the last few weeks. The euphoria of finally being free from prison. The ache of her mother's death. The confusion of finding her father. At least, she thought she had.

Unless this was another lie from her mother.

"You okay?"

Ian's concerned voice broke through her reverie. Blinking back the tears, Asia pasted on as bland an expression as she could manage and lifted her head. She couldn't let her news slip to Ian when she hadn't even talked with Cinda. That wouldn't be fair. "My mom passed away. A few months ago." Her throat ached as she swallowed against a tight knot.

"I'm sorry." Ian looked stricken, but she waved her hand, pushing away unwanted emotions.

"You didn't know." She smoothed a napkin in her lap and took a deep breath. "This smells incredible." She picked up one of the crisp chips and bit off a taste, more than the first sliver. Once again, flavor exploded in her mouth. "Oh!" She met Ian's I-told-you-so gaze. "These are even better than the chips we used to get at the fair when I visited. Remember those? Where we watched them take the ginormous potatoes and put them through that slicer and deep fry them?"

Ian nodded as he put veggies on his sandwich and lifted the whole thing in his hands. Pork, drenched in sauce, threatened to slip-slide out of the bun. "That's where I got the idea. I added some changes." He grinned at her. "Secret changes, before you ask. And, these are the result." He bit off a hunk of sandwich.

She popped the rest of the chip into her mouth. The savory, slightly toasted taste made her mouth water for more. She rearranged the half sandwich, picked it up, and took a bite. Once again, her eyes closed as her taste buds danced.

"Ian, you should market this sauce. It's better than anything I've eaten." She swallowed a second bite. "Not that I'm an expert. I haven't tried every barbecue place between here and Texas."

His deep chuckle warmed her.

They ate in silence, the murmur of voices in the restaurant drifting back to them. Meat sizzled on the central open pit grill, and Asia enjoyed watching the cook through the open doorway as he worked with a synchronized rhythm to fix plates of food. Everyone here seemed to enjoy what they were doing. Happy employees meant Ian must be an excellent boss.

She studied the man across from her. He'd changed. He was no longer the angry teen lashing out at the world. Devastated by his past. Cast aside by the system.

Had her friendship helped him at all that last summer? Where everyone else had seen a troubled youth, she'd seen a hurting young man who needed someone to care. It so happened she'd needed the same thing, and they bonded over their shared need.

"Penny for your thoughts." Ian had finished his sandwich and held one of his last chips between his finger and thumb. "Or is that too little? With inflation, you know."

She opened her paper menu and brought out the plastic bags. "I think you just paid way more than a penny by providing this meal." She slipped the leftover chips and sandwich inside the sack. "Two meals, I should add. This was excellent. When you have a chain of barbecue places across the world, I can say I ate at the first one." She wiped her mouth with a napkin one last time. The pile of used napkins on the table resembled a downed tree.

"Is there a place to wash my hands?" She glanced around for a bathroom sign.

"Back there." Ian pointed toward a hallway. "I'll order dessert."

Asia stopped in the act of standing. She gaped at him. "Where in the world would I put dessert? Where would *you* put it? You ate everything on your plate."

Ian laughed, that deep throaty rumble that made her knees tremble and shivers skitter up and down her spine. And those eyes. The blue. Now crinkled at the corners, but still heart-stopping.

"I'll order something to share then." He raised his hand to gesture to Meg.

Asia shook her head as she headed for the restroom.

By the time she returned, Meg was on her way to their table. She placed a plate with a huge slab of peach pie á la mode between them. "I brought you a fork and a spoon since I didn't know which you would prefer." She winked at Asia. "You might want to use the spoon for the food and keep the fork in your other hand to protect your half from the boss. I've seen him devour this in one gulp."

She sauntered away to Ian's growled objection, although his eyes glimmered.

He pursed his lips as he nudged the plate closer to her. "Meg could be right, you know. I'll give you a head start."

Asia stared at the pie and tried to blink away the memories stinging her tear ducts. "You remembered." She couldn't stop the words, and her face began a slow burn.

"Of course, I remembered." Ian leaned as close as the wide table would allow. "How many of these did we share? When I opened my restaurant, this pie was my specialty dessert." He shrugged. "I guess in the back of my mind I hoped to share it with you again one day."

Her throat closed. She didn't want to disappoint him. Again. She picked up her fork, cut off a small bit of pie with melted ice cream running over the peaches. Amusement glinted in his eyes as he watched her take that first taste. This time she didn't close her eyes. Instead, she watched him take a similar bite only several times larger. A drip of ice cream caught on his lip. Her heart stalled.

She had to get out of here.

"This is delicious, but I really need to get over to Cinda's shop. Plus, I'm so stuffed I won't be able to waddle that distance if I don't quit now." She wiped her mouth one last time and stood up. Slinging her backpack over one shoulder, she tried to ignore the hurt that flashed across his face. "Thank you so much for the meal. I enjoyed catching up with you."

"Don't forget your food." Ian gestured to the paper bag. "I'll have Meg save this pie for us to eat later. I'll walk you over. I wanted to see Cinda too." He licked the drop of ice cream from his lip as he stood up. "I can't wait to see her reaction when you walk through the door."

There had to be a way to keep him from going with her. Something that wouldn't hurt his feelings, but her mind went blank.

This would be an interesting reunion. Cinda never did anything low key. Maybe that's why they had always gotten along so well. Asia could be her quiet self, while Cinda made up for that in her abundant enthusiasm.

The distance across the parking lot felt like the walk she'd taken two years ago.

The walk that put a black mark on her record.

The walk she didn't want anyone here to know about.

Her stomach threatened to reject all the food she'd just eaten.

This time when she approached the quilt shop, there was no chance to hesitate. Ian reached around her to open the door. For a moment, she wanted to lean back against him. To draw comfort from his solid strength. She straightened her shoulders and stepped inside.

She could do this.

"Ian Kittredge. Where *were* you? You were supposed to be here an hour ago." Cinda, more mature but still looking like a high schooler, stood behind a counter not far from the door. She frowned at Ian. Then her gaze came to rest on Asia.

Her eyes rounded. Her red-lipsticked mouth formed an O. She dropped the cloth she'd been holding and slapped her palm to her chest. "Asia." Her hand came up to cover her mouth. "Asia, is that you?"

Faster than a runaway freight train, Cinda rounded the counter and had her arms wrapped around Asia, bouncing up and down on her toes. "I can't believe you're here. Girl, I've missed you so much! Where did you go? Why did you quit writing to me? Why didn't you come see us? Why are you here? Did you drive?"

The questions whirled by so fast Asia couldn't keep up. She wanted to stay in Cinda's warm embrace almost as much as she wanted to disappear. She'd missed Cinda. The way they would talk for hours, even after lights out. Cinda's sister, Glenna, would get so annoyed at them.

But then, Glenna never liked her much. Why, Asia never understood.

"We have so much catching up to do." Cinda shoved Asia back to arm's length. "How long can you stay?"

A woman walked past and said goodbye.

"Stella, this is my long-lost cousin, Asia. She used to come visit, and I haven't seen her in years." Cinda bounced as she said the words, morning glory eyes glowing as if she'd just won the lottery.

Asia's news would take about one second to wipe away that joy.

~

"Cinda Loo, let the girl take a breath." Ian stepped up beside Asia. He rested his palm on her shoulder just above Cinda's hand. The simple touch rocked through him.

"Oh, I'm so sorry." Cinda clapped her palms to her cheeks, eyes wide. Her long curls bobbed as she continued to lift up and down on her toes, a classic Cinda move. Dark bangs framed expressive blue eyes. Eyes that told the whole world every emotion she felt. And there were plenty of them. Cinda bounced through life higher than Winnie the Pooh's friend, Tigger.

"Tansie." Cinda waved at the young woman putting bolts of cloth on a shelf. Tansie turned as she slipped a bolt into a slot.

"Can you watch the front for a little while?" Cinda's question had every head in the shop turning toward them. Ian could almost feel the discomfort resonating off of Asia. What had happened to her? Whatever she'd been through had changed her.

He intended to find out why.

At Tansie's nod, Cinda grabbed Asia's arm and motioned for Ian to follow them. She swept them into the back room where a class had finished. Bits of cloth, cutting tools, thread, and other quilting paraphernalia littered the tabletops.

Ian suppressed a shudder. He'd agreed to take this class so Cinda could get some men to participate. Not that he wanted to learn to sew. Figuring out how tiny pieces of material fit together in some strange pattern and color scheme boggled his brain. He'd rather think up a new menu item any day than come here to learn quilting. Only for Cinda.

"I need a cup of coffee. Want something?" Cinda looked first at Asia, then Ian. "We have the machine over here, as Ian knows." She led Asia to the counter at the side of the large room. She had one of those useless one-cup-at-a-time machines with a carousel of individual coffees to choose from. There was also hot chocolate and tea. Everything the quilter might want to drink while she tortured her fingers with needle pricks.

"Tea might be nice." Asia stared at the variety of tiny cups.

"Coffee, Ian?" Cinda picked up the cup he usually chose and started the brewing process. She always knew what her patrons liked. Not that *he* was a patron.

"I apologize for the mess." Cinda led the way toward the back of the room where a few easy chairs sat. "We just finished a class that proved a bit challenging." She frowned at Ian again.

"Now, Cinda, you should thank me for not being here. I would have made it even more difficult." Ian gave her a cocky grin, hoping to charm her into forgiving him. She sighed and shook her head, and he knew he'd won.

"You're taking a quilting class?" Asia slipped her backpack to the floor beside one of the chairs, balanced the cup Cinda handed her, and sat down. Her disbelief mirrored the feelings Ian had on the subject.

"He's helping me out." Cinda chuckled. "I had the bright idea that I wanted to reach out to some of the husbands of my quilters. A few of them are retired, and they don't like their wives going off all the time. I thought if they heard Ian was in the class, they wouldn't mind coming along with their wives. It could be mutually beneficial because they might go to I-BBQ for lunch afterwards."

"I never thought about men sewing quilts." Asia sipped her tea. "How is that working?"

"Well." Cinda frowned at Ian. Again. He shifted in his chair, took a gulp of coffee, and felt the burn all the way down his throat.

"Today was the first class. Without Ian in attendance, we had a lot of grumbling men. I promised them that you planned to be here." Cinda flipped a long curl back over her shoulder before returning for her own cup as the coffee finished dripping.

"I ran into Asia."

Asia's look was clear: why didn't he tell her he was supposed to be someplace?

"I took her to lunch at the restaurant. I knew you would be busy, and I didn't want to leave her on her own."

"Isn't his barbecue amazing?" Cinda licked her lips. "I think it's just wrong how he pipes that smell into the air." She laughed. "Enough about us. Where have you been, Asia?"

She shifted in the chair. Took a sip of tea. Took another sip of tea.

"Dad said your mom moved away and he didn't know where you'd gone. You wrote me for a while, but then, nothing."

"My mom wanted to cut all ties." Asia shrugged. "She found out I was emailing you and made me quit. I'm sorry. I didn't want to, but she said..." She trailed off and stared down at her tea. Her shoulders had hunched inward as she talked.

It took all his will to stay seated.

"How is your mother?" Cinda leaned forward. He winced. Opened his mouth to say something but kept quiet. He could see the compassion in Cinda's eyes. Maybe Asia needed to talk about her mom.

"My mother died. A few months ago." Asia didn't look up. She put her cup to her lips but lowered it without sipping and cradled it in her hand.

"I'm so sorry." Cinda touched Asia's arm. "What about your other family? I can't remember if you had anyone else, other than us."

"If we had other family, I don't know about them." Asia rubbed her palm up and down the leg of her jeans.

"Well, I'm glad you came here." Cinda patted Asia's arm again and sat back. "How long can you stay? Do you have a job to get back to?"

Ian relaxed and sipped his coffee. Trust Cinda to ask all the questions he wanted answered. Asia might even answer her instead of hedging like she'd done with him.

"I'm sort of traveling around." Asia set her empty cup on the table beside her.

"No job?" Cinda's question had Asia rubbing both palms on her jeans. So she still did that when she wasn't comfortable. Any minute now she'd jump up to leave.

"Where are you staying while you're here?" He frowned at the look Asia sent him. Was she…hiding something? But why?

"You could stay with me." Cinda clapped her hands and bounced in her chair so hard her coffee on the table next to her sloshed in the cup. "Martin is coming for dinner tonight. I know he would love to meet you. I've talked so much about our summers together."

"Who is Martin?" Asia tugged her braid over her shoulder to rub the end between her fingers. How many times had that action tantalized him? He couldn't quit staring at her. As a teen, she'd been striking, but nothing like the beautiful woman she'd become. Her gorgeous face, with those huge eyes, was enough to stop traffic.

Cinda straightened in her seat. "Martin is my fiancé." She grinned at the look of astonishment on Asia's face. Of course, she didn't look at Ian. She knew he didn't approve of her choice of men. Martin Hannah had to be the most manipulative, narcissistic person to draw breath. How could Cinda have fallen for the man?

"Ian, you should come too."

When would Cinda give up on him learning to like Martin? Or vice versa? Asia turned imploring eyes in his direction. Had she sensed his reluctance?

He shrugged. He'd have to come up with a valid excuse to avoid dinner. Although…

Spending time with Asia might be worth suffering through Martin's latest thoughts on himself.

"How long can you stay?" Cinda turned back to Asia. "We need plenty of time to catch up?"

"I don't have any real plans." Asia fumbled with the strap of her backpack.

"Then let me show you around my shop. I'll ask if Tansie needs help out there, but she's probably fine. If you want, I can give you the key and directions to my house and you can drive on over there." Cinda scooted forward on the chair. "If you have a lot of luggage, Ian or Martin can help you carry it in tonight. Where are you parked?"

"Um, I don't have a car." Asia twisted the braid tight around her finger. "I don't have luggage either."

Cinda seemed shocked speechless. Well, that was a first. She stared at Asia, her mouth gaping, then sucked in a deep breath.

"What about clothes? Shoes?" Cinda glanced at Ian. "Necessities."

"I have a change of clothes in my backpack. It's all I need." Asia dragged said bag forward from the side of the chair as if presenting evidence. Ian almost laughed at the look on Cinda's face. When *she* traveled, she had to pay extra bag fees. Every time. She probably couldn't fit her makeup in that backpack.

Asia fidgeted. "What I'd really like is to see your dad. Does he live with you, or is he still in the old house?"

Uh-oh. Asia wasn't going to like Cinda's answer.

3

ASIA'S SHOULDERS drooped as she listened to Cinda talk about her father. Ian wanted to reach out and take Asia's hand, to lend support, but his touch probably wouldn't be welcomed right now. So much had changed since she'd last visited.

Alzheimer's. The term weighed heavy as Cinda talked. Asia clasped her hands together between her knees and stared at the floor, blinking, as moisture shimmered on her lashes.

"So, you see, we don't allow him visitors anymore." Cinda leaned forward, her hands weaving an expressive pattern in the air. "The past few times he's had visitors other than Glenna and me, he's become violent. That's why we have him in the Alzheimer's facility. We had to move him to the lockdown area. For his safety." Cinda's voice caught. She bit her lip.

Asia's mouth opened and shut as if she wanted to say something but had no idea what to say. Ian knew the feeling all too well. He'd been here for Cinda's struggle with her dad's disease. Walter's struggle too.

Cinda had tried so many ways to halt the progression of her dad's disease, to no avail. Ian made sure he was there as her friend, listening when needed, but nothing he could say or do could make anything better.

But then, who wanted advice from him on family issues? He shuddered at the memory of his father's red face as he stood over Ian's mother where she cowered on the kitchen floor. He could still see the fresh bruises blooming on Mom's cheek and arm. Her shaking fingers as she tried to pull herself to safety. He closed his eyes and forced his thoughts back to the present. He would *not* dwell on the horror of his past.

Cinda picked at some stray threads on her slacks. "Dad struggled after Mom died. That would have been after you left that last summer. A few times, he said something about being guilty, but I don't know what he meant. He never said." She lifted her hands, palms up, before clasping them together again.

"When he first got Alzheimer's, he became angry. As the disease progressed, he would wander off or become violent toward whoever happened to be his caregiver at the time." She swiped at a tear on her cheek.

"I don't remember him ever being angry at anything." Asia's voice quavered.

"Right?" Cinda shook her head. "He rarely raised his voice at us. Not even at Randall, who deserved it." She huffed a sad laugh.

"Is Randall still here?" Asia asked. "You haven't mentioned him."

Cinda shook her head. "He couldn't deal with Dad's disease. He got in some trouble. Went off to college. Dropped out and disappeared."

"Disappeared?" Asia's brows knit together. "Where is he now?"

"We don't know." Cinda's eyes glazed with tears. "We haven't heard from him in a few years. I've tried to find him. So has Ian. You'd think with all the internet capabilities he would be easy to find, but so far nothing."

Ian could almost see the thoughts circulating in Asia's head. This had been her place of sanctuary where she escaped the difficult life with her mother. She always said her summers here were perfect. The family life she longed for. How disappointing the reality must be compared to the memory. To realize the imperfection of a man, even if that man had no choice when disease stole his memories.

He'd struggled with some of the same issues when he came back here. To see those he loved in a different light. Maybe he could talk with her, help her deal with it all.

Asia looked at Cinda. "Does Randall know your dad's Alzheimer's has progressed so far?"

Cinda's eyes blinked closed, then open. "When we last heard from him Dad was living with Glenna. We told Randall we needed to discuss moving Dad to a facility when the time came. Then Randall disappeared." Cinda plucked a tissue from a box on the end table beside her and patted her eyes. "The police searched but couldn't find a trace of him. He's still a missing person, but they aren't really looking anymore. It's been too long."

Her breath shuddered. She closed her eyes. "The thing is, I keep hoping he will show up and talk to Dad. Maybe the father-son connection will bring Dad back. I know that's stupid to think, but I can't help it."

He hated seeing her hurt like this. "We all need hope, Cinda. You know that."

"You're right." Cinda's shoulders straightened. "Enough of the sad stuff." She smiled at Asia. "I hope you understand why you can't see Dad. I have no idea how he would react, and the last time he not only hurt the visitor, he hurt himself and one of the nurses."

"Maybe if you went with me. I really need to talk to him." Asia shifted in her chair.

He held back a frown. Why couldn't Asia just let it go?

"Why?" Cinda tilted her head to the side. "He doesn't even know who I am anymore."

"I guess it's that hope you talked about." Asia shrugged. "I wanted to ask him about my mom and how they were... related." She chewed her lip. "Maybe I could find other family if I talked to him."

"I see." Cinda stared down at her clasped hands. "I'll discuss this with Glenna and the staff at the Driftwood Cove Care Center. I'll let you know what they say, okay?"

Asia nodded.

Maybe the conversation would lighten up now. He hated seeing the sadness in his best friend and in the woman he once cared for. Maybe even loved. Asia might not know it, but she'd been his salvation that summer. Without her intervention and friendship, without her listening and understanding…

His life would be very different.

"Let me show you around the shop." Cinda jumped to her feet and tugged the hem of her top. "Oh, I forgot. Ian said you ate at his restaurant. I'm sure you have leftovers. I have a refrigerator back here." She waited until Asia dug the paper bag from her backpack and then stored the leftovers where they would keep.

"I think this is where I bow out." Ian stood and gave Cinda a hug. When he hugged Asia, he had trouble letting go. He sensed she had something she needed to talk about, but she was holding back.

"Are you coming for dinner tonight?" Cinda narrowed her eyes at him.

He tried not to sigh. He really did. "What time?"

"I'll close here at 6:00 pm. I have a roast in the crockpot. Say 6:30?" Cinda's eyes glowed, and she bounced up on her toes.

"I'll be there. Anything you want me to bring?"

"Weeellll." Cinda winked at Asia. "I don't have any dessert for tonight. I was going to stop somewhere on my way home, but..."

"Okay." He gave an exaggerated sigh. "I'll bring four peanut butter cookies for dessert." Martin hated peanut butter and made sure everyone around knew. He claimed to have an allergy, but Ian had never seen any evidence of that. Far more likely that Martin liked the sympathy an allergy evoked.

"Don't you dare!" Cinda crossed her arms over her chest.

"Okay, peanut butter pie then. I have a great recipe."

"Ian!" Cinda's eyes sparked fire.

Asia's head swiveled between the two of them, her brow furrowed.

"Gotcha." Ian pinched Cinda's cheek and grinned at Asia. "Martin *claims* to have an allergy to peanut butter, and I always want to see if it's true. You know, a science experiment." He laughed at the outrage in Cinda's expression. Asia smiled.

She had always understood him.

He said his good-byes and headed for the door as Cinda began to give her shop spiel to Asia. He'd heard the speech a thousand times and could probably give the talk as well as Cinda. He almost backed out the door, to keep Asia in sight as long as possible. He couldn't get enough of looking at her.

Tonight was going to be a good time. Even if he had to endure Martin.

"THIS IS our classroom where we teach quilting." Cinda gestured at the array of tables and machines. "We have classes every day, sometimes two a day. Keeps us hopping." She picked up a small trashcan and went around sweeping scraps into the bag as she talked.

"This morning we had a beginner's class. This afternoon is our more advanced group. We're doing a mystery pattern."

"Mystery pattern?" Asia helped Cinda gather the bits of cloth and thread for the trash.

"Each week I give them a section of a pattern to make. At the end we will put the whole quilt together and they will see the design. It's fun and the attendees love to see the different quilts they can make." Cinda paused to smile. "It's one of my favorite classes."

"How many come to your classes?" Asia did a mental count of the tables and chairs. How on earth did Cinda keep up with them all?

"The starter class is limited to ten people. They take more work since they don't know what they are doing. We have two different first-time groups going this round. One is full. The other, this morning's, still has one opening." She froze in the act of dropping a handful of debris into the trashcan. Threads and bits of material dripped from her hand. Asia shifted. When Cinda had one of these flashes of genius, she always believed everyone should agree with her.

Asia braced herself. That look meant trouble, usually for her.

"Asia!" Cinda dropped the basket with a loud clang and whirled toward her. Eyes glowing, she bounced in place and clapped her hands.

This would be bad. Asia backed up a step.

"You can be the last person." Cinda tipped her head back and laughed. "This is perfect."

"Last person?" Asia edged toward the door. "Last person for what?"

"The last person to fill out the class. The beginner's class." Cinda clapped her hands again. Bits of thread sprayed out to stick to her top. She didn't seem to notice. "I'm pretty sure you haven't done any quilting before. You said you're not in a hurry to leave."

"I don't... I can't do that." Asia bumped into a chair, rattling it against the table. "I can't pay for a class. I..."

What could she say? That she had no money, no home, no future? Well, why not? It was the truth.

"Yes, you'll need a job to stay here." Cinda almost leapt off the floor when she bounced this time. "You couldn't know, but I've been looking for someone else to help out, especially with the classes. You can be my assistant."

"Hello! Cinda!" Was she crazy? "You already said it. I know nothing about quilting. How can I assist in something I know nothing about?"

Cinda waved away her objection. "You were always a quick learner. Besides, how hard is it to cut pieces of material? Or pass out items to participants? Or tell them they are doing a good job?" She lowered her voice as she glanced toward the store area. "Even when some of them aren't that good. In my shop, they still get encouragement."

Asia had no words. Helping out with a quilting class was impossible. Still...encouragement she could do. And maybe handing out what was needed. But the rest? Not happening. She'd never been that great with scissors. Give her a computer and an illustrator program and she could work miracles. Cloth and scissors?

Disaster.

"You know what else?" Cinda clapped her hands again.

Maybe she should tape them to Cinda's sides so she couldn't do that anymore. Because every time she'd done it today, things got a little scarier. "Um, what?" Asia's fingers ached as she gripped the chair she'd almost knocked over.

"You're welcome to stay with me, but I know you'd like a place more your own. It just so happens we have an apartment attached to the quilt shop. It will need to be cleaned up but come on. Let's take a look." Without waiting to see if Asia would follow, Cinda swept around the tables, making for a door in the side wall.

Asia followed after Cinda into the apartment. A small chamber ran along the wall of the shop. Where they stood could be a living room. In the corner was a kitchenette. All small and in desperate need of cleaning, but livable. Was there a bathroom with a shower? Oh, how she wanted to climb in and get clean.

"Look at this." Cinda motioned to Asia from the kitchen. "Here's the bedroom. The storage has been nice, and we use it for the shop, but we can move everything out for you." Her gaze strayed to Asia's backpack.

The bedroom area had a four-drawer dresser and a full-size bed. There wasn't much room to maneuver, but it would do. Asia turned to see where Cinda pointed and saw an old-fashioned armoire against the wall to the kitchen. The piece of furniture would be perfect for holding any clothes or necessities.

This place was three times the size of her former residence, and she'd had to *share* that room. Plus, there were no bars or locked doors. No guards. It would be so wonderful to stay here, but she couldn't. Cinda wouldn't want her around after she shared her discovery.

"There's a bathroom here." Cinda leaned through the opening that led to the storage area. "It's tiny. No bathtub, just a shower, sink, and toilet." She turned back to Asia, seeming much more subdued. "I know it isn't great."

"Cinda." Asia held up her hand to stop the apology. "This would be wonderful, but I can't stay here. I'll be honest with you. I have no money. No job to pay rent. I can't take advantage of you like that. I'm not even sure how long I'll stay."

"Asia." Cinda grasped her hands. "You have no family that you know of other than us. Stay. Work in the shop with me. You can use the apartment. It will be nice to have someone on the premises to watch the shop or to open up if I'm running late. I'll pay you a little extra too. We can get reacquainted. I want to know you again."

The plea in her voice cut deep. Would Cinda beg her to stay if she knew what Asia planned to do while she was here?

She looked around again. If only she could accept the offer...but what would happen when she hurt the only people who cared at all about her?

"Come on. You don't have to decide now." Cinda led the way back to the classroom. "I'll give you the rest of the tour. You can stay with me until Saturday, and then we can clean up the apartment. I'll have Martin bring some of the kids from his school to help. He's a teacher at the high school." Her brilliant smile had returned when she glanced back at Asia. "Martin loves working with the kids. I can't wait for you to meet him."

Cinda brushed her hands together as if all were settled. Asia almost smiled. She'd forgotten how her cousin could be so determined and yet so sweet at the same time. Cinda always managed to get her way. When Asia had been staying with Cinda and her family, she'd seen Cinda manipulate everyone from her parents to the clerk at the grocery store. And she did it without even realizing what she was doing.

"Come on. Let me show you the shop." Cinda ushered Asia into the store. There weren't as many customers here now. A few ladies browsed the shelves lined with bolts of material in order of color. The neatness was beyond Asia's comprehension or ability. She liked color, but not in such order. She wanted to pull cloth off the shelves and rearrange.

Tansie stood at the cash register ringing up an order. Another woman waited at a table in the middle of the room with several bolts of cloth piled beside her. On a second table a mountain of material threatened to tumble and squash customers if one more bolt was added. Tansie must have been interrupted in her quest to straighten the shop.

"You okay, Tansie?" Cinda called.

Tansie waved a hand and finished ringing up the order.

Cinda led Asia around the shop. "We have a variety of materials to use in quilts. I stock a range of colors and patterns, plus the ladies can order anything we don't carry." She brushed her fingers along the bolts of cloth. "That doesn't happen very often."

"Who makes these?" Asia motioned to the quilts lining the upper half of the walls. They ranged from simple appliqués to quilts with such tiny pieces she couldn't imagine how a person could stitch them together. There must be names for the different patterns, but she had no idea what they were.

"I made most of them." Cinda pointed to one quilt, done all in blue satin with the pattern in white stitching. The contrast and design were breathtaking. A work of art. "That one is my favorite. I made it for a quilt show by special request."

"Do you sell your quilts? They're incredible." Asia edged around the room studying the masterpieces.

"Come look at these." Cinda took her arm and dragged her to another room. "Over here is the material for baby quilts."

Asia gasped. The array of stitched blankets was incredible. Baby animals. Farm animals. Zoo animals. Noah's Ark. Bright colors. Pastels. One quilt was in the shape of a dog, and some of the pieces were made like bones and balls. She could picture a child's delight or a new mother's joy at receiving one of these.

"This is amazing, Cinda. You were always artsy, but I didn't know you had all this talent. I don't even remember you sewing when I visited." Nothing like feeling like the least talented member of the family. Yes, she had a degree, and she was good at design, but who would ever hire her to work for them? Not with her background.

"Several of these were made by Tansie. She can whip out quilts faster than a person can sneeze. She gives quilts to all the new moms and still has time to make some for the walls here. The dog quilt over there is her design and creation. We get a lot of requests for the pattern, but so far she hasn't put it up for sale." Cinda lowered her voice. "She's working on a cat one like that. It has little mice and fish. It's adorable."

"So she can sell the patterns?"

"Yes, she would like to make a book of patterns to sell. Quilts of different animals like this. I think it would be perfect for her."

They looked around a little more and then Asia helped Cinda clean the classroom so it would be ready for her upcoming advanced class.

ASIA STRETCHED HER TIRED MUSCLES. Sitting in on the advanced class proved exhausting. It was closing time now, and good thing. She was ready for something to eat. The smell of barbecue seemed even stronger when she stepped outside than it had been at lunchtime. She pulled in a deep breath.

"I know. It's heavenly, isn't it?" Cinda jingled her keys. "I should have had Ian bring barbecue for dinner." She laughed and unlocked a red sedan, tossing her purse in the back seat. Asia climbed in on the passenger side. Boy, did it feel good to sit.

"I didn't ask if you're okay with roast and vegetables." Cinda glanced at Asia before turning onto the street. "Everyone seems to have some sort of dietary restrictions these days. Do you?"

"None that I know of." Her accommodations for the past couple of years wouldn't have allowed for any.

"Oh, look, Martin's here." Cinda waved at a man seated on the porch as she turned into the driveway. She parked in the shade of a large tree, and they stepped out. Martin rose and strode toward them.

"Who's this?" He smiled and his gaze slid over Asia.

It took all her willpower to suppress a shudder.

This was the wonderful Martin?

4

Ian threw his truck in park, grabbed the bag with the pie and ice cream, and hopped out. He could tell from Asia's stance she wanted to retreat from Martin's advance. As he rounded the front of his Ford, he noted Martin taking Asia's hand in both of his. She hunched her shoulders and yanked her hand.

The urge to intervene hit him so hard, Ian almost stopped cold. Was this from his dislike of Martin or from his almost instant reconnection with Asia? Maybe a bit of both.

"Ian, I didn't know you would be here tonight." Martin's face smoothed into a façade as he released Asia's hand and she stepped back. Except for the slight flare of his nostrils. He wasn't happy.

"I meant to text you, Martin, but the time got away from me." Cinda stepped close and put her arm around Asia's shoulders. "Remember me talking about my cousin, Asia. Well, she surprised us with a visit today, so this is a celebration. I invited Ian to join us."

"We may bore you with our reminiscing." Here was hoping his comment would convince Martin to leave the dinner early. Or back out entirely.

"I am so glad to meet you, Asia. I've heard so much." Martin crowded Ian and reached for Asia's arm. She didn't let him touch her. Martin frowned but didn't pause for long. "I was just telling my classes today I felt like something monumental was about to happen." His smile broadened. "And here you are."

He led the way toward Cinda's house as if he owned the place. Asia followed behind. Cinda's expression showed her hurt. The bum hadn't even greeted her. The man was Cinda's fiancé. Of four years! If he didn't intend to marry Cinda, he should let her go.

Ian held up thc bag as he patted Cinda's shoulder. "There's always the opportunity for a little pie in the face. I knew I should have brought the peanut butter one." He winked at Cinda as she tried to look annoyed and ended up grinning at him instead.

"Come on. I need to check the roast and get dinner on the table." Cinda's hair bounced in rhythm to her jaunty walk as she strode toward her door, keys in hand.

"Cinda, it smells amazing in here." Asia stepped away from Martin, who hovered at her side, and reached for the bag Ian carried. "Let me take that to the kitchen for you. I'll help Cinda."

"I'll come with you." Martin grabbed the paper sack and the handle tore.

Ian snatched the dessert from midair before it turned into a disaster on the entryway floor.

"Martin." Cinda's sharp tone froze them all in place. She cleared her throat, her cheeks pinking up. "Martin, why don't you and Ian have a seat in the living room. Asia and I will get the food on the table in a few minutes. We'll call you."

Ian read the pleading in Cinda's gaze as she looked at him. The last thing he wanted was to hear a monologue on Martin's surefire teaching methods. Listening to the bore always left Ian wondering why they needed any other teachers at the high school. According to Martin, he could handle it on his own.

Martin's eyes strayed to the kitchen. Why was he so fascinated with Asia? Did she remind him of his students? She certainly looked like she could be in high school.

Martin was on the third rendition of I-started-this-incredible-program-that-should-catch-on-nationwide when Asia came to the doorway to announce dinner. She hurried away before Martin could reach her. Ian did his best to emulate a herd dog, winding his way around Martin to keep him from touching Asia. If the man laid his hands on her again…

"So, Asia, what is your degree in? What college did you go to?" Martin took a sip of tea and continued on as if he hadn't noticed Asia's panic. Maybe he hadn't.

"I have my degrees from UCLA. I thought about Harvard or Yale, but I prefer the weather in Southern California. None of that snow and ice for me." He brushed his fingertips over his ever-perfect hair. "I have a master's degree in higher education and a doctorate in psychology. I wanted to help my students who are troubled. And, if I tire of teaching, I can go into counseling and have a challenging career there."

He finally paused to take a bite of food. Ian almost laughed at the obvious relief on Asia's face. He knew from experience how hard it could be to derail Martin once he started on his favorite topic—himself. Still, he needed to try.

"Asia, is there anything you'd like to do while you're here?" Maybe that would cut short Martin's monologue.

Apparently Martin had swallowed and ignored Ian's question to Asia, because he just kept going. "I spent a lot of my younger years doing extreme sports, but I realized that wouldn't get me the necessities of life: home, car, family. So, I buckled down to study."

"How did you end up in Driftwood Cove?" Asia barely glanced at Martin as she asked the question. She stirred her potatoes and cut her carrots into minuscule pieces.

"Oh, that's quite a story." Martin patted his mouth with his napkin. Ian tuned him out, finished his meal, and helped Cinda clear the table. Ian had heard this story so many times he could tell it better than Martin.

"Shall we call Asia in to give Martin time to finish his meal?" Ian nudged Cinda with his elbow as he placed dishes next to the sink. "If we don't, he'll still be pontificating at midnight."

Cinda snorted. "Ian, be nice. He's always excited to meet someone new."

Ian glanced back into the dining room. Asia had scooted her chair a few inches farther from Martin's reach. The man caught Ian watching and pulled his hand back, picking up his fork again.

What was *wrong* with that idiot? "Cinda, why don't I work on the dessert, and you can ask Asia to help clear the rest of the table?" He turned back to find Cinda at the sink where she'd been scraping dishes, shoulders slumped.

"Hey, you okay?"

"I am." Cinda's smile when she looked up seemed forced. "Just a lot of thoughts running through my head. Thoughts about...just thoughts."

"Scary." Ian raised his hands and backed away. Cinda laughed, just as he'd intended. "Here, I'll finish this. Show me where the bowls or plates are for the pie and ice cream, and I'll bring them out in a few minutes."

Cinda showed him what he needed and went back into the dining room. Martin was still eating as he regaled the women with more of his exploits. He kept asking Asia questions, even though she blanched as if answering was the worst idea in the world. Good thing Martin didn't wait for an answer before going off on another story of himself. A true narcissist.

Oh, Cinda.

Ian warmed the pie, cut the pieces, and put them on plates. He glanced at the pantry. Hmmm. Cinda kept a jar of peanut butter there...just a bit on Martin's pie...

Stop it!

He grabbed the first plate and the softened French vanilla ice cream and carried them into the dining room.

"I'll let you dish up the ice cream, Cinda." He set what she needed in front of her and returned to the kitchen, then brought out the other three plates of pie.

"Mmmmmm. Peach pie and ice cream." Cinda leaned forward and drew in a breath. "Do you remember this, Asia?"

Asia's green eyes sparkled as she watched Cinda spoon out the ice cream. "We almost had some at lunch, but I was so stuffed from the barbecue, I could only manage one bite. I remember though." Her shy smile stole Ian's breath.

"Is the diner still there?" Asia asked.

So she still remembered the small diner they all used to hang out at, the one on the back road to the beach.

"Oh, it closed years ago." Cinda frowned as she passed a plate to Ian. "They had the best food, but the owner got sick. Cancer, I think. His wife couldn't take care of him and run the business too."

Ian nodded. "I remember when they closed their doors. That was a hard day for all of us who used to be regulars. Even if we only split a piece of pie because we didn't have much money."

"Mabel used to give us an extra piece. Remember that. She didn't charge us and sometimes gave us an extra scoop of ice cream. She was a sweetheart." Cinda capped the ice cream and set it away.

Asia smiled at Cinda. "I loved that place."

"We all did." Ian shared a smile with the girls, then made the mistake of looking at Martin.

He looked like a thundercloud had moved in over his head.

~

BY THE TIME the men left and Cinda showed her to her room, Asia wanted to crawl under the covers and hide. She loved reconnecting with Ian and Cinda, but the tension tonight had been over the top. The knot in her stomach had expanded with every bite she ingested.

The weight of her secrets all but crushed her. She *had* to tell Cinda, but what would happen? How would Cinda react to Asia's real reason for wanting to see her father. What would happen if they found out about her stint in prison? Even though Mother was dead, she didn't want to say anything against her. So she couldn't tell the truth about what happened.

Could she?

Asia shuddered. And then there was Martin. No wonder Ian didn't like the man. From the moment Martin approached her, she just wanted to leave. How many times had she seen the same look in the eyes of the men her mother brought home? How many times had she hidden to avoid their grasping touches and lecherous gazes? He might be Cinda's fiancé, and her cousin deserved respect, but that man wasn't touching her again.

Asia sat on the bed, her elbows on her knees, and rubbed the heel of her hands against her burning eyes. Too tired. She needed sleep. A shower first. Then sleep.

A light knock sounded on the door.

Cinda opened the door a crack and peered at her. "Hey, can I come in?"

"Always." Asia straightened.

"I put out a towel and washcloth, plus some other items you might need. The hall bathroom is all yours. I have mine off my bedroom." Cinda paused, leaning her shoulder against the doorframe as if deciding whether to say more.

"I brought these too." She held up some folded clothes. "A pajama set and some undies if you need them. We can wash your clothes tomorrow if you want." Her face flushed.

"Thank you." Asia crossed to take the proffered pjs. "I appreciate you letting me stay and…everything. I've missed this place. You. It's been a long time." Asia bit her lip to stop from spilling more than she wanted to. This wasn't the time. She was so tired a light breeze would topple her to the ground.

"Grab a shower. Get some sleep. Tomorrow Tansie is opening the shop. I don't go in until noon usually, but I messaged Ian just now to see about going in an hour earlier. We can make up the quilt class you didn't get today so you'll be caught up for Friday's class."

Cinda's thick curls slipped over her shoulder as she pulled Asia in for a hug. "We are going to have so much fun catching up. I'm so glad you came. Family is important."

Asia clutched the soft pjs to her as Cinda disappeared into her bedroom and the door clicked shut. Cinda had no idea how true her statement was. Family was important, something Asia didn't have until she found those documents. Cinda's family was a lifeline, and Asia was alone and in danger of drowning. Their connection, although tenuous, seemed to be her only hope right now.

Leaving her bag in her room, Asia stepped into the hall bathroom to find that Cinda had provided everything she would need. Toothpaste, toothbrush, soap, shampoo, conditioner. She'd forgotten Aunt Mary used to do the same thing in her guest bathroom. Clearly, some people didn't live day-to-day like she and her mother had. Another gift of family—the right family.

The bathroom decor was a beach theme with seafoam green walls, beach prints, and embroidered towels. Little shells decorated the counter, including a basket made of tiny shells, which held small bottles of lotion and other items.

The warm water in the shower felt so good. Asia lifted her face and let the droplets wash away the tears she couldn't hold back any longer. She pressed a washcloth to her face to muffle the sobs. Couldn't face Cinda's sympathy if she heard. Asia just couldn't give in to the temptation to spill all her secrets. If she did, she might land on the street for the night.

Back in the bedroom, she climbed in between crisp sheets that smelled like sunshine and soap. Once again, the color combinations in the room were perfect. Ivory walls with sky-blue trim, quilted wall hangings in varied blues, browns, and ivories, and a quilt on the bed that brought in yellows and oranges with the blue and brown to add a dollop of color. A few colorful pillows were on the bed and the easy chair by the window. Cinda should have become an interior decorator.

Asia reached over to click off the light and eased back on the pillow. She wanted to pray. Needed to pray. But the thoughts didn't come. She didn't know what to ask for that didn't sound selfish and wouldn't cause anyone pain. If she got what she wanted, Cinda and her family would be hurt. If she left without finding out the truth, she would always be lost and alone. There wasn't a solution she could present to God for Him to answer. Maybe once she had some rest, she would be able to think of something.

As she drifted to sleep, the picture of Ian smiling at her sent warmth through her, and then apprehension. He too would be hurt by her reason for being here. Contrary to her customary role, she wasn't here to be a peacemaker…

But to possibly start a war that would leave casualties on both sides.

~

THE SMELL of coffee and something baking woke her. Sunlight streamed through the sheer curtains, lighting her room. Asia swung out of bed, stretching to ease the tightness in her muscles. She finger-combed her hair, used the bathroom, and padded down the hall to the kitchen in her bare feet and pajamas.

She stopped in the kitchen doorway and drew in a deep breath. "What smells so good?"

Cinda glanced up from the iPad she had propped up in front of her on the table. "You mean besides the coffee?"

"Yes. Coffee." Asia imitated a zombie as she headed for the coffeemaker. It looked like the one Cinda had at the shop. Asia bent over to study the device. "I have never used one of these machines. Is there a magic word I need to say?"

Cinda laughed and came over to stand beside her. "Thank goodness, no. Because I'm so muddled in the morning I couldn't do anything intricate to make coffee. This is so simple."

She pointed to a rack beside the pot. "You can choose your coffee type here. You don't open it or anything, just put the little container in the machine." She demonstrated how. "Put your coffee cup under here and press the size cup you want here. This shows you the water level on the side." Cinda indicated the markings showing there was plenty of water available.

Asia picked a strong blend, popped it in the machine, chose a cup from the cupboard, and got the coffee started. She breathed in the scent, her mouth watering.

"Creamer? If you want some, it's in the fridge." Cinda pointed as she grabbed a hot pad and opened the oven door. Steam wafted out, and Asia could see the source of the delightful cinnamon smell. Muffins.

"Are those your mom's cinnamon-apple-ginger muffins?" She stepped closer to stare at the perfect golden tops as Cinda set the pan on the stovetop.

"I thought you would remember. These were your absolute favorite. Right?" Tears misted Cinda's eyes. She blinked and hugged Asia. "I'm just so glad you're here. Have I said that already?"

Fighting past the lump in her throat, Asia returned the hug. "I think you have. I'm so glad to be here."

They chatted about old times as they drank coffee and ate the best muffins she'd ever tasted.

After breakfast, Asia grabbed her clothes and ran them through the washer and dryer so she'd have something clean to wear to the quilt shop.

They were finishing dishes and getting ready to leave when the front door opened, and footsteps clicked on the hardwood floor.

"Cinda, are you here? Do you know what I heard?"

Glenna.

Asia would recognize that harpy tone anywhere. She shrank behind Cinda as her other cousin strode into the kitchen, put her hands on her hips, and glared at Cinda, not seeming to notice Asia.

"I heard that gold digger is back in town. I don't want you to have anything to do with her."

5

"I'll be back in an hour. You know where I'll be if you need me." Ian waved at Meg as he left the restaurant to go to the quilt shop. He smoothed his hair back from his face again and shook out his arms. His stomach did a little flip when he saw Cinda pull into the lot, Asia in the passenger seat beside her. He could almost walk on air today.

"Good morning, ladies. I hope you had a..." Ian halted midstride as Asia and Cinda climbed out of the car. Cinda pasted on a fake smile and attempted a spring in her step. Asia's shoulders were bowed forward as she studied the ground.

What had happened?

"Is everything okay?" He spoke low to Cinda.

"The Iron Queen paid a visit this morning." Cinda blinked fast, and her lips twisted.

Glenna. The polar opposite of Cinda, yet they were sisters. Glenna took the good out of good morning. He could just imagine what happened when she discovered Asia at Cinda's house.

Glenna had hated Asia since they were teens. She did and said the meanest things to get her to leave and never come back.

Adulthood hadn't helped. Glenna wasn't a nice person. Oh, she could pour on the charm when she wanted to. Pity she rarely wanted to.

"Come on. Let's go inside and we can talk." Cinda led the way into the shop, waving greetings to a few customers and stopping for a moment to talk with Tansie.

Asia looked so fragile. He'd never seen her so pale. Even her dark hair, usually so shiny, didn't gleam the near blue-black of yesterday. She didn't relax until they were in the back room with the door closed and the chatter of voices out front dimmed.

"Hey." Ian touched her shoulder and felt an instant of tension before she relaxed. "I hear you had a run-in this morning. Want to talk about it?"

She shrugged. "Not much to say. She still hates me. Maybe more so. I don't know why."

"Asia, sweetie." Cinda enfolded her in a hug before stepping back. "I don't understand it either. I used to try to talk to her about you, but she would only get angry. I'm not even sure how she found out you were here. I know she didn't realize you'd be at my house. The things she said. She didn't...."

"Don't say she didn't mean them. You know she did."

Ian stared at Asia. Cinda's mouth fell open.

Asia closed her eyes, and her lips pressed into a tight line. "I'm sorry. I didn't mean to snap. But you know she meant what she said."

They were quiet until they all settled in chairs with their coffee. Ian glanced between Cinda and Asia. "Why don't you tell me what happened?"

"Glenna didn't expect me to be at Cinda's. She said some things…." Asia ran her finger around the rim of her cup without looking up.

"My sister." Cinda twisted a strand of hair around her finger. "Glenna hasn't ever accepted Asia. You know that. She isn't happy about her being here, and finding her in my house didn't help."

"I see." Ian debated how much to say. "I'm concerned about her attitude. I know she's going through a tough time right now."

"What do you know?" Cinda's focus turned intense.

At her alarm, he raised his hand, palm out. "I can't say why, but I saw something a few weeks ago that has disturbed me. I'm praying about it and will let you know when I can say more."

"But she's my sister. I should know." Cinda's hand trembled as she set her coffee down.

She seemed to be searching for clues she'd overlooked. Trying to piece together thoughts much the same way she pieced together the beautiful quilts she made.

Cinda's eyes widened. "Jeffrey."

"Jeffrey?" Asia tilted her head, looking back and forth between them. "Who is Jeffrey?"

Cinda swallowed hard. Pressed her palms to her eyes. Met Asia's gaze. "Jeffrey is Glenna's husband. He travels for his job but has been out of town a lot more lately. I hadn't even put that together with the change in Glenna. He's away more than he's at home."

Cinda turned to Ian. "Is that what you mean? Did you see something with Jeffrey?"

He hesitated. Blew out a breath. How should he put this? "I have a...concern about him, but that's all I can say. Please don't ask for more." He thought of the dim corner of the restaurant in Santa Barbara. The booth in the corner with the couple snuggled close together. Jeffrey. He didn't know the woman. He shook away the memory.

"Okay." She nodded, pushed her fingertips against her forehead, and paused.

Asia glanced at Ian. He shook his head and steepled his fingers. This wasn't a time for words.

Cinda was praying.

She sat upright, rubbing her palms on her jeans. "All right. Let's breathe for a couple of minutes to get this bad out of us, and then we'll get to work." She led them in deep breathing. Ian always wanted to laugh when she did this--but he *did* feel more relaxed afterwards.

Cinda smiled at Asia. "We're getting a late start, so I don't have time to show you everything we did yesterday. I can talk to you about the different fabrics later. We are doing a small quilt first that can be a wall hanging or a baby quilt. It's simple to make and will show you how fun quilting can be."

Ian almost snorted. Fun? Her idea of fun wasn't the same as his.

Cinda led them to the side of the room to a table cluttered with material at one end and a bunch of, he had no idea what, at the other end. Ian rolled his eyes at Asia. She pressed her lips together, but he knew she wanted to laugh. That was good.

Cinda pointed to the material. "Yesterday, the class chose their fabrics. Some of the ladies know how to quilt and are here with their husbands. Those ladies picked out materials they could cut, but the new ones all picked out charm packs to use."

"Charm packs?" Ian winced. "Is this some cheerleader thing that's going to be all pink and girlie?" He edged toward the door, ready to make a break.

Cinda gave an exaggerated sigh and pointed to the piles of material. "Charm packs are materials that go together by their colors or patterns. They have variety. Yes, some are pink. But I also have some fall colors, some animals or hunting designs, some are definitely baby patterns. They are precut 5-inch squares, so that work is all done for you."

She rifled through the packs of fabric pieces bundled together and set several along the table. "Go ahead and look. See if there is something you like, and then we'll lay it out in a pattern."

Ian almost groaned. But hey, this was a chance to be close to Asia. And to gauge if she'd recovered from Glenna's attack. He stopped beside her, stared down at the colorful pieces of cloth, and snorted. Softly.

Asia thumped him on the arm with the back of her hand. His breath caught at the familiar gesture. All those years ago, he said inappropriate things, and her well placed backhand thumps became his filter.

"This one looks like you." Asia picked up a bundle of white cloth with strawberries on the top piece. "You like food."

"Maybe you could do this one." He showed her one with bears and woods.

"Be serious." Cinda came up beside them. "Asia, you used to like animals. What about this one with the cats and dogs? I like the colors in the pack."

Asia took the charm pack from Cinda to check the different colors and patterns. Ian turned over the strawberry batch and noticed one of the other pieces in the bundle had pie. Asia was right. This one was for him.

Cinda led them to large tables pushed together in the center of the room. Along the wall were sewing machines. He shuddered. *What was he doing here?*

From Asia's expression, she was wondering the same thing about herself.

"I want you to open your packs and lay out the pieces in the pattern you want." Cinda explained how they would lay them out. "See what catches your eye. And remember, there isn't a wrong way to do this." Cinda clapped as they freed what felt like a million scraps of cloth.

Ian slipped off the paper holding the fabric together and promptly dropped the pieces. Asia laughed and then lost her hold on hers too. They rained down on top of his.

"Looks like your cats and dogs are eating my pie." Ian chuckled, and they grinned at each other. For a moment, the years fell away, and they were teens again.

ASIA PRESSED her hand against her aching side as she wiped a tear from her lashes. She didn't know when she'd laughed so hard. Maybe not since she'd been here as a teen.

"Well, we can sort this out." Cinda knelt to divide the pieces back into their proper packs.

"Wait." Asia knelt beside her. "I think we should share these. I'd like some strawberries and pie for my cats and dogs. What do you think, Ian? The colors are similar."

"I think my stomach is ready for pie." Ian peered down. "Yeah, I'll see your cats and dogs and raise you some strawberries and pie."

Asia groaned. She and Cinda scooped up the squares and plopped them on the table. They spent the next twenty minutes laying out material and figuring out their pattern. Ian pretty much went along with whatever Cinda said.

"Think of it this way, Ian." Cinda waved a pie square under his nose. "When you put a plate of food in front of a customer, you have it laid out a certain way to be appealing. You don't just mash it all together. Right?"

"Nope. The customer does that when they put the top on the sandwich." Ian grinned as Cinda rolled her eyes.

"But you plate the food to be attractive. That's what we're doing here." She grabbed the pie cloth from him as he started to bite it. "Stop that."

Asia hiccupped a laugh.

Once they each finished arranging their quilt, Cinda showed them how to organize the pieces. They put right sides together and stacked them from the top down. She promised this would make it easier when they started sewing tomorrow.

Asia wasn't so sure. She'd never used a sewing machine before. How was she supposed to do this? Still, anything for Cinda. And for an excuse to not share her secret. Not yet.

"Let's go next door for some lunch." Ian rubbed his stomach. "All this hard work makes a man weak. I need food."

Cinda snorted. Asia grinned. She could eat, but even more, she wanted to get out of the quilt shop for a few minutes.

When they were seated at the restaurant, Meg took their order.

Asia inhaled the wonderful smells, mouth watering. No matter how hungry she was, though, she was grateful Cinda agreed to share a plate with her.

Cinda glanced at Ian as she twirled the ice in her diet soda. "I heard you're thinking about adding in a night of music. Or is that just a rumor?"

"Well, I know where that came from. I only mentioned it to one person." Ian shook his head. "I've thought about it, but I don't think it would draw a crowd. Even if I make room for a dance floor, who would come here when they can party at a place that serves alcohol?"

I would. Asia's mother used to go to bars. And Asia had to show up in the alleys in back of the bars, where the stench of alcohol and vomit almost made *her* sick. She shuddered.

She'd take coming to Ian's place any day.

"I don't agree. I think there are a number of families who would appreciate music or even dancing without worrying about some drunk ruining their evening." Cinda sat back as Meg slid the plates of food in front of them.

They were quiet as they ate. Oh man! It tasted as good as the first time she'd tried it. Ian was right. She could eat this food every day and not get tired of the taste.

Her mind drifted back to the idea of a music night at the restaurant. "You know, there are plenty of ways to market a fun music night when you don't have alcohol." Asia swallowed hard when Ian and Cinda both looked at her.

"There are ball teams or other groups that include kids who don't want to go to a place where there's drinking. You could market to them for starters. Families that want to get out for the night and do something different would want a safe place to take their kids. You could even have a game night. Maybe have a trivia night. Or put in a dartboard. Have board games and an area where people could sit and play--" Why were they still staring at her? She swallowed hard, not wanting to admit some of the ideas came from her mother's talk of what the bars she frequented offered.

"Asia, that's genius!" Cinda's face glowed as she took a bite of a chip. "There are a lot of church groups that would love a place like this to meet."

"I don't have any kid friendly food on my menu." Ian frowned. "It's a good idea, but I'm not sure it would work."

"A menu is easy to change." Asia bumped his arm with her shoulder. "Even for someone who doesn't like change. You could add a peanut butter and jelly sandwich. Or some macaroni and cheese. The kids would love these chips."

"And a kid-sized barbecue sandwich might work." Cinda cocked her head to the side. "Maybe one that's not quite as messy."

They all laughed.

Ian leaned back, the blond scruff on his face showing in the light. "Those are good ideas, but I have no idea how to market them. I have trouble with a simple flyer that we pass out at events around here."

"Same." Cinda nodded. "I'd love to put out some ads, but hiring someone is expensive, and I don't have the skills to make them myself. Tansie tried, but we both agreed that type of design isn't her strong point either."

Asia took a bite of sandwich and chewed slowly. Should she tell them? She wanted to, but if they ended up sending her away... Maybe she should wait a bit longer. If she was ever going to make her dream of having a design and marketing business happen, doing Ian's ads would be a start. Would he trust her with that? Maybe Cinda too?

She took another bite. She had no computer or program to work with. And no money to buy the equipment she needed. How could she ever go into business on the limited funds she would make at the quilt shop?

Ian nudged her. "You are thinking entirely too hard."

Meg stood beside them, looking at Asia. She smiled. "Would you like a refill of your drink?"

Asia's face burned. She must have been so lost in thought she hadn't heard Meg ask the first time. "Yes, thank you."

She listened as Cinda and Ian talked about ideas for their businesses.

Say something.

The inner nudge reminded her of the way Cinda jumped to give her both a job and a place to stay. How Ian had provided meals for her. Of course, neither of them knew her past. What she'd done. Where she'd been.

Still, she could help them out for as long as they accepted her assistance. Maybe one of them would have a computer she could borrow. There were some free programs that would work for making ads.

Meg returned to see if they wanted pie. Ian shook his head. He was foregoing dessert? Wow. With no leftovers, they handed Meg the empty bag menus.

Asia jumped in before she could stop herself. "Before we go, I'd like to mention something." This could go so wrong. What if they wanted to know where she'd studied? What if they asked questions she couldn't answer? Or wouldn't answer.

“What is it?” Ian settled back down beside her. The warmth of his response gave her the confidence she needed.

“Look, I don’t have a computer, but if one of you would loan me one, I could make some ads for you to use for your business.” The end of her statement came out in a rush. Did it even make sense?

Ian’s eyebrows rose.

Cinda leaned closer. “You know how to make ads and do marketing?”

“How?” Ian’s fingers thumped a rhythm on the table. “Forget that. I don’t *care* how. I have a computer you can use. It’s not real fancy but should work. Have you done this before?”

“I haven’t actually done design and marketing for a company yet, but I have a degree in it.” She cleared her throat. “A graphic design and marketing degree.”

“That is an excellent degree to have, Asia.” Martin’s nasal tone from behind her made her jump. Did he sneak up on everyone that way?

He sat down beside Cinda. “Tell me where you studied. I know all the best schools and can tell if you have a good education or not. I stay informed on the best colleges to help my students make the best choices. They all listen to me when I give advice.” Martin pursed his lips and nodded.

Man! She’d love to kick him under the table. Instead, she rubbed her suddenly moist palms on her jeans.

“So, where did you study, my dear?” Martin’s gaze slithered over her as he leaned close.

Yup, she was definitely going to kick him.

6

An ocean breeze ruffled Ian's hair as he crossed the parking lot to Cinda's shop late the next morning. No dragging his feet to get to the class this time.

Asia was there.

He drew in a long breath of salt-laden air, calming his rambling thoughts. He wanted to know everything about her. Especially if they still fit together.

Even though that wasn't a possibility.

She was like a mystery that needed unraveling. Cinda told him Asia didn't have a cell phone. Who in this day and age didn't carry one? Every woman he knew had a phone and spent hours a day taking pictures and posting to social media.

Then there was her knowledge of marketing and design. Why didn't she have a job in her field? When Martin hounded her about her school last night, Asia excused herself to the bathroom. To avoid the subject? Why? By the time she returned, Martin had moved on to enlightening them about the finer points of his teaching method. Ian shook his head as he reached for the doorknob.

Cinda, what do you see in him?

As quiet as the parking lot had been, the inside of the quilt shop was sheer pandemonium. Women chattered and oohed and aaahed over materials and quilts. Cinda bustled about, or bounced in typical Cinda fashion, helping customers decide on colors and patterns. He swallowed hard to stifle his gag reflex.

Six weeks stretched to an eternity.

In the corner near the classroom door, the two husbands who were taking the beginning class huddled together. They were trying to be nonchalant, but Ian recognized the hunch of their shoulders and the slight jerkiness to their motions. Yep, totally stressed.

He didn't see the one person he'd been waiting all morning to talk to. Asia. His stomach did the rollercoaster drop. Had she left town? Had Martin so intimidated her she didn't want to stay?

"Beginner class. Time to head to the classroom." Cinda clapped her hands, motioning to the open doorway. "We need to get started."

Most of the people in the shop followed her like little ducklings in a row. The two husbands got in line with their wives. A couple of women were at the register checking out their purchases with Tansie. She waved to Ian and pointed to the classroom with her thumb. He got the hint.

Where was Asia?

Sure, he'd managed the private lesson with just Cinda and Asia. He'd loved their company, especially Asia's. But the whole sewing concept? Not his thing. Yes, quilts keep you warm at night, but why not just buy one rather than spend hours putting tiny pieces of cloth together?

"Your starters are all laid out on the table by the south windows." Cinda gestured to a table piled with colored cloth. "They have your names on them in case you forgot the pattern. Grab your project and head for your machine. If you leave your quilt at your machines and gather around, I'll demonstrate how to sew the pieces together. For those who already know, feel free to get started."

Movement from the other side of the room caught Ian's attention. He glanced over--and couldn't stop the smile.

Asia. Now it was a good day.

She had leaned over to brush at her jeans. When she straightened, she met his gaze. Her expression softened, and her lips lifted at the corners.

A *very* good day.

She crossed the room to him. Her loose hair drifted over her shoulder in a shining mass. She leaned close, glancing toward where Cinda was engaged in animated conversation with one of their classmates. "Ready for torture session number two?"

"My fingers are cringing in anticipation of the contact with needles." He chuckled along with her soft laugh.

At the table, they found their projects side by side, only the colors were different. Good grief! He was noticing colors now.

They dropped off their quilt pieces by two of the vacant machines and then joined the semi-circle of students around Cinda.

Asia stood close enough for him to feel her warmth. He fought the urge to touch her. To take her hand.

"Today, we're going to sew your quilt top. If we have time, we will set up the backing and pin the binding in place. The sewing part is easy." Cinda picked up the top cloth and waved it in the air. She showed them how to pick up the pieces to keep them in order. "All of our seams will be one-quarter inch."

A dour man shoved his hands in his pockets. He appeared even less enthusiastic about the class than Ian. "How are we supposed to know where to sew? I didn't bring my measuring tape."

Cinda's lips pressed together as if she hid a laugh. "That is an excellent question. Let me show you how simple this is. Most of the machines are set up with a foot that will help. If they don't have the special quarter-inch foot, there's a marking in this silver needle plate to the right of the foot. If you keep to this first line, your seam will be a quarter inch. Very easy." She waited for them all to get a turn watching her sew.

Cinda sat in the chair, took two pieces of cloth, and demonstrated the sewing technique. The line of her stitching was straight enough to use for a ruler. Ian shook his head. He'd never be able to do that, not even with a straight edge to guide him.

Asia edged closer until her arm brushed against his. He'd hardly have to move at all to slip his arm around her...pull her close. There was a time he would have done that without thinking. Before he'd gone to college, and his true colors had manifested.

Like father, like son.

Cinda's voice cut through his thoughts. "Okay, I want you all to go to your machines and sew your pieces together to form the rows. Remember to keep them in order to maintain the pattern you've chosen. If you need help, raise your hand. Tansie will be in here if the shop is clear. She and I are both available to help."

The class dispersed. Some of the students strode to their machines. Ian noted the two husbands, he, and Asia moved slower. He approached his machine like St. George must have approached the dragon. So where was his sword to slay this beast? Seemed like this time the dragon had all the tiny daggers.

He dropped into the chair and leaned toward Asia. She grasped the edges of her own chair and grimaced at him. He held up his hands and inspected his fingers. "One last look at them whole and healthy."

Asia laughed, then slapped her hand over her mouth. Shook her head at him. "Did you write out your last will and testament before this class? I'm thinking it might be necessary in case you bleed to death." She bit her lower lip, tilted her head, and studied him.

He shook his focus from her lips. "I *should* have done that. My brain was in fear mode though. Maybe Cinda keeps pints of blood in that refrigerator. You know, in case someone needs a transfusion." He grinned and sat back in his chair--just in time to catch Cinda glowering at him from across the table.

When did she come up?

"Ian, stop bothering Asia, or I'll make you sit elsewhere." Cinda's hands fisted on her hips, but her lips twitched as she fought a smile.

"Do I have to wear a dunce hat too?" He twisted his face.

"You could quilt him a dunce hat." Asia snickered. Then started to laugh. Everyone who heard the exchange laughed. The two husbands were now relaxed in front of their machines.

"Okay, enough antics." Cinda came around to their side of the table and lifted the squares of cloth Ian needed to sew. "I'm beginning to think, Mr. Kittredge--" She tapped Ian on the back of his head. "--that having you take this class was *not* one of my better ideas."

"IAN. *IAN.*"

Asia closed her eyes as the cool of the sewing machine warmed against her temple. She tugged again at her scarf. Did he hear her whisper? She didn't want to alert anyone else to her problem. Not the class. Not Cinda. Not even Ian. But she needed help from someone.

Why me? Why do these things always happen to me?

"Ian." She tried again, a little louder. The hum of machines and the buzz of conversation probably drowned her out. Plus, if Ian looked at her, all he would see was her head leaning against her machine. He'd probably think he was hearing things.

She heard the scrape of a chair. Close by. *Please let him come help.*

Ian's face swam into view as he rounded her chair. He leaned down. "Need some help?"

"Yes. I don't know what to do."

"What's wrong? It can't be all that bad. Sit up and let's take a look. I think I'm getting the hang of this thing." He brushed a strand of hair back over her shoulder.

"I can't." Her face heated. Oh, this was ridiculous!

"Can't what?" His brow furrowed and he knelt next to her.

"Can't sit up."

"Why not?" His hand on her shoulder would have been nice in other circumstances. Right now, she wanted the floor to open up and swallow her whole. Not the machine though. She wanted to be far away from this demon device.

"My scarf. My hair." She closed her eyes. Swallowed. Met his gaze. "I sewed my scarf and my hair into the quilt pieces. I can't move."

His expression would have been comical any other time. His mouth dropped open. His gaze flew to the sewing machine needle. His mouth closed into a tight line, but his dimples told the truth.

The rat wanted to laugh.

"Stop it." She glared at him, or tried from her uncomfortable position. "I don't want everyone to know."

"Need some help?" Cinda's perky question made Asia groan. Now she was doomed. To total humiliation.

"I think Asia has a little problem." Ian's dimples deepened. "I'm not sure I know how to help."

Cinda's smile came into view. "Nothing is this bad, Asia. Sit up and let me look." Cinda patted her on the back like she was some second grader who messed up her homework.

"That's the problem." A low chuckle escaped as Ian looked up at Cinda. "She can't sit up." His grin spread wider as he explained what she'd done. Asia wanted to duct tape his mouth.

"Oh, my. That's new." Cinda pressed her fingertips to her mouth. "Okay, let me in here, Ian. I'll see what can be done. We can't have Asia walking around attached to a sewing machine for the rest of her life. Right?" They both chuckled.

Asia closed her eyes. They were trying hard not to laugh at her expense, but she *had* to look ridiculous. Who did something this stupid? She'd been so focused on keeping the seams straight, she'd caught her scarf underneath the fabric and hadn't noticed the strands of hair mixed in. Not until the momentum tugged her downward and she couldn't see anything.

"Asia, I'm going to lift the foot and pull the squares out to clip the thread. Then we'll talk about how to separate you from your work." Cinda grinned when Ian snorted.

In no time at all, she was free. Asia sat up as Cinda released the fabric and thread. Colorful squares connected by strands of thread trailed down one side of Asia's hair like some strange 60s accessory.

"Okay, class." Cinda clapped her hands, and everyone stopped sewing to look their way.

Could this get any worse? Asia checked to see if there might be a crack in the floor that would open. Nothing. Nada. No help there.

"I haven't mentioned one of the essential tools you will learn to use. Maybe you could all gather around, and we'll talk about the seam ripper or unpicker." The eight people around the tables stood and gathered close. Tansie joined them, her hand over her mouth as she noted Asia's hair.

"When you make a mistake, and all of you will, you'll need to take out the seam and start over. One of the tips I usually give, and forgot this time, is to pull your hair back in a clip or a band instead of having long hair hang free. If you are wearing a scarf, make sure it is out of the way or remove it. You'll see why when you notice what happened with Asia." Cinda patted her shoulder and urged her to stand.

"Asia was kind enough to demonstrate what can go wrong with long hair. Or a filmy scarf. Or anything that hangs down and can get in the way of your sewing without you noticing."

A few of the ladies gasped when they noticed the quilt pieces in Asia's hair. One of the husbands laughed out loud and patted his bald head.

"This is an unpicker." Cinda held up a wicked looking tool with a two-pronged end, one a sharp point and the other a point with a little red ball on it. Between the two was a dip with a sharp edge.

"This tool will make taking out seams pretty easy, and there are several ways to use it. How you use it will depend on what you're ripping out. In this instance, we want to take out the seam without cutting Asia's hair." Cinda slid that sharp tool way too close to Asia's face, snipping threads and dangling pieces of cloth. The worst fashion statement ever.

Cinda lifted a square, turning it so everyone could see what she'd done as she explained the technique. Asia leaned forward as her hair was tugged one way and then another. Total humiliation.

Cinda grinned at her. "Sorry. I want to make sure they understand."

Asia's face was hot enough to combust. Ian moved behind her and squeezed her shoulders. His support warmed her.

Cinda went on to explain the different ways to extract the seam and then the best one to do in this case and save Asia's hair in the process. When Asia was free, the whole class applauded.

By the time class ended, Asia had recovered her dignity. Sort of. Cinda helped her get back on track. She even provided a hair scrunchie. Asia remove her scarf, just to be safe.

Cinda reminded them they could come in on Mondays to work on their projects, but it wouldn't be an actual class time. They also had the option to take their work home if they felt comfortable enough to do so.

Asia smirked at Ian. "Are you taking your quilt home to work on?"

Eyes wide, he slapped his hand to his chest and choked on a cough. "Since you're moving into the shop apartment this weekend, you can spend all night sewing and making hundreds of quilts." He grinned at her.

"Like that's happening." Asia's stomach grumbled, and she pressed her hand to her middle.

Cinda came over. "Asia, I'd like to go to lunch with you and Ian and finish what we were discussing last night, but I have to clean up." She lifted on to her toes, her hands clasped in front of her. "Maybe we could order something, bring the food here, and plan while we eat. I'm excited about the ads and social media."

Thank You, God! Maybe eating here and talking would keep Martin from finding them. Asia didn't think she could stomach another meal with that man.

"Sounds good. If you want food from my place, I'll call it in and bring it here for us." Ian pulled out his phone.

"Okay. I'll help Cinda clean up in here while you get the food." Asia grabbed a trashcan and began to pick up scraps and pieces of thread.

By the time Ian returned with lunch, they had finished. He brought food for Tansie, too, but she took hers out front so she could watch for customers.

Asia explained some of her ideas and listened to what they needed. Inside she bounced like Cinda, but outside she focused to breathe, eat, and talk while ideas spun circles in her head.

"Well, this is cozy."

Glenna stood inside the door, hands fisted on her hips. She glared at Asia. "I thought I made it clear you should leave town."

A burn crept along Asia's nerves. Seriously? What made Glenna, or anyone for that matter, think she could tell Asia what to do? And what gave her the right to spew hatred at her? She'd never done anything to Glenna. Not ever!

She opened her mouth to tell Glenna so, but Cinda beat her to it.

"Glenna, I invited Asia here. She has some great ideas for helping Ian and me with our businesses. You should join us and listen in." Cinda wiped sauce from her hands as she spoke, jumped up, and pulled another chair over.

"I don't want to listen to anything except why she's really here. Because, mark my words, she has an agenda." Glenna stalked closer. "What is it, Asia?"

"Glenna." Cinda slammed her hand on the table beside her. "Lay off. She's our cousin."

Asia came to her feet.

So. It was time. She drew a breath, then looked into Glenna's icy green eyes. "I came to see your father."

7

"WHAT DO you mean you came here to see my father?" Glenna's eyes narrowed to pale green slits. Her hands curled into fists as she leaned close.

Her cloying perfume almost made Asia gag, but she refused to retreat.

"My father doesn't want to see you. Understand?" Glenna's lips thinned to a line.

"Glenna." Cinda stood and took a step toward her sister, one hand outstretched, the other touching Asia's arm. "Please. Sit down and let's talk about this."

Ian joined them, his hand resting on Asia's shoulder.

"I don't need to talk about anything." Glenna turned her glare on Cinda, and Asia almost stepped between them. "Did you know she wanted to see Dad?"

"Yes. She told me." Cinda shot a glance at Asia. "I told her his condition and that I would talk to you."

"The answer is no." Glenna swung back to face Asia. "You can't see him. Just leave. Go back to where you came from."

"Glenna!" Cinda raised her chin as she snapped her sister's name. "There is no reason to be rude."

"I have *plenty* of reasons." Glenna's nostrils flared. "Plenty of them."

What could she say to convince them without saying the whole truth? She wanted to talk to Walter first. What if her mom lied... again? What if she wanted family so much she believed a lie?

She squeezed Cinda's arm to thank her for coming to her rescue. "I know you don't think seeing him is a good idea, but I need some answers." Asia wanted to blurt out what she hoped was the truth, that Glenna's father was *her* father. But with Glenna so angry already, what would happen when she heard that?

What could she say to convince the sisters to let her visit their dad? Maybe her dad?

"Maybe you could talk with his doctor." Ian's calm voice settled over Asia. "Or the nurse at the home where he's living. They know his situation and might be able to offer a suggestion."

Asia glanced at Ian. He closed his eyes, his chin lowered. Was he praying? Wishing he was anywhere but here? Asia couldn't blame him. Right now, she wished *she* was somewhere else.

Everywhere she went, people wanted to say what she could and couldn't do. Freedom had always been a joke for her. She'd gotten a glimpse of what it might be like in the last couple of days, but that was an illusion.

She did have the hope of a business she could build, but first, she had to settle the issue of her parentage. If Cinda and Glenna wouldn't give her permission, she would find a way to see Walter Bryant.

She had to.

Asia met Glenna's glare. "I'll give you time to consult with the doctor or nurse, if you want."

Cinda's breath whooshed out.

Glenna didn't relax. "No matter what they say, I won't let you see him. His health is too fragile." She glanced away.

Wait. Was that...could that have been the glint of tears in her eyes? So she wasn't a complete ice queen. Had Ian been right? Was her anger about another hurt in her life, and Asia simply a convenient target?

Glenna fixed her sister with a look. "I need to talk with you. I'll be back later when we can speak freely." She spun and marched toward the door, the click of her shoes loud in the silence.

When the front door of the shop shut with a decisive slam, Tansie peeked around the doorway, her eyes like saucers. "Are you okay in here?"

"We're fine." Cinda rolled her shoulders. "I'm sorry you had to hear that Tansie. Can you shut the door, please?"

Cinda headed for the coffee machine. "Anyone else need some coffee or tea after that?" The comforting hiss of hot water and the scent of roasted coffee soon filled the air.

Asia sank back into her chair. This might not compare to what soldiers faced, but she could almost understand the term battle weary. A verbal battle. She certainly understood verbal scars. So did Ian. Why couldn't life be easy?

They were quiet for a few minutes as they sipped coffee. Asia appreciated the silence so she could think. She did *not* want to alienate Cinda or Glenna. If they were her family, she wanted them to love her. She wanted to love them. To have the relationship she'd only dreamed of having. To spend time together. To have meals together. To share recipes…or whatever family did.

Yet, if she pushed ahead, all that might vanish as a possibility. What if she saw Walter and something horrible happened? Could she live with that? Knowing she'd been the cause of more hurt to some of the only people to ever show her kindness. Her shoulders sagged under the weight of her choices. Her mind spun with possibilities and disasters.

"Cinda." Ian slapped his palm against his pant leg, and Asia and Cinda both jumped. "Can you take a couple hours off? Why don't we go down to the beach? Like we used to do when we were kids?"

Cinda's face lit up for a moment, then fell. "I can't. My mystery block class is coming in at three. I have to be here to teach. Tansie can't manage the class and the shop."

Asia shook her head. "I would love to do that, but I can't go either. I promised to help Cinda, so I need to be here."

Ian nodded. "What about after closing? Oh…never mind. By then it will be busy at the restaurant. I won't have time."

"Tell you what." Cinda rose and went to rinse out her cup. "It's only one-thirty. Why don't you take Asia for a quick trip to the beach? She hasn't been there in years."

She held up her hand as Asia started to protest. "I can get ready for the class. If you're back here by two-forty-five, you can pass out materials and help with anything else I need. Will that work?"

"We'll take it." Ian jumped up, grabbed their mugs, and took them to the sink. "I'll let Meg know, grab my truck keys, and be ready in three minutes. Does that work for you?" He stopped beside Asia. Those deadly dimples flashed. His gaze warmed the cold places in her heart, and she nodded.

Yes, that worked for her. Big time.

Five minutes later she was buckled up in the cab of Ian's pickup as they traveled the streets of Driftwood Cove. So much had changed, but there were also many places she recognized from years ago.

"What happened to the little ice cream stand we used to go to?" She stared out at a run-down pizza place. The one where she first met Ian....

"They've moved out near the mall. They still have the best ice cream. All they're missing is the pie to go with it." Ian grinned at her as she rolled her eyes.

Outside of town, near the bluff overlooking the Pacific, Ian turned onto a dirt road she remembered well. Of course, then they'd ridden their bicycles here. She'd loved riding down to the beach. Going back home, she'd had to push the bicycle up the steep hill. Not so much fun, but worth the trip.

A few wildflowers poked up around the chaparral on the hillsides. The yellow and purple added a beautiful touch. God's handiwork. If only He found her worthy enough to help. She would have to try harder.

They turned a curve in the road. Ahead, the ocean stretched to the horizon, a few rocks sticking up offshore farther down the beach. Oh, good. The cove was deserted. She could hardly wait to climb out of the truck, take off her shoes, and let the waves wash over her toes. That had been her absolute delight to do when she was here last.

She hadn't seen the ocean since.

"Ready to get your feet wet?" Ian shut off the truck and pocketed the keys. He reached over to squeeze her hand before climbing from the cab and coming around to open her door.

They walked onto the sand. She'd forgotten the tickling sensation of the tide pulling the sand from under her feet as the water receded. She laughed. She trotted along the hard line of wet sand, stopping to let the waves wash up almost to her calves.

Laughter escaped her again.

"I remember you doing this over and over that last summer you were here." Ian caught her hand in his. "You gave me new insight into the wonders of the ocean, something I'd come to take for granted. You gave me new insight on a lot of things. Mostly on life."

He put her hand to his chest, and the rapid thud of his heart hit against her palm.

~

STANDING HERE with Asia touching him, looking up into his eyes. The trust. The longing… Memories swamped him. He cleared his throat. He'd better say something before he did something stupid —like pull her in for a kiss. Bad idea. Very bad idea. He. Could. Not. Be trusted with a woman.

Like father, like son.

"Shall we walk down to the tide pool? I remember you loved the anemones."

“I forgot.” Her face lit with a smile. “I hope there are starfish too. Let’s go.” She turned and tugged his hand as if he might be left behind. No way. He might not be able to have a relationship with her, but he would cherish every moment of this time with her.

While Asia climbed the rocks to the tide pool, Ian set an alarm on his phone so they’d be sure to leave when they needed to. It was too easy to lose track of time out here.

“Look, a sea hare.” Asia scooped up the giant slug and brought it close to her face. The hare’s tentacles with the bulbous points waved. Asia returned it to the water and moved to a different spot. “Ooohhh! Star fish.” She bent close to the water, totally absorbed in the gentle motion of the sea creatures.

This was the Asia he’d fallen in love with years ago. The one who delighted in the new and unique. The one who taught him to see life through a lens of wonder instead of the lens of despair. The one who helped him hear more than the angry voice of his father echoing in his head.

Now he had a Father’s voice that didn’t scream hatred, but whispered love.

“Ian, have you seen the color on these anemones? The green and pink are amazing. Cinda should make a quilt with these colors.” Asia smiled up at him, and his heart stuttered. How he’d missed her. With a soul deep ache he hadn’t realized had been there until now.

He dropped to his knees beside her, ignoring the damp seeping into his jeans. They would dry. If he was damp when he went to work, no one around here would think anything of it.

“It’s like they’re dancing.” Asia spoke in a whisper, fumbling for his hand. The awe in her tone drew him in, and he wanted this moment to last for eternity.

No. No. No.

He jerked his focus from Asia and stared down at the pool. One of the starfish slithered to the side, its arms elongating to pull in the direction it wanted to go. The rippling water strengthened the orangish-yellow to an almost surreal color.

Starfish. Anemone. Sea hare. Think about those, not Asia.

He closed his eyes and breathed out slowly. Cinda must be rubbing off on him if he was using her method of calming breaths to bring his thoughts under control.

"Why do you want to see Walter so much?" Ian moved to the dry rocks and sat down. Maybe she would explain some of the mystery of her past while they were alone.

She shrugged. Poked her finger in the water to touch the starfish. Didn't look at him. "My mom died. I don't have any family, and I have some questions for him."

He gentled his voice. "He's not able to answer questions. The Alzheimer's keeps him from carrying on a conversation." Emotion played tug-of-war with his stomach. He wanted to be supportive of Cinda, but he also understood Asia's desire to connect with family. With her uncle. What would he give to have family? Family worth mentioning.

"I've heard they live in the past. Maybe the past he remembers will tell me what I need to know." Asia crossed to sit on the dryer rocks on the far side of the pool, facing him. She tapped the bottoms of her feet in the water. Little droplets danced in the air.

"Your mother didn't mention other family? Not at all?"

"No." Asia pulled the scrunchie from her hair, ran her fingers through it, and started to braid. "She had Kim, her friend, but no family. She had men." She wound the hair tie around the end of her braid. "Lots of men."

Her movements became jerky. He'd heard rumors about her mother when they were teens. But now...now he understood that so often, when a woman lived that lifestyle, the beautiful daughter was at the mercy of the scum who chased after the mother. He shuddered at the thought.

They'd both been damaged by their childhoods.

"Can you tell me why you have nothing? Not even a cell phone? Or clothes?" He kept his tone low and even. He had a feeling she needed to talk, needed a friend.

Needed a fresh start.

When she looked up and met his gaze, the hollows in her cheeks spoke volumes. The pain in her life, the pain she must have experienced, shone through. "I can't talk about it. I'm sorry." She swiped at her eyes. "Maybe someday, but not today."

Silence stretched as they watched the starfish climb above the water line. The tiny fibers on its legs moved like a millipede's legs. Or seemed to from this vantage point.

"What about you? How did you escape?"

In other words, why had he come back? Wasn't that the real question? If he'd escaped the horror of his childhood, why would he want to return to the scene of the crime, so to speak.

"After you were here, I worked hard at school." He picked up some pebbles and lobbed them one at a time into the water beyond the pool. "I guess I could feel you there encouraging me to do better and become the best me possible."

She huffed a laugh. "I did used to say that, didn't I?"

"You did." He chuckled. "I had a teacher my junior year who encouraged me to go to college. We picked out a major and put in applications. Because my grades improved, I landed a scholarship. I now have a worthless degree in history, but I also figured out I had a talent for cooking."

"Do you ever think about your mom? Or dad?" Her question danced on the breeze, and he almost missed hearing it. But he did, and his chest tried to collapse.

Did he think of his parents? Of the day when his whole life imploded? *Like father, like son.* His father's dying words, spoken only for his ears as his mother's body lay in a broken heap on the kitchen floor.

Of course he thought of them. Every time he stepped in a kitchen.

"Yes. I can't escape." He blinked against the burn in his eyes.

"I'm sorry. I shouldn't have asked." She sniffed. "I hoped maybe the past would fade away. Maybe not to the point of nonexistence but at least to the point of mild discomfort." She reached into the water to run her fingertip along the side of the sea hare.

His phone began to chirp. "Time to head back." He swung his feet around and stood. Offered her his hand, which she took as she navigated out of the pool.

They walked in silence back to their shoes and then on to the truck. The ocean waves continued to lap at the beach. Coming in to deposit detritus and sucking some back into the depths.

She fidgeted on the way back to town, her hands never still. What could he say to put her at ease? Was she nervous about helping Cinda? Had their talk and his admission stressed her or reminded her of something in her past? He couldn't think of a thing to say. Gone were the days when they could talk for hours. Would they be able to resurrect that relationship?

Did he even want to?

There were several cars in front of the quilt shop, probably early class participants arriving. Asia urged him to park in his spot at the restaurant and she would walk back.

He turned off the truck, climbed out, and went around to open her door. She turned in the seat but didn't get down, not even when he took her hand. She studied the ground, her teeth nibbling at her lower lip, a very distracting movement.

"Ian, I..." She glanced up at him. Looked back down. Drew in a deep breath, breathed out. Met his gaze. "I think Walter is my father."

8

IAN PASSED the evening at work in robotic mode. After Asia dropped her bombshell, she'd teared up, jumped from his truck, and jogged to the quilt shop. As for him…

He'd been unable to put a coherent thought together since then. He'd come to his office to work. Not that he'd gotten much done.

He'd updated his bookkeeping but would probably have to check the figures again later. The last thing he needed was to have his accounts in arrears because of some thoughtless mistake.

Walter. Asia's father.

Ian and Asia had long talks about her father when they were teens. She wanted to know him, but her mother claimed he'd died. Or she said he left them. Asia figured her mother didn't know who her father was.

Ian's heart had been heavy when he heard that, but now it felt like a boulder in his chest. How could he face Cinda with this bit of news? She could always tell when something was wrong with him.

This could tear their family apart.

How had Asia discovered this? If her mother hadn't remembered or known, what new piece of information had been discovered? He groaned and dropped his head against his palms. He had to do something other than work on the computer or he would go crazy. Crazier.

A soft knock on his office door had him looking up. Meg peeked inside. "Boss, you're never going to believe who's here." Her wide grin faded. "You okay? Something wrong?"

"I'm fine." He pushed back from the desk and stood. "Something came up that I'm sorting through. Who's here?"

She slipped inside. "They don't know you're here, so if you don't want to socialize, stay in here."

"Who's here? Must be someone important. I don't mind socializing." He didn't want to admit the distraction would be nice. He needed to get away from his morbid thoughts.

"Harold and Vanna Nevins."

"The head of the Chamber of Commerce? He's here?" Thank goodness he'd been out of sight when he received the news. After his parents died, the man had told him to leave town and never show up again. He hadn't been welcoming when Ian returned. What was it he'd said? Oh, yes. "Bad eggs breed bad eggs."

So why were Harold and his wife visiting I-BBQ?

"I'll be out in a few minutes. Thanks, Meg."

She nodded and left, pulling the door shut behind her. Ian sank back down in his chair, folded his hands, and prayed to let bygones be bygones. The man may have been mean to a hurting teenager, but he probably had reason. Ian hadn't been a decent person back then, and Harold had been a father with a daughter drawn to bad boys.

When he stepped out of his office, the scent of barbecue sizzled in the air. The hiss of cooking meat underlay the buzz of conversation and the bustle of waitresses with the dinner hour in full swing. For once, his restaurant was full almost to capacity. He hadn't realized they'd filled up so much while he was in his office whining to himself. He should have been out here working or greeting guests.

He strode into the main dining room and made his way around to all the tables, greeting the diners and asking about their meals. He usually enjoyed this part of his ritual, but today he had too much on his mind. Plus the flutter in his gut at the thought of speaking with Harold kept him on edge.

Harold, Mr. President of the Driftwood Cove Chamber, was seated in the overflow room near the fireplace at the back. The seating there was cozy. Harold and his wife were staring at their phones.

Ian started at one side of the room, stopping at each table. No point making Harold think he was being singled out because he was important. Ian smiled and spoke to an older couple, then frowned. They were members of the Chamber, too. He looked around. More members of the Chamber were in the room. Some he knew, some he'd only seen around. He chatted with each of them, doing his best to put them at ease and make sure they were enjoying their dining experience.

"Mr. Nevins. Mrs. Nevins. Good to see you." Ian stopped by the table and waited for the couple to disengage from their devices. Why would you go out to eat with someone and not talk or interact in any way?

"Ian." Harold held out his beefy paw to shake hands. "I've heard about the barbecue here, and we decided to try it out tonight. You have a simple menu and a different presentation."

"I do." Ian forced a smile. "I may be adding to the menu soon. I'm talking with some people who are helping me develop a business plan." It was true. He, Asia, and Cinda had certainly discussed the ideas enough in the last couple of days.

"You need to add something to drink that's more interesting than iced tea." Harold picked up the paper bag and studied the print. "When people go out in the evening, they want something with a little kick to keep them awake." Harold winked at Ian.

"If you're thinking along the lines of alcoholic drinks, those won't be served here. This will be a family establishment with plenty of good food." Though he made sure his tone was friendly, Ian's neck muscles tightened. Not many people stood up to Harold Nevins. If he said jump, folks in this town would leap the Grand Canyon.

Harold frowned. "Just because your daddy couldn't handle his liquor doesn't mean others can't." His loud voice carried across the room, hushing conversations.

Stay calm, Ian. "My father has nothing to do with this. It's my decision. If you'll excuse me." Ian backed up a step. He had to get away from this man before he said something he shouldn't.

"Your daddy was dead drunk when he beat your mama to death. When he beat you within an inch of your life. If you can't handle alcohol, maybe you're just like him. Who are you going to beat to death?" Harold shook his finger at Ian.

Ian shoved his hands in his pockets, swiveled around, and strode from the room.

His stomach churned. Sweat broke out on his forehead. His jaw ached, and he tried to relax his muscles. Couldn't even remember how to breathe.

Meg's eyes were huge as she stood near the massive grill, tray in hand. The restaurant had quieted, only low murmurs to be heard. He had to leave.

Now.

He could feel the gazes on his back as he strode out the door and turned toward his truck parked to the side of the restaurant. But he stopped. He couldn't drive. Every muscle in his body was stretched taut enough to explode. He couldn't trust himself behind the wheel.

Skirting the yarn shop, he rounded the building. Across the alley was a break in the fence that surrounded a small park. He turned sideways to get through without snagging his clothes and went deep into the trees at the back of the park.

His vision darkened. He wound around some bushes to what, over the years, had become his private spot. He sank to the ground as memories flooded him. The pain. The horror. The agony, both physical and mental. His father, beating his mother again. His futile attempt to save her. He'd tried. As best a young teenage boy could.

It hadn't been enough.

More memories assaulted him, but these were from college--

No. He couldn't bear to revisit that horror.

Now, just when his life had taken a turn for the better, would he lose everything? People would be reminded of his past, something most never acknowledged. Would this be the end of his restaurant? His good name? He could only imagine Harold carrying on, telling everyone in the restaurant what his father had done and how the son would follow in those steps. Who would want to be around him then?

He reined in his penchant for negativity. People knew. They accepted him. Right?

"God, I know you said there would be trials, but why this? Why now?" He drew up his knees and rested his forehead there. Asia asked earlier why he'd come back here. Right now, he wondered the same thing. Why hadn't he started over in another town, a place where no one knew him or his history? Why here, when this town held almost every bad memory he'd lived through?

No, he chose to return to Driftwood Cove. But he couldn't tell Asia why. Not when what drew him back here was the hope that she would someday return.

~

WHAT HAD SHE BEEN *THINKING?* How could she have blurted out that truth to Ian without even asking him to keep it to himself and not talk to Cinda? He had one of those faces that let everyone know he had a secret. And this one was a whopper.

Asia ran the noisy vacuum in the deserted classroom, watching the machine suck up tiny bits of cloth and thread. The mindless job gave her time to think. To plan. Except she couldn't think of a plan that would have all of them coming together as a happy family. And now she was on a shortened timeline. Because Ian would let the truth slip.

She had to do it first.

She shut off the vacuum and wheeled it to the closet. The classroom was ready for tomorrow, if Cinda had a class on Saturday. She didn't think so, but some women liked to come in and sew at the shop. Cinda said she always encouraged that because they also bought their material and notions from her. They all benefited from being a community.

"Asia." Cinda stepped through the door. "I've closed the shop. The last customer just left. Instead of going home for dinner, would you be okay with going to I-BBQ again? I know you've eaten there a lot. Something happened. Meg called. We're going to support Ian."

"What happened?" Asia grabbed her backpack from under a counter and hurried to the front of the shop. "Is Ian okay?"

"Evidently one of the town bigwigs stopped by with his wife. They were at a table when Ian stopped to talk. Harold's voice carries, and he said things that were hurtful. Some of the customers left. Not many, but some. It was the dinner rush or the start of it."

"What could he have said?" No one could have anything negative to say about the restaurant. "The restaurant and everyone there is amazing. What's to criticize?"

Cinda straightened an already perfectly aligned stack of quilting magazines. "I think the comment was directed at Ian, not the restaurant. Meg didn't say for sure."

"Where's Ian now?"

Tansie finished counting the register and closed it up. Her usual smile was gone, a worried frown creasing her brow. This must be serious.

"Meg said he disappeared for a while but is back now. He's in his office instead of talking with customers or helping in the kitchen as he usually does." Cinda snagged her purse, fluffed her hair, and headed for the door. "I called Martin. He's going to join us. Ready?"

Asia pasted on a smile and nodded. Not Martin again. At least she wouldn't have to worry about what to say. He wouldn't give her a chance to talk at all.

When they stepped through the front door of I-BBQ, the normal restaurant cacophony was absent. The front room wasn't packed, but fairly full, with only a few vacant tables.

Meg motioned them into the back room, where she had a table set up. Asia followed Cinda and Tansie through the doorway. Meg spoke in a low voice to tell them what the Chamber president said to Ian. Her cheeks flushed, and anger sparked in her eyes as she talked.

"I don't know where Ian went, but when he came back, he didn't talk to anyone. Went straight to his office and has been there ever since. The door is locked, and he won't answer. I'm hoping one of you can talk to him." Meg glanced in the direction of the office, as if hoping the door would spring open and a smiling Ian would come out.

"I'll go." Asia took a step in that direction. "Do you have a key? Should I just knock?" She would do what she could to show him the love he needed. To be his friend. And yes...she'd ask him not to say anything to Cinda or Glenna--

Oh! That was terrible! How could she be so selfish? How could she be thinking about her own worries? That man, Mr. Nevins, had hit Ian with the pain of his past. A low blow if there ever was one. Her throat ached. She pushed her concerns away and focused on the best way to talk to Ian.

Cinda glanced around. "What did Nevins do when Ian left?"

Meg grimaced. "I was so angry. I may have made a mistake. Sometimes I speak without thinking first." Most of the tables in the back room were empty. Asia didn't recognize any of the people, but Cinda nodded at a few before turning her attention back to Meg.

"I'm sure you did the right thing." Cinda patted Meg's arm. "You're one of Ian's staunchest supporters. What did you say?"

"He wanted to order. Beckoned me over. He was so condescending and not at all remorseful about dragging Ian through the mud." Meg swiped away a tear. "I told him we didn't need his business and to go find somewhere to eat that catered to venomous creatures like him." She hesitated. "I may have said that loud enough to carry through the restaurant. It was pretty quiet at that point."

Cinda snorted. Then started to laugh. Asia grinned. She knew Meg had spunk but had no idea the woman would let someone have it like that.

"Way to go, Meg!" Cinda pulled out a tissue and blotted at her eyes. Tansie pushed a hand against her chest as if she couldn't get her breath because she was laughing so hard. Meg finally relaxed and grinned.

"Meg, we have some others joining us. We'll order drinks but wait until they get here to order food. Set aside a pie and ice cream for us for after the meal. We're going to celebrate, and you are going to join us." She turned to Asia. "Talk to him. We'll see that the restaurant fills up tonight. But if anyone can bring him out of this, you can. He still sees you as that teenage girl he had feelings for."

Asia nodded and strode toward the office door. Her soft knock went unanswered. She tried the knob. Locked. She rapped a little harder. Waited.

The office door was in a corner of the back room, near the hallway leading to the restrooms. She didn't want to make a scene, but she needed Ian to answer the door. She knocked louder. A few heads turned at the sound.

"Ian. It's Asia. Can we talk?" She held her breath and listened for any sound. Memories pressed in on her, those days in his teens when he turned to alcohol to cover the pain. Surely he'd gotten past that...

She rested her forehead against the door. That last summer she visited, Ian had finally opened up to her one night, telling her the whole ordeal with his father. The night his mother died, and he had almost died. He bared his soul that day, and she doubted he'd done so for any other person. The revelation had been too painful. She could almost hear him thinking about his father's last words.

The lock clicked. The doorknob turned, but the door didn't swing open. An invitation. She tried to pray. All she could come up with was *Jesus, help*. She pushed the door open, glanced back at Cinda, who had her hands together in a gesture of prayer, and walked into the office.

Ian looked like he'd been run over by a steamroller. One that had backed up and run over him again. She closed the door, making sure it latched. She crossed the room to where he stood by the desk and wrapped her arms around him.

He stiffened. Shuddered. Blew out a breath--and deflated against her. His arms came around her in a hold so tight she had to sip air. His head pressed against hers. He shuddered again, just holding on to her, not speaking.

Just as they'd done so often that summer long ago.

He would hit a slump. Come looking for her. He had no words to express his hurt or grief, so she would hold him until he reached a point where he could talk.

That must be what he needed tonight. A friend to love him unconditionally. He had God, but right now he needed someone in the flesh. Someone who cared. Someone who knew his past and loved him anyway.

Loved like a sister, right? Because this could never be more. Ian wanted to fit in with Driftwood Cove. Wasn't that why he came back? He didn't need to be saddled with someone who'd been incarcerated and would tarnish any reputation he'd been building.

He had her for a friend. And that's all she'd ever be to him.

9

IAN TEETERED on the edge of an abyss. He could let the darkness below swallow him up or walk away. Since he'd returned to the restaurant from the park, he'd taken minuscule steps toward the gaping hole. The bottomless pit. His father's hateful words bounced around his skull like a prophesy of doom. Was there any way to escape his fate? He tried to pray but couldn't feel God's presence.

Nevins had struck home. Reminded him of the fragility of his place here. What had he been thinking? That his past would be forgotten. No, he'd never fit in. Maybe with a few people like Cinda. But his being here...her being his friend...could hurt her.

When Asia knocked on the door and called out to him, his heart and mind leapt toward her. He'd been dying of thirst, and she offered sweet relief. She knew him. At least, she knew the real him of years ago. She would be the only one to understand. That she'd shown up at this critical time in his life didn't escape him. This was a God moment. God orchestrated. Because He knew Ian would need her.

He trudged to the door. Flipped the lock. Couldn't make himself swing it open but went back to lean against the front of the desk. It felt like his heart had been ripped open, leaving him vulnerable to every dart the enemy might choose to sling.

She stepped in. Closed the door and leaned back, studying him. He could see the understanding in the nod of her head. She crossed the room, put her arms around him, and rested her forehead against his chest. Stood there. Not speaking. Simply offering herself. The one thing he needed most at the moment.

His throat tightened to the point of pain. He shuddered, fighting for the strength to continue to stand, grateful for the solid support of the desk. Otherwise, he would have tumbled to the ground, taking her with him. He wrapped his arms around her, reveling in the feel of her hair against his cheek and the soft scent of her shampoo.

He had no idea how long they stood there. He knew she prayed for him. He could feel peace flowing in, pushing away the darkness. He walked away from the abyss. From the darkness.

From the idea he was like his father.

"Thank you." He kissed the top of her head. Wished he could do more, but just loosened his hold so she could step back.

Tears moistened her cheeks. Her mossy green eyes glistened like a forest in the rain. His heart cracked at the sight of her. She'd rescued him again. And in that moment, it hit him.

He would never love another woman. Not like this.

"Are you okay?" Her long hair, loose about her shoulders, glinted in the light. "Never mind. Of course, you aren't okay." She sighed and scrubbed at her cheeks. "Let me try again. What can I do to help? I'm so sorry that pompous south-end-of-a-horse-headed-north said that to you."

Ian couldn't help laughing. "I haven't heard that phrase in years. Walter used to say that, didn't he?"

"Not often." She grinned. "But when he was really aggravated with someone, that's what slipped out. I never forgot."

He nodded. Cupped her cheek. He had to touch her.

"Is the south-end still out there? I didn't look when I came back." He let his hand drop to his side. She would understand that he didn't have the strength to look when he came back. He did know people had left because there wasn't the usual noise.

"I believe he's long gone. And he won't return." Asia chuckled as she repeated what Meg said to the man.

Ian shook his head. He shouldn't doubt his friends. He might not have many, but the ones he had were there for him. He wasn't alone.

"What are you doing here?" Ian hadn't expected her. The quilt shop would be closed by now, and Cinda usually went out with Martin on Friday nights. He figured Asia would go with them or stay at the house by herself.

"We're here to eat." Her mouth twisted in a cross between a smile and a grimace. "I'm getting seriously interested in updating your menu. If you're okay with it, I'll get together with you and Meg and talk about some new items."

"Such as?" He crossed his arms over his chest. His menu was pretty perfect.

Asia mimicked his stance. "Salads. You can put a couple of salads on the menu. People can add meat to the salad as an option, but there are a lot of people who would love to have a salad instead of a heavy meat meal. You could attract some vegetarians that way."

"Vegetarians?" Ian slapped his palm to his chest, trying for a look of horror. "In a barbecue restaurant?"

"I know. Perish the thought." She put her hands on her hips. "But think of all those people who might want to come here, but their better half won't eat anything on the menu. Salads would be a good addition." She tilted her head and raised her eyebrows. "You know I'm right."

He frowned. Stared at the ceiling. He couldn't give in too fast, even though he knew she spoke truth. "Okay. We'll talk to Meg about the salad idea. She's been hounding me on that front too. What else?"

He was stalling. He didn't want to talk menu, but he also didn't want to have to walk out that door and face any whispers or looks from customers. He wasn't quite ready to see the mostly empty rooms he'd been picturing.

"One more thing and then we're going out there for some dinner. Right?" Asia dipped her head.

He nodded. The look of satisfaction on her face made him want to pull her in for a hug. Maybe for more. He gripped the edge of the desk to keep from acting on the urge. She wasn't ready.

"We mentioned a kid's menu but need to firm that up." She held up one hand when he started to speak. "This is pretty simple. Add some mac n' cheese or a grilled cheese sandwich. Maybe even peanut butter and jelly. Those are very simple options for kids. The barbecue might be too messy for them, but the other items are simple and easy to fix. Some adults would enjoy the grilled cheese too."

"Those vegetarians?" He gave a mock shudder.

"Yes, the vegetarians." She rolled her eyes.

“You are a hard taskmaster.” He tugged a strand of her hair. “I’ll consider it. Those are a lot of changes.”

“Oh, we haven’t even started.” Her eyes narrowed as she grinned. “I haven’t mentioned the gluten-free crowd or vegans.”

“No.” He put his hands over his ears. “You’re going to ruin my establishment.” He couldn’t help himself. He pulled her close for a quick hug.

“Thank you.” He trailed his fingers down her arm. “You have a way of understanding me and making everything seem better than it is. I think I’m ready to face the ravening hordes.” His hand shook as he reached for the doorknob. “Maybe I should say the ravening few. I imagine the restaurant is mostly empty.”

“Let’s go see.” Asia half turned toward the door and held out her hand to him. Sending her out there while he hid out in his office until closing tempted him. But that just wasn’t him. Not really.

Wrapping her small hand in his, he walked with her to the door and swung it open. What was all that noise? He’d expected quiet. Instead, he stepped into a room with the tables filled. From the level of noise, the front room was full as well.

How had this happened?

He glanced down at Asia, noting her delight as she watched him. She hadn’t expected this. Had there been as many people when she entered his office? He hadn’t noticed the chatter.

Calls of “Hey, Ian,” rang out. People waved. People he knew. People he hadn’t seen in a while and some he saw on a regular basis. At a table not too far from them, Cinda stood beside a chair, her hands clasped together, bouncing up and down on her toes as only Cinda could do.

Asia tugged his hand. He met her gaze. Saw the joy shining there. "And you thought no one would care, didn't you? You thought everyone would desert you for that no-good south-end? Looks to me like you have a lot of friends who care more about you than about some hoity-toity guy's opinion."

~

Asia couldn't stop the laughter that bubbled up. "Did I just say hoity-toity? That sounds like something a grandmother or great-grandmother might say."

"That's okay. It goes right along with *south-end*." Ian laughed and seemed to relax.

She squeezed his hand and let go. "Go say hello to everyone. I'm sure Meg can figure out what you want to eat. I'm told there is a pie and ice cream set aside for dessert for all of our table."

She made her way to the table and sank into a chair beside Tansie, who sat across from Cinda. Putting Asia across from Martin. "I can't believe you got all these people here. How did you do this?"

Cinda lifted her chin. "A woman has her ways. And doesn't tell."

"Don't let her kid you." Tansie snorted. "She knows every friend everyone has in this town. She's been on the phone nonstop, making calls and convincing people Ian needs them."

"It wasn't hard." Cinda leaned across the table to be heard over the din of voices. "Ian does a lot for the community. A lot. Especially for the churches and youth events. I'm sure Mr. High-and-Mighty will hear from several people about his comments in this establishment."

"I called people, too." The slight frown on Martin's sculpted face said exactly what he thought about not being in the limelight.

The nerve.

Meg fast walked to their table. "Let me take your order, and then I'm letting the other crew have the evening. I'll join you." She leaned down to sling an arm around Asia's shoulders and hug her. "Thank you. Thank you for bringing him out like that. I don't know what you did, but that black mood is gone. Plus this crowd is excited to see him and help him out. Thanks."

She took their bags, grabbed an extra one to mark for Ian, and then one for herself, and hurried away. The evening flew by. Ian finally returned to the table. He brought a chair over to sit at the end of the table beside her. Thank goodness! Martin kept trying to rub his foot against her leg. Creepy.

She lifted her chair to move and give Ian some space. At the same time, Martin sank lower in his chair, his questing toe searching for her. Opportunity. She glanced down, let the chair leg land on his toe, and plopped back down before he could jerk his foot back.

Martin yelped. She lifted enough to free his toe. He sat up, made some ridiculous excuse for his cry of pain, and continued with some story no one wanted to hear.

Somehow she was going to find a way to tell Cinda she was engaged to an obnoxious toad.

When they stepped outside, the cool night air felt good after the warmth of the restaurant. Asia blinked at the dark. It was closing time, but Ian said his head cook would take care of morning prep and closing up.

"I'm ready to be home." Cinda reached over her head to stretch. "It's been a busy day, and tomorrow we're cleaning out the back room for Asia. Martin, are your students still coming to help?"

"Two or three of them will." Martin tapped his fingers against his leg, the keys he held making an annoying jangle. "They need some extra credit, so they said they would show up."

"You give extra school credit for something that isn't class related?" Ian sounded incredulous.

"They have to give a report. It's like a community service with schoolwork involved. It's close to the end of the school year. A few are struggling to stay with their class."

He gave Cinda a hug. "I'll see you all here tomorrow morning." He strode across the lot to his car, and they watched as he pulled out on the street.

"Ready to go, Asia? I'd like to get a shower and put my feet up. Maybe read for a while." Cinda stepped close to slip her arm around Ian's waist. "You have a lot of friends who love you. Don't forget."

"After tonight, how could I?" Ian hugged her back. "Asia, would you like to go out to the point for a while? I know we went to the beach today, but the sky tonight will be amazing."

Yes, she wanted more time with Ian. But, no, she didn't. If she went, he would probably quiz her about her earlier remark. Was she ready to trust him with all her secrets?

Maybe she would pray on the way there and see where the conversation went. She was still too keyed up to sit and read. Listening to the ocean and watching the stars sounded like a great way to end this day.

She glanced at Cinda. "Do you mind? Or do you want to come too?" She hoped Ian didn't mind her inviting Cinda.

"No, I'm really beat. You guys go ahead. One of these days we'll have a little more time and do a bonfire picnic on the beach at night. Like we used to." Cinda waved and turned away.

Ian led the way to his truck, and they followed Cinda from the lot, turning toward the coast when she turned toward her home.

The drive didn't take long. Not nearly long enough to pray like she needed to. "Hey, this can't be right." She leaned forward to peer out the windshield when Ian parked.

"Why not? This is exactly where we used to come." Ian pulled the keys from the ignition and cracked open the door.

"But it took so much longer to get here then." Asia wrinkled her nose at him.

"Maybe because bicycles are a little slower than trucks. If I'd known you wanted fast back then, I would probably have stolen a truck to drive." He laughed as he climbed out.

He swung her door open, and she hopped down. "You *would* have stolen a truck. Rascal." She slipped her hand in his as they walked to a bench overlooking the ocean. Had the seagulls left any offerings on the seat?

Happily, the bench was spotless. From here they could see the waves lapping at the beach below. The moonlight danced on the water. The colors and sound of the ocean always soothed her. The tension of the day finally started draining away, as if being washed out to sea with the tug of the tide.

Asia tilted her head back and studied the expanse of sky. "Those stars. I'd forgotten how amazing they are." Pinpoints of light spun out in an amazing array. The soothing rhythm of the ocean waves rolling onto the beach made a perfect soundtrack.

"Do you see the dippers?" Ian pointed upward. "How many of the star formations do you remember? We used to be able to pick out several of them."

"It's been so long. I haven't had the chance to look up at the night sky in forever, it seems." She snapped her teeth together. Now he would wonder why she hadn't seen the sky. She fumbled for a logical explanation.

"Where have you been that you couldn't see the stars?"

The inquisition had begun.

"City lights often mask the night sky. The stars have to be very bright to show through." It wasn't a lie exactly, and it helped her to avoid the real answer. *Please don't let Ian catch on to that.*

"Okay, I'm going to quiz you. If you get enough right, you will get extra credit."

"Oohhh. Does that mean I'll graduate ahead of everyone?" She tilted her head to the side looking at him. "What exactly does extra credit get me?"

"Why does it matter?" He picked up a strand of her hair rubbing it between his fingers. His touch was electric.

"It determines how hard I'll try." She crossed her arms and gave him a mock glare. "If all I get is a pat on the back, I may not try very hard. On the other hand, if I get a trip to the Ice Cream Shack, I'll amaze and mystify you with my knowledge."

He laughed. Scooted closer. Put his arm around her and his face next to hers. Her pulse surged.

Ian lifted his arm and pointed, going from one constellation to the next, reminding her what they were and waiting for her to find them. If she played dumb, she could stay this close to him. Have the years fall away. Have him kiss her like he'd done the last time they met here.

Whoa! Time to go home. "I'd better head back. Cinda will want to lock up, and I don't want to sleep on the porch." She stood and tugged his hand.

They ambled back toward the truck. Ian opened the door for her, and she swung into the cab. He leaned in toward her. She could see the moonlight reflected in his eyes and couldn't breathe.

"Asia, I need to talk about the bombshell you dropped earlier. Why do you think Walter is your father? I need to know."

10

The sun peeked over the horizon, lighting Asia's bedroom. She groaned and pulled the sheet over her face. What? Was all the grit of the Sahara in her eyes?

Today was clean-out-the-back-room-of-the-quilt-shop day, and all she wanted to do was sleep. And hide.

From the world. From responsibility.

From Ian.

She'd told him last night. Sitting in his truck as he stood beside her, they were eye-to-eye. The pleading in his gaze, begging her to be honest, had been her undoing. She told him part of the truth. Not everything. Just about her father. The box her mother left her. The birth certificate. The letters from Walter to her mother that she still hadn't read. Reading them would be an invasion of privacy. She needed to talk to Walter first.

Ian listened to all she had to say. She could see the weight of her words bearing down on him. They talked about what this would mean to Cinda, to Glenna. How much the knowledge would hurt them. She and Cinda were almost the same age, which meant Walter cheated on their mother while she was pregnant with Cinda. After he'd been married. Asia wasn't the product of some fling when he'd been single. She was the product of adultery.

How sordid could it get?

"Did you ask your mom about this?"

Oh, if only she'd been able. "How could I? She was already buried when I found out. All those years she never said a word. Like she couldn't face me with the truth." Asia had ducked her head to hide her tears.

She wouldn't blame Ian if he wanted nothing more to do with her ever. Her whole life was a mistake. Something that should have been erased long ago.

"Hey." He'd lifted her chin with one finger. "You are not at fault in any of this. You are the innocent bystander caught in the fallout."

She smiled even now, with the sun lighting up the dust motes in her bedroom. She'd said those very words to Ian many times when he talked about being worthless and the heritage of his parents.

Weren't they a pair?

Asia sat up and plumped a pillow behind her. She didn't want to get up before Cinda. Or disturb Cinda's morning routine. They still had a couple of hours before they left for the shop. No classes today. Only the running of the shop and cleaning out the back room.

Asia didn't mind staying here, but she would be glad to have her own space. Once she moved, she had a plan for sneaking out to visit Walter. Yesterday, she'd seen Cinda's mail, which included a letter from a care center. She'd looked the center up when no one was using the computer at the shop and found they had an Alzheimer's wing. That had to be where Walter lived.

She leaned over the side of the bed and dug the box from her backpack. Maybe it was time to read a couple of the letters. She hadn't even taken the ribbon off of them. They seemed cherished. Private. Something her mother wouldn't want anyone to see. Yet she'd left them for Asia. And now…

Walter wouldn't care.

The ribbon had raveled on the ends and yellowed with age. Asia tugged gently, and the tie came loose. The stack of letters shifted as the ribbon fell away. Her mother's name, Kim Jessup, no address. In the upper left corner the initials, *W. B.*, Walter Bryant. These had to be from him.

Asia picked up the top letter. No postmark, so she had no idea of the order. He must have hand delivered the notes or had some other system for getting these to her mother. The letter was slit open at the top, and Asia slid the paper from within.

My Dearest Kim,

I am sorry to be away from you for so long. I miss you more than I can say. You have my heart, but I also have a responsibility to my family here. I am so torn with what I should do and what I want to do. Choices are not always cut and dried. They can be nasty pieces of business with no easy solution.

Asia wiped a tear from the page. When had she started crying? How hard this must have been for her mother and for Walter. Did her mother want him to marry her? Had she begun her life of addiction and men because of her failed love with Walter?

If only she had answers.

At least these letters would provide something, but with no letters from her mom, she would never be able to hear her mother's side of the story.

She glanced at the top of the page. This letter was dated six months before Asia's birth. She skimmed the note and realized Walter was responding to the news that he and Kim would be having a child. He sounded so happy. Yet so sad. He mentioned his wife was due to give birth any day, which rang true. She and Cinda were not quite six months apart.

Oh, Cinda. Asia dropped the letter and pressed the heels of her palms to her eyes trying to stop the flood of tears. How she would have loved being Cinda's sister. Being claimed as such all those years ago. How different her life would have been if Walter had acknowledged her and given her a place to live where she wasn't in fear for her life or of being raped. Where drugs weren't an everyday occurrence.

She folded the pages and put them back in the envelope. She would have to read these later. Maybe when she lived in the shop and didn't have to worry about someone seeing her with eyes reddened from crying. She picked up the bundle to try to put the ribbon back on. One of the letters slipped free. This one wasn't flat like the others but rounded as if it contained more than paper.

Asia picked it up, setting the others aside. She heard the creak of a door and the pad of Cinda's slippers in the hall. She froze, holding her breath. The letter rattled the tiniest bit. Had Cinda paused? Continued on?

She relaxed at the clink of glass in the kitchen. That had to be the coffeepot bumping the mug Cinda used. The faintest scent of fresh coffee wafted in the air.

She started to put the envelopes back in the box, but the one that was different made her pause. The top of this envelope and the ones after it were closed. Had her mother never opened them to read? Why?

Asia worked her finger under the tab and pried the old glue of the envelope free. One page of paper came out along with something wrapped in old tissue paper. She glanced at the letter first.

My Dearest Kim,

I know you are upset with me. My choice is not easy although I wish it were. I will continue to send messages via Joy. She refuses to tell me where you are, but says she is delivering my letters. Please answer me. My heart is heavy without you. I want to know how little Asia is doing. Please write back. I would love a picture.

I am enclosing a gift for you to remember me by. Please think of me as you wear it.

Forever your love,

Walter

Maybe her mother hadn't read any of the letters. Joy, the friend who gave Asia the box, could have slipped them inside with the other mementos and Asia would never be the wiser. From the tone of these letters, Walter loved her mom. He wanted to know Asia. So how was it that Asia spent summers with Walter when these letters were unread? How had that happened?

She closed her eyes and thought back. Angry words echoed... words spoken in the kitchen while she stayed in her room, unsure why her mother was so upset. Joy telling her to pack for an extended stay with her uncle and cousins. Joy taking her to meet

Uncle Walter. Joy picking her up at the end of the summer. Joy keeping her because her mother went to prison--

Bumps raised on her arms. The paper rattled in her hand.

How had she blocked that out?

If only she could talk to Joy again, but when she gave Asia the box, she told her she was leaving town and wouldn't see her again. She'd left no contact information.

Asia unwrapped the gift her father enclosed. A necklace fell into her hand. The beautiful black and white stone heart shot through with gold stole her breath. A piece of paper fluttered to her lap from the tissue.

Kintsugi necklace. Black and white agate. Broken hearts made stronger.

She frowned. What did that even mean? She flipped the paper over.

Kintsugi: Japanese art of repairing broken things with lacquer infused with powdered gold, silver, or platinum to make the piece stronger.

Her stomach growled at the aroma of breakfast cooking. She needed to get out there and help Cinda. To get ready for the day. She stuffed everything back in the box and shoved it in her backpack. She pulled the necklace back out. The design called to her. She put it on the nightstand. After breakfast, she would shower and wear this under her shirt.

Something of her dad's to get her through the day.

"ALL THE TRASH IS OUT, and the boxes for your garage are in the back of my pickup." Ian stood in the doorway of the small apartment in the quilt shop. He had to admit he'd had doubts about this being a decent place to live, even after they cleaned it up. But he'd been wrong. Cinda brought a few things, including bed linens and a couple of quilted wall hangings, which made the place downright homey.

Martin's two high school students showed up in the afternoon, then spoke with Martin and must have gotten permission to leave. They almost mowed Ian down trying to get through the door. They hadn't been a lot of help but had done some of the work. Cinda and Asia were grateful for everyone who helped out.

Well, maybe not Martin.

The man shadowed Asia at first. Ian had taken him aside earlier and told him to leave her alone, but Martin was persistent. Grabbing the blowhard by the lapels—not that he had any today—and reminding him again of his upcoming nuptials would be so satisfying. He clenched his fists until his knuckles ached. He'd tried to talk to Cinda about her fiancé, but she wouldn't listen.

How could she be so blind?

Ian narrowed his eyes. Asia was across the room talking with Cinda, maybe about the kitchen area since they were gesturing to cabinets and the stove. Probably figuring out what she would need for cooking.

Martin stood behind Asia. Cinda must know he was there, but she wasn't paying attention to him. He very slowly ran his hand down Asia's braid. Asia gasped. Jumped away and whirled around. Raised her fist as if to deck the guy. If only she would.

Enough!

Ian stalked forward as Cinda, whose back had been turned, asked Asia some questions, and Martin edged behind Asia again.

"I have a couple of pans and at least one skillet I can bring over. You'll need a coffeepot and a toaster. Plates, cups, silverware. I should be making a list." Cinda laughed and put her arm around Asia's shoulders. Her hand bumped Martin's. Ian paused as Cinda turned to look at her fiancé, a frown creasing her brow.

"Martin, what are you doing?"

"Um, I thought I saw an ant on her. I was going to brush it off." Martin perused the floor as if looking for the insect.

"Ants?" Cinda gasped. She pulled out her cell phone and switched on the flashlight. "I've never had ants in the shop. That would be a disaster." She moved the light one stripe at a time searching the floor for something that was a lie.

Ian stood behind Martin, tapped him on the shoulder, and glowered when the man turned around. Ian motioned with his thumb to the door and mouthed the word *Now*.

Apparently, Martin knew Ian was serious. He made his excuses and beat a hasty retreat. The relief on Asia's face made the demand worthwhile.

"It was probably a trick of the light, Cinda. I'm sure Martin only thought he saw something." Asia opened one of the cupboards. "Shall we make that list? I don't need much of anything."

"Do you have a list app on your phone?" Cinda glanced up from scrolling through her apps and made a comical face at Asia. "Of course you don't. You don't have a cell phone. We need to remedy that. I'll need a way to contact you."

"Cinda, I can't afford a phone. I've gone without one this long. I can get by. Don't you have a landline in the shop? I could use that." Asia turned to Ian, her back to Cinda, and mouthed *Thank you* to Ian.

He thought he'd been so discreet, but she must have caught his interaction with Martin.

"You know what?" Cinda waved her phone. "I still have my old phone. It's paid off. A little slow, but I can add it to my plan, and you could have a cheap phone. Let's go do that."

She put her hands together under her chin, mouth stretched in a Cheshire cat grin. "Seriously, I don't want you staying here alone without a way to call out. What if someone broke into the shop? You couldn't go out there and say, 'Excuse me, I need to use this phone to call the police, because I don't have one of my own like every other person my age. And younger.'" Cinda's foot sounded like a sewing machine on high speed.

Ian laughed. He couldn't help it. Cinda manipulated everyone around her but did it in such a way you were happy to be manipulated. He didn't know a single person who didn't love Cinda. Well, maybe Martin. Asia's soft laugh made him think she read his mind.

"If you're sure. And if it won't be expensive. I'm only working part-time, so my paycheck will be slim."

"You should talk to your boss." Ian nudged her with his elbow. "Ask for a raise."

Cinda glared at him.

"Why don't we take those boxes to Cinda's. We can gather what you need to bring back here and stop at the thrift store to see if there's an old coffeepot or toaster to buy. You mentioned that earlier. We have to go soon, or they'll be closed." Ian glanced at his phone. Yup, they still had time.

"Better idea." Cinda glanced at her list. "I have an old coffeepot at my house. I know which items I have there and which I don't. I'll give you the house keys, and you can put everything in the garage while I do the shopping and meet you there. When we're done, we can grab something to eat other than barbecue. Then we'll go see about the phone."

"What?" Ian slammed his hands on his hips. "You're tired of barbecue? You must not be an American. I'm glad you didn't say that in Texas."

Cinda and Asia preceded him out the door, laughing and chatting about what Cinda thought necessary in Asia's kitchen versus what Asia considered necessary. They would never agree, and Asia should just give up before Cinda steamrolled over the top of her.

They parted ways as soon as Cinda gave Tansie instructions for locking up. There weren't many customers this late on a Saturday afternoon, so Tansie would spend the time re-shelving material and doing general clean up.

He held the door while Asia climbed in the truck. She moved with the grace of a ballet dancer. Wow.

On the way to Cinda's they chatted about some ideas Asia had for ads and a new menu layout for the restaurant. Tomorrow afternoon they planned to sit down with Meg and finalize the new menu options. After the surge of community support last night, Ian was ready to try something new. Maybe a community event. Risky, but it could be worth it.

He carried the larger boxes into Cinda's garage while Asia moved around yard equipment and other paraphernalia to make room for what they'd brought over. There wasn't much, but Cinda didn't have a lot of excess room here.

"That should be good. You think?" Asia stepped back as he slid the larger boxes into the space she'd prepared. They would stack them, but not too high.

"I think it's perfect." He smiled at her, doing his best to slow his galloping pulse when she smiled back. She had the perfect face. Rounded cheeks, sparkling eyes, a beautiful smile. He could spend hours staring at her.

Days. Weeks.

A lifetime.

He jerked away from that thought train. No way could he do anything about this attraction.

They finished and stepped back to view their handiwork. "I don't know about you, but I'm about ready for something to eat." Ian pressed his hand to his stomach. "I think I can feel my backbone." He winked at Asia.

She quirked her mouth. "Do I need to carry you? Are you too weak to walk?"

He laughed, slung his arm around her shoulder, and gave her a hug.

"Asia, I appreciate you opening up to me last night. I know it wasn't easy." He felt her tense, but he didn't let go. He squeezed her upper arm and she relaxed. The faint scent of spilled oil and dust filled the air. Somewhere outside he heard a lawnmower running. A car door slammed down the street.

"I understand your reasoning now. I'm not sure how Cinda and Glenna will feel about you seeing Walter, but I will do my best to support you."

"I know how Glenna would feel about it." Asia gave a soft snort of laughter. "I think you know too."

He nodded. Leaned his chin against the top of her head. "You know what you need to do. It will be hard, but there's only one way to do this."

"I don't want to hurt anyone." The pain in her whisper broke his heart.

"If you didn't want to hurt anyone, you shouldn't have come back." He felt her tense again but had to put that out there. "I'm glad you're here. Very glad. But you need to tell Cinda."

"Tell Cinda what?"

Glenna's sharp tone echoed in the garage.

11

"I'm back and starving." Cinda strode into the garage on her sister's heels, curls bouncing, almost vibrating with energy.

Then she hit the wall of tension. She paused. Took a hesitant step. Met Ian's gaze with her questioning one. Glanced at Asia, who stood rigid, her back against his chest.

Oh boy. Ian braced himself. This could get ugly fast.

"Glenna, I didn't know you'd be here. What's up? Want to go to dinner with us?" Cinda stepped up beside her sister, who hadn't taken her laser-beam gaze from Asia.

"I want to hear what Asia has to tell you." Glenna's lips stretched taut as she spoke through gritted teeth.

"Asia has something to tell me?" Cinda glanced at Ian and Asia, tilted her head to the side and looked back at her sister. "Why do you think that? What's the big deal?"

"I came to see who was in your garage and heard them talking. Ian told her she should talk to you about something. I want to know what it is." Glenna took a step forward but stopped when Cinda put her hand on her arm.

"So you were eavesdropping and now you want to know the whole story. Is that right?" When Glenna didn't answer, Cinda went on. "I'm sure if Asia has something to tell me, she will do it at the right time." She turned back to Ian and Asia. "Let's go eat. We've worked hard today and still aren't done. After we eat, we need to do the phone and take everything I picked up back to Asia's apartment. Give me a minute to get the coffeepot and other things from here."

"Wait." Glenna grabbed Cinda's arm. "Asia's apartment? What apartment? How does someone who doesn't even have a car or phone afford an apartment?" She glared across the garage.

Ian thought sure some of the dust began to smolder.

Asia didn't waver or step back.

"Stop." Cinda removed her sister's hand and rubbed her arm. "Asia is staying in the rooms attached to my shop. She'll be helping out there and watching the place for me. She can open up if Tansie and I are running late."

"She knows nothing about quilting or the shop." Glenna's eyes narrowed. "Why would you do this? I told you she needs to leave town."

"Because she's *family.*" Cinda held up her hand when Glenna began to sputter. "I know we looked into where she came from and couldn't find a connection. Dad wouldn't say either. But he introduced her as a cousin, and to me she will always be family."

Ian felt a tremble thread through Asia. What did she think of Cinda's defense of her? He glanced down and caught the glint of tears in her eyes.

Cinda stepped in front of Glenna. "You can either go with us to dinner or go on home. I'm too tired to put up with any argument."

"I have to get home in case Jeffrey comes home tonight."

"He didn't tell you when he'd be home?" Cinda's soft inquiry barely carried to the back of the garage.

"No." Glenna's shoulders rose and fell. She stared out into the night. "I've got to go." She strode down the drive toward her car.

Tension bled out of Asia. For the first time since the confrontation started, Ian realized he had his hands on her shoulders, holding her against him, supporting her.

"I'm sorry." Cinda seemed to have deflated. "She's going through a rough patch with Jeffrey right now. I'm sure they'll work it out, but she's gotten a little prickly."

Ian snorted. Cinda huffed a laugh. Asia straightened away from him, and he dropped his hands from her shoulders. He wanted to draw her back, to protect her from any more hurt. But could he protect her from himself?

Like father, like son.

Cinda went inside and returned with a coffeepot and a few other kitchen items. "Let's go." She twirled her keys on her fingers. "Not that I don't love your barbecue, Ian, but I have a hankering for pizza. Anyone else?"

"A hankering?" Ian snorted. Asia flashed him a grin that wavered.

"Yep, a hankering. My dad used to say that all the time."

"I remember that." Asia chuckled. "I never could figure out where that came from."

"I think it had to do with his roots in the Midwest." Cinda grinned and gestured at the pile of boxes behind them. "Thank you for doing that. My garage looks better now than it did before more stuff was piled in here. Someone is more organized than me." She edged toward the door.

"I don't know." Asia rounded a box and walked toward her. "The material in your shop is so organized I'm always wanting to move the bolts around."

Cinda threw back her head and laughed. "That is not me. If you do it, you will face the wrath of Tansie. Trust me, she can be scary."

Asia went to Ian's truck. He couldn't stop the thrill that chased through him. She could have ridden with Cinda, but she'd chosen him. He almost didn't feel the ground as he hurried to open the door for her.

"Hey, Ian, let's take Asia to Ashes Pizza. Sound good?" Cinda opened her car door but waited for his reply. He laughed and gave her the thumbs up and rounded his truck to climb in. The garage door rumbled down as he started his engine.

"Ashes?" Asia frowned. "Is that new? I don't recognize the name."

"It's outside of town. A renovated place. They have some excellent pizza, although they also have some weird pizza, if you're a barbecue sort of person." He winked at her. Her cheeks flushed pink. Oh, he would have to be careful. Just a few days around her and he already wanted more.

Much more.

That horrible memory from college slipped into his mind as he drove. The wrong he'd done. The hurt he'd caused. Sure, he'd tried to make amends. Regretted his choice. But hadn't that been the way his dad behaved too? He'd hurt Ian or his mom and then the next day do something kind to make amends. Until the day he went too far and there wasn't a way to make anything right again.

"The pizza place is up here?" Asia had removed the tie holding her braid and loosened her hair. It swung in a dark curtain as she turned toward him. His mouth went dry. The way his heart kept responding to her, he needed the upcoming distraction to keep from falling deeper for her.

"I can't believe this." Her mouth twisted in a grimace. He held his breath to keep from snorting. This place housed a horror when they were teens.

"Yep. Up here." He turned the final curve and drove into the parking area. Off to the side stood a brick edifice with a steeple and an old smokestack at the back of the long side building.

"Is this a joke?" Asia's mystified look made him grin.

"No joke. This place closed down a long time ago. Then it sold about two years ago. The new owners refurbished the place. Repurposed it, I guess you could say." He pulled in beside Cinda, climbed out, and walked around to open Asia's door. She was still gaping at the building and hadn't taken off her seat belt.

"I don't know if I can eat here. They call it Ashes?" She swallowed hard. "Isn't that a little morbid?"

Cinda rounded the end of his truck and must have heard the question. Her lilting laugh echoed in the evening air. "I love it. It's an amazing place, and they have great pizza. Come on. You'll have fun."

Asia unbuckled and slipped out. A little shudder rippled through her. Ian locked the truck and followed the women toward the front door. Asia and Cinda might be half sisters. He studied them. The roundness in both their faces was similar. They were both beautiful. They had similar hair color and texture. He could see them being sisters.

How would Cinda take the news? Asia needed to summon the courage to tell her soon.

Right now, he wanted to watch Asia's reaction when they entered the pizza place and were seated. She remembered this building from her time here. When the kids avoided the place or snuck close for a peek and bragged later.

They were seated in a corner of the room. Red bricks lined one wall. Gleaming wood arches added a touch of magnificence. Framed historical photos were artfully arranged on the walls.

Asia's eyes were huge. Her skin had paled, and she didn't look like she would enjoy the experience. Had this been a mistake?

"Good evening. I'm Chad. I'll be your waiter tonight. Can I get your drinks? Are you ready to order?" The waiter was young, with short blond hair and an engaging smile.

Asia spoke in a hushed tone. "Didn't this place used to be a crematorium?"

Chad must have heard the horror in her tone. His grin widened. He waved his hand in the air. "Yep, but no worries. We changed out the ovens."

~

Asia's sides ached. Tiny hiccups of laughter still bubbled up. She'd been so horrified to find out the crematorium they feared long ago—said to be haunted—was now a popular pizza restaurant. And a good one at that.

When the waiter made his oven comment, she and her friends lost it. Chad ended up saying he would bring them water and then get their order.

Maybe they were just tired, or maybe some of the stress of the past few days had overwhelmed. Whatever happened, the laughter brought relief.

Different ovens.

Just thinking about that made a giggle bubble up. She bit her lip to keep from exploding again. She couldn't begin to look at Ian. Or Cinda.

By the time the food arrived, they'd all calmed down and were able to chat. Cinda told them all about the history of this building and how it came to be for sale. At one point the new owner stopped by their table to chat. He knew Ian from eating at I-BBQ, and they shared a couple of funny stories.

Ian had been right. She hadn't wanted to listen to him. Hadn't wanted to break this fragile peace between herself and Cinda. But she needed to tell Cinda the truth.

Tonight.

Maybe Cinda wouldn't react in a negative way. Maybe she would agree that Asia needed to visit Walter. Then she wouldn't have to sneak out to the care center like some thief in the night.

"I am so stuffed." Cinda picked up the box with her leftover pizza. They each had one since they all ordered different pies. Asia was grateful her new place had a toaster oven. A little old-fashioned, but the leftovers would taste good heated in there.

"Ian, do you want to go with us to get Asia's phone?" Cinda clicked her key fob and the lights on her car lit as the locks clicked open.

Asia hadn't considered they would part ways now. She liked riding in the truck with Ian. She appreciated being there with him and the comfortable camaraderie they shared. Since she'd shared the truth about Walter with him last night, that release of tension had given her some freedom.

Would he react the same when he found out about her past? Would he forgive her indiscretions? Would he still care for her when he knew the whole truth?

"I should go check the restaurant. I know my people are good, but I've been gone a lot today. I'll watch for you to get back to the shop. I can come over and see what Asia's number is so I can harass her whenever I want." He nudged her with his shoulder. "It will be nice to have you in the twenty-first century." He grabbed her in a side hug and squeezed. Without Cinda, would Ian give her a different kind of hug? The hairs on her arms prickled.

The interaction between Ian and the owner of Ashes flitted across her memory. Oh, right, bad idea. Ian needed someone who would benefit his standing in the community, not an ex-con.

Getting the phone activated and switched to her took forever. Who knew there would be so many people waiting to get phones?

Asia leaned over to whisper to Cinda. "We could always come back at a better time."

"It won't be too much longer. Once someone can help us, the change will be quick. I charged the cell so it's all ready to go."

The salesman who helped them knew Martin. They lived in the same apartment complex. They must be good friends because he had the same slimy feel. He hit on Asia several times, touching her —by "accident"—and when Cinda went to the bathroom, he stopped typing.

"How about you and I go out tomorrow night? I'm off work. I can show you a good time." Gordon, as his nametag read, wiggled his eyebrows, probably thinking that made him sexy. It didn't work. Asia took a step away.

He leaned over. "I heard about your mom. What she was like." Her stomach churned. His gaze traveled over her leaving a layer of filth behind.

"Like mother, like daughter, right? We'll have some fun." His dark eyes had an unmistakable gleam of lust.

"Instead of hurting you in front of all these customers, I'll pretend you didn't speak." Asia's jaw ached. "If you say another word to me, I'll make such a scene that you'll be looking for work in another state."

She couldn't wait to leave the store. She had to talk to Cinda about Martin. Soon.

After she talked to her about Walter.

"Are we done?" Cinda popped up at Asia's shoulder, startling her. She'd been so focused on staying away from the salesman's clutches, she hadn't noticed Cinda's return.

"Just a few more minutes." Gordon clicked away on his computer, his eyes straying to Asia every few seconds. She made a show of looking around at all the people. He focused on his work.

After Cinda had signed a sufficient number of places, Gordon handed Asia the phone. He grabbed her hand, holding even when she tried to tug free. She almost slapped him upside the head with her new cell.

"Keep in mind if you want to upgrade any time, you come see me. I'll help you get a good deal." Once again, his eyes swept over her. Asia shuddered and yanked her hand away. Hadn't he learned anything? She would never come in this store again.

"He was certainly taken with you but a little creepy." Cinda slid the key into the ignition. "Martin has mentioned him before. In fact, he's the one who told me to bring you here to get the phone taken care of because Gordon would be expecting us. I'll mention to Martin that his friend wasn't a great help." She backed out of the parking space.

"Cinda, the man is a troll. He kept touching me when he shouldn't. He leered at me, and when you were gone, he said he figured I was like my mom."

"Your mom? He wouldn't even know your mom." Cinda's lips pursed. "I didn't know your mom. I never met her. Why would he say that?"

"I have no idea. The only other person he could have gotten anything from is Martin. What does he know about my past? And why would he share anything about me?" Asia stared at the lights going by. Businesses were starting to close, and the traffic had increased as people headed home for the night. She had to distract her thoughts, or she would start in on a diatribe about Martin and the way he treated her. Cinda wouldn't want to hear *that* news.

"Well, Martin certainly never met your mom. He only met you a couple of days ago. I have no idea what Gordon meant. Maybe he had you mixed up with someone else. That must be why he acted so stalkerish." The blinker clicked on as Cinda slowed to turn into the quilt shop parking lot.

She had to let this go. Cinda's head was firmly buried in the sand as far as Martin was concerned. Asia would pray and see if a time presented where they could have a frank conversation.

Before talking about Cinda's fiancé, they needed to talk about family connections. Would she even believe Asia if she told her about her birth certificate? If she didn't listen about a virtual stranger, how would she ever believe the truth about the father she adored?

"There you are." Ian hurried over as they got out. "I was just leaving. They are closing up. All the customers are gone. Let's get Asia's things inside, and then you two can relax."

Cinda punched the button, and Ian lifted the lid of the trunk. He handed a couple of small things to Cinda, who went to unlock the door. He grabbed the toaster and a bag that clanked with silverware as Asia grabbed the last bag while balancing her pizza leftovers.

"How did it go with the phone? Are you all set up?" Ian's smile chased away the remnants of Gordon's sliminess. She stood there mesmerized, the scent of barbecue in the air and the ocean breeze cooling her face.

Asia glanced toward the shop. Cinda had gone inside and turned on the lights. "The salesman was a friend of Martin's."

Ian's smile faded, replaced by a grim scowl.

"He knew we were coming." She shuddered. "I won't be going back there. Trust me."

The noise Ian made sounded like a growl. "Let's get this stuff inside. I want to check the locks and make sure they're sturdy."

She shuddered again. The thought of one of those men coming here in the middle of the night made her glad she had phone access. She felt the weight of the locket under her shirt and wondered what Walter would have said or done.

Ian held the door for her and followed her through to the back rooms. In the kitchen, he set the toaster and the bag on a small cleared space. Asia put her bag down and turned to open the refrigerator for the pizza.

"Asia, I knocked over your backpack and this box fell out." Cinda gestured to the letters and scarf on the floor. "What *is* this?"

Her hand trembled as she held up Asia's birth certificate.

12

"Is this your birth certificate?" Cinda rattled the paper. Or maybe the shaking of her hand caused the trembling. "Why is my dad's name on here?" Cinda swiveled toward Asia. "I want to know what's going on." Her voice cracked.

Chills skittered up Asia's back. She meant to tell Cinda. She did. But not this way.

"Cinda." Asia took a step toward her cousin—sister—friend. Cinda stepped back, bumping up against the wall. Tears streaked down her face.

"I wanted to tell you. I wasn't sure how." Asia swallowed against the lump in her throat.

"How long have you known? Is this real? Did you know when you spent the summers here and went on about how you wanted to know your father?" Cinda shook the birth certificate. Asia feared she would ruin the fragile paper.

"No. I had no idea." Weight pressed against Asia's chest. Her vision swam.

"But you knew when you came here this week. Right?" Cinda's face reddened. Her voice turned shrill.

"Yes." How to explain her actions, her reluctance to share the truth? As she thought about her choice to conceal her reason for being here, Asia realized how manipulative it would sound. Would Cinda believe her? "I found out the week before, when my mother's friend gave me the box my mother left for me. I had no idea before then. None at all." Asia pressed her hand over her mouth at the look of utter disbelief on Cinda's face.

"Stop." Ian came forward to stand beside Asia. His low voice brought a note of calm to the chaotic scene. "Asia told me last night, Cinda. She wanted to tell you but was afraid to."

"Afraid? Why? Of what? That Glenna would be right? That I should have just told you to leave?" Cinda dashed the back of her hand across her cheek. "You expect me to believe that after all these years your mother never told you who your father was? How am I supposed to believe that? Why do you want to see my father?"

Asia twisted her fingers together, and her knuckles popped. "I can't tell you what to believe. I only know I saw my birth certificate for the first time when Joy gave me the box. I prayed about what to do and came here to see if I could find the truth. I have no idea why Walter's name is on my birth certificate. My mother was already several months dead. I can't ask her. I can only ask your father." Asia bit her lip to stop before she said something she would regret. Think. Think. Her thoughts refused to coalesce.

Ian touched her back, the warmth from his hand flooding through her, settling in her heart.

She glanced up to see the kindness in his gaze. "Cinda, I didn't want to hurt you. That's why I didn't say anything. I guess I hoped to see your dad and find out what he knew." Asia fought to keep from leaning against Ian.

Why had she come back here? All she did was cause pain. What had she been thinking? When she prayed, had she heard wrong? This Christian thing was so new to her, so maybe she misunderstood and wasn't supposed to be here. Maybe family didn't matter.

But family did matter. That longing of a little girl seeing other girls with their daddies had never gone away. Seeing them with siblings. Seeing them with a special connection she'd never had. Yes, she had a mother. But a mother who was needier than a young child. A mother who sucked the joy out of life.

Cinda stepped over to the table. Put the birth certificate down and picked up her purse. "I have to go."

"Wait." Asia held up her hand.

"No." Cinda wouldn't even look at her. "I have to sort through this." When she looked up, the utter anguish in her eyes cut deep.

"I'm so sorry." Ian's warm touch on her back tethered her. He had such strength. How could she draw him into this mess she'd started any more than she had already? He should leave and not look back. She needed to make him understand that being associated with her would only bring him trouble and heartache.

Just like with Cinda.

Just like her mother had with her.

She stood frozen as Cinda left without looking back.

Without giving her any hope of forgiveness.

"Ian, you need to leave." Her throat ached as she forced the words out. She didn't want him to go, but she couldn't face him being here any longer. She needed to be alone. Completely alone. That's what she deserved.

"Asia." Ian's hands tightened on her shoulders. "Give her some time. Cinda loves you. Finding out her father cheated on her mother and that you are her sister is a lot to take in."

"She doesn't believe it." Asia held her breath against the sob clawing to get out.

Ian pulled her against his chest. Leaned his head against hers. "You didn't either."

She gasped. Stiffened. He didn't let go.

"Am I right?" His breath whispered past her ear, making her hair tickle against her cheek. "If you believed it to be the truth, you would have spoken up right away. Instead, you wanted to talk to Walter first. Why is that?" His question cut deep. The truth poked at wounded places she wanted to keep covered.

"Because my mom never once told me the truth about anything." This time the sob wracked her body. Ian turned her around to pull her tight against him. She buried her face, unable to stop the avalanche of tears and grief.

Had adding Walter's name been a joke? How had Mom even known him? Where had they met? Did they have a mutual friend or family member? The questions raked through her mind, stirring up memories long forgotten. Memories that tore at the walls around her heart.

Her mother and Joy fighting in the kitchen:

"Kim, you need to tell him where you are. This girl needs a father."

"No. He's never going to get her. If I let him know, he'll take her away. We have to do it this way."

Joy's tone softened. "Maybe that's for the best."

"No. If I give her up, I'll never get anything more from him." Her mother sounded so angry.

Had they been talking about her? About Walter being her father? She couldn't remember more. She'd been so young. Hadn't seen Joy again for a long time—maybe two or three years.

"Kim, he wants to see her. Don't you think it's time?"

Asia sat on the bleachers in front of her mother and Joy, eating popcorn, ignoring the circus performers in front of her to listen to the conversation behind her. Eavesdropping. Something her mother forbade her to do.

"No. She's happy as she is." Loud cheers drowned out the rest. Asia quit chewing. Leaned back to hear better.

"What if he hires someone to track her down? Track you *down."*

She remembered asking her mother about that conversation. Her inquiry earned her a sharp slap and a lecture about not listening in on private conversations. She must have been a preteen then. Remembered her mutinous thoughts and increased probing about her father.

Then her mother went downhill into drugs and alcohol. Into one man after another. Years of horror. Years of hiding when the men came looking for her. Years of wanting to run away and being too afraid there would be worse things outside her home than inside.

When her mother was arrested, Asia went to live with Joy. She wouldn't see her mother for years. That first summer she spent in Driftwood Cove with an uncle she'd never heard of and cousins she didn't know.

Family. A real family.

Her tears slowed. "I'm sorry." She pushed back from Ian. Brushed at his damp shirt. Couldn't look at him knowing her tear-ravaged face would be ugly.

"Hey, no problem." He rubbed her back as she turned away. "Let me help you put these things away. Then you can get some sleep. We'll talk in the morning. I'll bring some coffee and pastries since the shop is closed on Sunday. You're welcome to go to church with me if you want."

She didn't have the strength to argue. They worked in tandem, finding a place for the toaster and coffeepot, putting a few groceries in a shelf. Opening a box of much needed tissues.

"I think that's it." Ian finished putting the liner in the trash can and put it back out of the way. "Is there anything else?"

"No. Thank you. I..." She wanted to add something but had no idea what else to say. She waited until he left, watched through the window as his truck turned on the street, the taillights glowing red in the dark.

Alone. Always alone.

HE'D KNOWN it would be bad. Known Cinda would be second and third guessing what her father had done. What had happened between him and Asia's mom and why. If Cinda's mother knew. Would wish she could talk to her dad but couldn't. Would she be willing to take Asia there now, to see if her presence sparked anything in a man whose memories were only vapor?

He tossed and turned as he played possibilities over and over in his mind. He loved Cinda like a sister he never had. They'd spent hours together after that last summer with Asia, wondering where she'd gone. If they'd ever see her again. If she was okay without them because they sure weren't okay without her.

Not once had he and Cinda ever considered anything romantic between them, although the kids at school speculated. Without Asia around, rumors started. Even Walter had approached Ian at a football game to tell him to stay away from his daughter. Ian shrugged off the hurt. Sort of. But the pain still settled deep inside when he thought of Walter's angry gaze and forceful threats. They had come to terms, but it had taken time.

He finally gave up at five in the morning, got up, dressed, and sat down in the living room with his Bible and that first cup of coffee. Scripture verses chased away the disquiet. Even when he didn't know the question he wanted to ask, God always led him to an answer he needed.

"Peace I leave with you, My peace I give to you; not as the world gives do I give to you. Let not your heart be troubled, neither let it be afraid." The words *let not your heart be troubled* leapt off the page from the verses in John 14. Peace trickled through him. God knew. He knew what Asia needed. He knew what Cinda needed. He even knew Ian's needs. And He offered peace. A release from worry.

Ian closed his eyes, tipped his head back against the chair, and listened. Listened for the whisper across his soul that told him all would be right. God, in His sovereignty, would see to that.

Asia had said she was a new Christian. Would she feel the same peace? Would these verses speak to her as they had to him? He didn't know, but he jotted the reference on a sticky note to put on her refrigerator if he got the chance.

After doing some clean up and some much neglected working out, he showered and grabbed what he needed for the day, including the scripture note for Asia. He stopped at a local coffee shop to grab coffee, egg sandwiches, and a couple of pastries. Maybe she'd agree to go to church.

Asia opened at his knock. She looked about sixteen, fresh and rested. How did she manage? Her damp hair told of a shower, and the running shoes by the door said she'd gone for a walk or a run. Barefoot, she greeted him and led him into the small kitchen/dining area.

"Something smells good." She gestured to a chair.

"Thanks. I just showered." He grinned as she rolled her eyes. He handed her a coffee, and she sniffed.

"You remembered. This is peppermint, isn't it?" She closed her eyes and inhaled deeply. He had to fight the need to grab her and pull her close. To touch her.

Fight against feelings he couldn't acknowledge.

"I also brought sustenance." He opened the bag and pulled out the sandwiches and pastries. Asia reached for the orange scone, his favorite. He gave her hand a light smack. "Not until you finish your sandwich. You know the rules."

They both laughed. On the few occasions Ian had been invited to Cinda's for a meal, he'd always wanted to go for the sweets first. Cinda's mom was adamant. Food first, dessert last.

Waiting had been sheer torture.

"So, about this morning. Would you like to go to church with me?" His heart thudded against his ribs as he waited for her response. Why did it matter so much to him?

He knew the answer. No matter how he tried to ignore his attraction, he wanted Asia to be on the same page spiritually. Because he couldn't go forward with anything until she was.

Oh, right. He couldn't go forward anyway, so what did it matter?

She picked at her food. "What's your church like?" While they ate, they chatted about various church experiences they had, both positive and negative.

They split the pastries. He gave her half of the orange scone and half of the lemon bread. While he recalled her coffee preference, he didn't think they'd ever bought pastries. As teens they hadn't been able to afford much.

"Are you drinking a peppermint mocha too?" Asia leaned forward to stare at the label on his cup. "I didn't know you liked them."

Ian chuckled. "I didn't use to. I got hooked when I met this girl several years ago. She liked peppermint mochas, and I couldn't afford to buy two drinks. We shared the one, and before the summer's end, I liked them too."

She stared at him. Memories swirled. The two of them seated in the coffee shop on the few days when the weather didn't beckon them outside. Sitting in the park on the beautiful days, counting the sips he took and the sips she took. Arguing over who drank the most. Laughing. Growing closer. Learning to love.

Healing his shattered heart.

She cleared her throat. Took a sip of coffee. "I'm glad to see I had a good influence in your life. What if you'd lived forever without knowing the beauty of this peppermint bliss?" She wrinkled her nose at him just as she had years ago.

Oh no. It was too late.

To protect his heart.

To keep from falling in love—again.

Ian threw away his trash. "So. Church?"

"Does Cinda go at the same time?" She folded the paper bag from the scone into a creased grid.

"She does sometimes, not always. Hey, if you're worried about fancy clothes, this isn't the church the Bryants attended when you went with them. Note what I'm wearing." He gestured to his jeans and polo. Nothing fancy.

She studied him, then shook her head. "Maybe another time. Thanks for the invite."

He'd attended church alone. As usual. Even the few of his teens who attended weren't there. He headed for work.

I-BBQ opened at noon on Sundays. Today there were people waiting to come inside. Ian greeted each customer, helped with setting tables, and even took a turn at the grill. He kept busy until the lunch rush ended. Asia should be here soon, as well as Meg, who agreed to come in on her day off to discuss a community event.

He went to his office and rummaged through some boxes on the shelves. He'd meant to do this before, but the past few days had been too busy. He found his old computer, plugged it in, and fired it up. He needed to get some of the files and extras off so it would be as fast as possible for Asia.

A knock on the door startled him. He glanced up as Meg stuck her head in. "Hey, Boss Man. We're here. Want to do this in your minuscule little office or out here where there's room to spread out and have pie." She grinned. "I went walking and am in danger of wasting away if I don't have something sweet."

"We can't have that." Ian unplugged the computer. "Is Asia here?"

"She just walked in. This room is empty, and it's quiet out front."

"Then grab a table in the back room. Let them know we need pie and peace and quiet. I'll be right there." He wound up the cord--the battery on this beast wouldn't last as long as they needed to use it--grabbed a pad of paper, and stepped into the dining area.

He breathed in the scent of grease from frying chips and walked over to join Asia. She also had a pad of paper that she'd been scribbling on. Well, maybe you didn't call the doodles of an artist scribbling. Hers had purpose to them.

"I put down some ideas already." Asia scooted her pad aside to make room for him to put the computer between them. "I absconded with one of your menus that didn't have sauce on the outside, and I think I've come up with some ideas that will fit on the same size bag." She seemed more subdued than she had this morning. Did talking to Walter seem more urgent now that Cinda knew?

"Asia, after we do this, why don't I take you to the care center."

Her widened eyes and open mouth mirrored his own reaction to his words.

Where had *that* come from?

13

THE AFTERNOON SUN hung low in the sky as Ian pulled his truck into a parking space at the Driftwood Cove Care Center. Surrounded by colorful flowers and tall trees, the *U*-shaped brick building looked attractive. He'd never been here before, but heard they housed about sixty residents.

"This is it." Asia's fingers twined together, the tips nearly white. Her lips had thinned, her eyes grown huge. He could almost feel the trepidation coming off of her in waves.

"Hey, you okay?" He pulled the keys out, switched them to his left hand, and rubbed at the stiffness in her shoulders. "We don't have to do this. We can wait."

"No." The word exploded from her. She looked at him, her eyes haunted, and swallowed. "Sorry. I'm a little nervous. I don't want to wait though. I have to do this." She fingered the birth certificate in her pocket. She'd brought it in case the personnel working here didn't want to let her in to see him. They'd talked about the proof of the document being the key to getting inside.

"Let's do it." He went around to her door, put his hand on her back, and walked with her to the entry. The feel of her small frame under his fingers called to him. Oh, to have the freedom to pull her in an alcove somewhere and hug her until the tension left her. Would she be able to relax as long as she didn't know the truth of her parentage? Why hadn't her mother been more forthcoming? Or Asia's mother's friend, Joy? Surely *she* had some answers.

"Do you think Cinda will be here?" Asia stopped under the portico to look over her shoulder at him. Her face paled. "Or Glenna?"

"I have no idea. I imagine they would have come earlier in the day though. This is mealtime, or close to it. They're probably home getting ready to eat." He hoped that made sense. He didn't want to run into either sister, and neither did Asia. That would cause more problems than either of them wanted to deal with right now.

"I wonder if Cinda said anything to Glenna." Asia swallowed hard. Faced the door and stepped forward without waiting for his response.

He didn't have one anyway. Cinda wouldn't have gone to Glenna, would she? The sisters hadn't been close lately. Maybe Cinda wanted to mull over the implications of Asia's birth certificate. He hoped she took time to consider the options.

Brenda Patterson greeted them at the check-in desk. He'd known her since high school. Her cheery smile didn't hide the way she perked up at the prospect of something interesting. Brenda could make anything sound like the juiciest gossip. He almost groaned aloud. If she got wind of Asia's connection to Walter, everyone in town would know.

Asia signed in and asked for Walter Bryant's room number.

"He's in 214." Brenda pushed the clipboard toward Ian and handed him the pen. "You can ask at the nurse's station to see if he can have visitors. The Alzheimer's unit is locked to prevent patients from wandering off." She studied Asia. "Didn't you use to visit the Bryants in the summer?"

"Yes, I did. I'm surprised you remember." Asia's smile didn't quite reach her eyes.

As they walked down the hallway, Ian breathed a sigh. So far, so good. "I feel like we're teens again, slipping out to meet after bedtime."

"You and me both." Asia shook her head. "I thought those days were behind me."

He caught her hand in his, and she didn't pull away. The chill in her fingers warmed as he held them. There weren't many residents in the hallway. They must be in the dining room, if they were able, or in their rooms awaiting their meals otherwise.

One white-haired woman sat in the wheelchair, nodding her head and talking to someone or something. "I want it." She kept saying it over and over as they walked past her. A nurse's aide came hurrying toward them and called out, "Mrs. Bradley, you're missing your dinner. Let's go." She grabbed the handles on the chair and wheeled the woman around, hurrying down the hallway. Maybe they needed seatbelts in those chairs.

Ian wrinkled his nose at the scent of astringent cleaners and the occasional whiff of urine. He'd been told the staff did a good job of keeping the facility clean. That must be difficult with residents unable to care for themselves.

He and Asia reached a locked door with a doorbell. Brenda had mentioned they would need to have someone let them in. Asia pushed the buzzer.

An older nurse Ian didn't know opened the door for them. Her gray hair poofed out in curls around her head. She pushed her glasses up as she studied him and Asia. "Come on back to the station and tell me who you're here to see." As they walked the short distance, she talked over her shoulder. "We're a little short-staffed today. We've just gotten over a bout of the flu. All the patients are eating in their rooms today to keep from spreading anything."

They passed a room, and a wizened old man, bent and gnarled, shuffled out.

"Mr. Benson, you get back in that room." The nurse—Ian hadn't caught the name on her tag—spun out a practiced move and got the man headed back into his room. He didn't even seem aware his path had changed.

The nurse rounded the desk and turned. Ah. Nurse Radcliff.

"Here we are. Who are you here to see?"

"I'd like to see Walter Bryant." Asia leaned against the desk. "He's in room 214."

"Yes, yes, he is." The nurse frowned as she studied something on her computer. "We have here that only family is allowed in to see him. I believe that's his two daughters. I don't recall you being here before." Her face filled with sympathy as she looked up at Asia. "Perhaps you could talk to one of the girls, and they will accompany you."

"But I'm his daughter." Asia fumbled in her pocket. Ian heard the rustle of paper as she pulled out her birth certificate. "I've been away, and this is the first opportunity I've had to come visit."

Nurse Radcliffe took the document and frowned as she studied the print. "This is highly unusual. His daughters were adamant that no one else be allowed in, but it says here he is your father." She studied Asia. "You don't look like his other daughters."

"Not really." Asia's hands were trembling the tiniest bit. Ian put his arm around her. Showing her birth certificate to this woman could get the news of her parentage spread throughout the small town. Walter Bryant had been a well-known person in his time. He'd even been the mayor at one point and served on the town council. This would be a juicy piece of gossip if Radcliffe was inclined to share.

"Maybe I should call Cinda." The nurse reached for the phone. "I'll just check to make sure it's okay for you to go in. Mr. Bryant gets so upset with new people."

"Please." Asia's lower lip trembled. "I haven't seen him in so long. You can call Cinda if you want, but let me go visit my father while you're calling." She drew in a ragged breath. "Please."

"Okay." Nurse Radcliffe handed back the certificate. "His room is right down the hall. He should be done with his meal by now. Please speak calmly to him. If he starts to get upset, leave right away. He will only escalate if you try to calm him."

Asia nodded. Glanced at Ian. Fear and excitement shone in her eyes. He followed her down the hall to the door marked 214. She put her palm on the wood, hesitated, closed her eyes for a moment, and pushed.

The room was brighter than Ian anticipated. The wall of windows had the curtains open, looking out toward the wooded area near the care center. A tray with leftovers sat beside the unmade bed. Walter stood at the window, his palm on the pane of glass as if trying to figure out how to get outside. He used to love the outdoors and must hate being made to stay inside.

Ian waited by the door as Asia took a few steps into the room. Walter turned to look at them. His haggard appearance shocked Ian. His white hair, once lush and well combed, now showed patches of baldness and stuck up in wild disarray.

His blue eyes were as vivid as ever. Even from across the small room, Ian could make out the color.

Walter noticed Asia, paused, and his face lit with a smile. “Kim.” He took a tottering step. “You’ve come back.”

~

SHE HADN’T KNOWN what to expect, but this emaciated man with the vacant expression left her dumbfounded. Uncle Walter had never been heavy, but he had been robust and healthy. The man standing before her was so thin a strong wind would knock him over. He had crevices in his face instead of wrinkles. His age-spotted hands trembled, and she feared he might fall to the floor before he could sit down.

He’d called her Kim.

Her mother.

“My Kim.” Walter stretched out his hand, and the shaking grew stronger.

She cleared her throat. Her time was short. “Walter.” Maybe if she pretended to be her mother, she would get some answers. “Can we talk?” She glanced over her shoulder at Ian. He nodded. Her heart beat against her ribs, her breathing grew rapid. The room swirled. She had to get hold of herself before she blew this chance.

“Kim. Does Mary know you’re here?” A look of panic chased across his features. His movements became jerky.

"No. She doesn't know." Asia kept her voice steady. Soothing. He seemed to calm. "I wanted to talk to you about Asia. Our daughter."

"Asia." Walter took a tottery step. "I went to Asia. Is that where we are?" He turned back to the window, shuffled closer, and put his palm back on the pane, staring out at the coming twilight.

"This is Driftwood Cove. Your daughter is Asia." Her throat ached. How could she make him understand? She thought he might say something when he believed her to be her mother, but now he didn't even turn around to look at her. Acted as if she weren't in the room.

She tried a different tack. "Walter, Asia needs you."

He turned around too fast. Stumbled. Caught himself on a chair situated between the bed and window. "I don't want to go to Asia. I've been there. I'm not going back. Get out." He waved his hand at her. Took a step toward her.

His patchy hair, funny looking at first, now made him look crazy and angry. Asia backed up a step.

She couldn't leave. Not without the truth. This was her chance. The only reason she'd come to Driftwood Cove. The only reason she'd put herself at risk.

"Walter, it's Kim. Remember me? You wrote me letters."

"He *what?*"

Asia spun at the snarled words.

Glenna. "What are you doing here? Get out." Glenna's fingers caught her arm, the tips digging into her flesh.

"Glenna, stop." Ian's strident tone made Walter jump. He began to wave his arms in the air. He turned in a circle. Came toward Asia, and she feared he would hurt her more than his daughter was doing. Wild cries came from his mouth, like a warrior on a rampage.

Nurse Radcliffe and a male nurse hustled through the door. "Okay, everyone out." The gray-haired nurse pushed at Asia as the man confronted Walter. Asia's eyes burned. What would she do now? How would she ever learn the truth? Even if she came back when Walter had calmed down, they would be on the lookout for her. She wouldn't get to see him again.

Ian caught her arm, tugging her out past Glenna. Asia glanced back one more time at the man who might be her father. Her last glimpse was of the male nurse wrestling Walter onto the bed while Nurse Radcliffe pulled out a needle to give him a shot.

"I can't believe you came here to see my father." Glenna's eyes snapped, her face so close Asia could count her eyelashes. "What gives you the right? How did you even convince them to let you in?" She raised her hand to slap Asia, but Ian caught her arm.

"Glenna. We'll leave." Ian had Asia pulled back against his chest. She tried to draw comfort from him, but only wanted to run. Back into Walter's room. Or away from this town.

Nurse Radcliffe came out of Walter's room and hurried them all out of the Alzheimer's wing. As the doors whooshed shut, Glenna rounded on Asia again.

Ian stepped between them. "We're leaving. We can talk about this another time." He urged Asia past Glenna.

"What happened? I got here as fast as I could." Cinda trotted down the hall, her long hair disheveled. Martin strode after her looking like a thundercloud.

"Somehow she got into the ward to see *our* father. In. His. Room." Glenna faced her sister but pointed one finger back at Asia. If she'd been closer, she could have poked Asia's eye out with the strength of the motion. Her shrill voice echoed in the hallway.

Brenda rushed toward them from the front desk. "People, you have to take this outside. We can't have you upsetting our residents. Now." Her firm tone left no room to argue. Cinda and Martin led the way, with Asia and Ian following them. Asia could feel the burn of Glenna's glare on her back. She hoped she wouldn't be turned to ash. Then again, maybe that wouldn't be so bad.

In the parking lot, well away from the building, Cinda swiveled to face Asia. "What were you *thinking?*"

"You wouldn't let me see him. I needed to, so I came here." Asia crossed her arms over her chest.

"And you came with her?" Hurt rang in Cinda's voice and reflected in her eyes as she gazed at Ian. "Why?"

"You know why." Ian's hands cupped Asia's shoulders. "She deserves to know the truth."

"The truth about what?" Glenna stomped over beside her sister, her hands curled into fists.

No one spoke. Fireworks would fly if Glenna heard about her birth certificate. She'd wanted to have something to back up the document before she confronted Glenna.

"The truth about what?" Glenna ground out the words.

She wouldn't let this go. She could pull out the proof, but Glenna would probably tear up her only link to Walter and the past.

"Glenna. Please." Cinda's shoulders slumped. Her mouth turned in an uncharacteristic frown. "I'll come over in a few minutes and talk to you. Please go home and let me deal with Asia."

Glenna humphed. "So what? You can give her a better job? More money?" She turned her back on Asia. A spine so taut she might crack. "Okay. But you'd better be at my house almost as soon as I am."

She strode away without waiting for a response. Asia heard a beep and then a car door slam. Tires squealed as Glenna left.

They all seemed to breathe a sigh. Cinda bowed her head. Reached back to fumble for Martin's hand. He still looked angrier than any of them.

Why should he be so upset?

"Asia." Cinda's cheeks were hollowed when she looked up. "I don't work tomorrow. Do you think we could go somewhere and talk? Just the two of us." She pressed her lips in a thin line and blinked. Moisture beaded on her lashes. "I want to understand. I'm trying. It just hurts so much."

"I know. I don't know how I could have made this any easier." Asia swallowed hard.

"I'll go see Glenna. I have no idea what will happen there." Cinda faced Martin. "Can you take me to my car? I'm sorry about dinner."

Martin's jaw clenched. He glared at Asia and Ian. Jerked a nod. Took Cinda's elbow and hurried her toward his vehicle.

The sun dipped to rest on the horizon. From here, Asia could glimpse the ocean. She wanted to be there, to dip her toes in the surf and feel the power of the tide. The breeze lifted her hair, chilling the sweat on her neck. She shivered.

"You cold?" Ian put his arm around her shoulders. He felt so strong, so comforting. She wanted all this to be resolved. She wanted Ian to still care for her when he knew the whole truth. She rolled the words around in her mouth wondering if this would be the time to say something.

The wounds opened by seeing Walter and confronting Glenna were raw and achy. She couldn't face any more strife right now.

Was she cold?

Yes. Chilled to the depths of her soul.

14

SHE'D HUDDLED in her bed most of the night, going over and over the scene at the care center. Asia tried to recall Walter's face from her teen years. Did she resemble him at all? Maybe the jawline and the shape of her face. Did she resemble Cinda or Glenna?

She groaned and rubbed at her eyes as she stumbled to the counter to start a cup of coffee. She had enough grit in her eyes to fill a second Sahara Desert. While the coffee brewed, she took a quick shower. What to do until lunch? Maybe pull out the computer Ian loaned her and work on some ads for him?

Meg had some great ideas, so while Asia munched a piece of toast, she reworked the designs. She would send them to the paper and other places in town for advertisement. Meg had the authority to approve the new menu bags and order them. They should be able to implement the new menu in a couple of weeks, in tandem with the announcement of the family night and night of dancing.

A tingle ran through her as she finalized the ad design. She could picture the increase of business for I-BBQ, from families wanting a safe place to take their kids to teens wanting a place to dance and listen to music. Ian and Meg needed to find a group to play who would draw a crowd.

She glanced at the clock as she emailed the designs to Meg and Ian. She still had over an hour before meeting Cinda for lunch. Her gaze fell on her backpack, partially hidden under her bed. Time for more letters.

She put away the computer and poured another cup of coffee. Sat down with the envelopes and undid the ribbon. She had tried to put them back in the order she found them but wasn't sure she was successful. Those she'd already read had a mark and a date on the envelope.

She opened the next letter in the pile and settled in the only comfy chair in her small apartment.

Kim. My love. Joy told me you listed me on Asia's birth certificate. If she is mine, please allow me to see her. I would like to know for sure. If I have another daughter, I want to be in her life. I want her to know my girls too. She would be almost the same age as my youngest daughter, Cinda. I picture them being friends.

The letter continued with Walter begging her mother to answer. To tell him where she lived so he could come and visit. At the end, he talked of his choices and his marriage. The damage he'd done to his faith by being unfaithful to his wife. And how, even though he tried to resist, he still loved Kim and wanted to have her in his life.

Asia's heart ached. He'd wanted to know her. Wanted her to know him. Yet he also sounded as if he wasn't positive she was his. Had her mother ever answered him? Had she ever acknowledged Asia as Walter's daughter other than on the birth certificate? If her mother wasn't sure, why had she put his name there?

A tear dripped on to Asia's cheek. She swiped it away, folded up the letter, and opened the next one.

She read several more that had never been opened. They were much shorter. Mostly begging for news. For confirmation. For a picture. How strange that her mother kept the letters when she didn't want to know what they said. What prompted her to leave Walter and never talk to him again when he so obviously loved her? She lifted the kintsugi necklace out and rubbed the cool stone with her fingers.

"Oh, Mom. What did you do?" Asia tied the ribbon and stuffed the packet back in the box. She couldn't read any more right now. Her whole body ached. She wanted to weep but the tears didn't come. Instead, she had a vast emptiness inside. An aching hole that might never be filled.

Closing her eyes, she saw Ian's face. His smile. Felt his touch again on her back. His steadiness. His strength.

She wanted him with all that was in her. To be his. Connected in a way no one else would be. His for the rest of her life.

That was never going to happen. Not with people like Harold Nevins and the other Chamber members around. They would never accept her. Not if they knew what she'd done. If the higher ups in town discovered her past, she would drag Ian down with her.

She simply had to maintain her distance. Was this what Walter felt about her mother? The bone-deep ache that sucked the very life from you, knowing if you chose what you wanted to do, you would hurt everyone you loved?

Asia cried out to God. She had no words. No plan to present. Just a wordless cry from her heart.

~

An hour later, seated on a bench outside, Asia watched Cinda pull up to the shop. She'd wanted to walk somewhere to meet, but Cinda insisted on picking her up.

"Ready?" Cinda's smile as Asia sank into the passenger seat didn't carry the usual buoyancy. Heavier makeup under her eyes tried to hide the shadows there. Her normal peaches-and-cream complexion had more cream than peaches today.

Asia nodded at her.

Cinda pulled out, maneuvered the streets, and turned west, heading out of town. "I packed us a picnic. I hope that's okay. I didn't want to eat anywhere we could be overheard." She blinked fast and a tear shimmered on her lashes.

Asia nodded.

They pulled off at the same spot where Asia had gone with Ian a few days ago. That seemed like a lifetime now with all that had happened. The car bumped over the dirt road leading down toward the beach. Cinda pulled off and put on the parking brake.

They stared out the windshield at the rolling waves. In the distance a dolphin jumped, coming down with a splash, followed by another doing the same. Asia couldn't stop her smile. She'd always loved watching the marine life, dolphins in particular.

"I don't know about you, but I'm grasping at anything and everything to keep from having this conversation." Asia could see the agreement in Cinda's hollow-eyed gaze. She stilled her own trembling and reached out her hand. "Can we agree to be friends no matter what? I didn't do anything to cause our parents to…to do what they did. I know you didn't either."

A tear dribbled down Cinda's cheek. "I know. I've been thinking. Part of me wants to blame you. I talked to Glenna last night, and I know she blames you. But how can a baby be at fault? You aren't the reason for your mom's and my dad's indiscretion. You are the result. I think we connected so well in our teens because deep down we knew we were sisters."

"But are we?" Asia wiped the moisture from her cheek with the back of her hand. She sniffed. "I'm not sure your dad believed me to be his daughter. He wanted proof, but my mom wouldn't talk to him."

"Why do you think that?" Cinda tipped her head to one side, her earrings winking in the light of the sun.

"I have some letters." She pressed her lips tight together for a moment before she could continue. "Letters your dad wrote to my mom, but she never answered."

The soft thunk of Cinda's head hitting against the window at her side sounded loud in the car. She winced. Rubbed at her head. "You have…letters." Her low statement carried a tone of disbelief. She shook her head. "Do you mind if I see them?"

Pulling her backpack around, Asia reached in for the box and placed it on Cinda's lap.

"Wait." Cinda held up one hand palm out. "Let's pray first. Maybe even get out the food." Her mouth twisted as she glanced out the windshield. "I think it's too windy to sit on the beach. I'm afraid the pages would blow away. Do you mind sitting in the car?"

Asia agreed. While Cinda brought out the lunch items--sandwiches, chips, and fruit--Asia took out the letters and removed the ribbon. She put the unopened letters back in the box. There were enough to look through without opening new ones.

She handed the first two to Cinda, took her sandwich, and waited, unable to take a bite as she watched her possible sister open the letter Walter had written.

THE KNOCK on the office door dragged Ian away from his paperwork. He'd been immersed in his accounting program trying to figure out a minor discrepancy in the books. He rubbed the back of his neck to ease the ache as Meg popped in and shut out the noise of the restaurant.

"Have you seen Asia's ads?" Meg grinned like she'd won a prize. "That girl has some talent."

"I haven't looked." He rolled his shoulders, blinked a couple of times, and minimized his accounting program to open his email.

"It's midafternoon. Have you even eaten lunch?" Meg frowned at him. "Breakfast?"

"Are you in charge of me?" He added a grin so his words wouldn't sting. Meg always wanted to micromanage everyone. It was the mother in her, and he loved that about her.

"I had a donut and coffee on the way here this morning." He winced. Meg wasn't going to like that.

"You should write a book on nutrition." Meg crossed her arms over her chest. "You look at the email, and I'll grab a plate for you. We're on the brink of an amazing change here. I don't want you to starve to death before that happens."

He laughed and patted his gut as she headed out the door. "I don't think I'm in any danger." While he hadn't gained much weight, he'd noticed a few pounds creeping onto his frame. He'd have to get back to running and be more determined to watch what he ate.

Meg was back in no time and set a plate of food before him. He leaned forward and breathed in the scent of fresh barbecue and deep-fried chips. He would watch every bite he put in his mouth. He bit back a laugh. He wouldn't say that out loud, or he'd get another mom lecture.

As he took his first bite of sandwich, he opened Asia's file and almost spit out the food. He swallowed the half-chewed bite, wiped his mouth, and stared at Meg. "Did she do this today? All of these?"

"Yep. She sent them midmorning. She wants to know what changes we want, but I think they're pretty perfect." Meg came around to lean down and peruse the images. She snatched one of his chips, and he glared at her before turning back to study the ads.

"Wow. These are amazing." His chair squeaked when he sat back. "Do you have any ideas for the game and music nights? How soon do you think we can be ready?"

"I've talked with a local band I know. They're free the second Saturday from now. I have another idea to run by you." Meg went around to the front of the desk and sat down. She curled her fingers over the edge of the seat. Licked her lips. Looked like she wanted to bolt out the door.

He put down the chip he'd picked up. "Okay. Let me have it. If you say you're quitting, I'm tying you to that chair and making you stay."

She grinned and shook her head. "No. Nothing like that." She rubbed her palms on her jeans. "My friends in the band had a suggestion I think is really good." Her words began to rush out as if she thought he would interrupt her. He listened, apprehensive at first, but could feel the thrumming in his veins as he pictured what she described.

She fell silent. He waited a beat for the objections to start popping up, but he had nothing. "I think that might work. Do you think we can pull it together in time to get ads up and the word out? You're talking less than two weeks."

"He suggested planning a little farther out. Maybe shoot for Memorial Day weekend. That would give you extra time to plan and implement." Meg leaned forward. "He also thinks he can get a second group if you want a longer event."

"Let me think. I'll finish my lunch. If I still think it's a good idea, I'll give you the go-ahead to contact him and go talk to Asia about changing the ad to reflect the different date and ideas."

Meg pointed at the food before she walked out and closed the door. "Eat. You need that."

He picked up the sandwich and took another bite. He hadn't wanted to change anything with the restaurant. He hadn't been doing a great business, but he'd kept in the black. This idea could change everything. While Meg had occasionally mentioned making improvements, Asia's suggestions had made him sit up and take notice. The time had come to make his mark in the community. He had some ideas of his own.

Wolfing down the rest of his food, Ian put his computer to sleep and carried his plate and utensils to the kitchen. "Meg, I'm going out. Be back before the rush."

The afternoon had warmed up. The breeze off the ocean kept the temperatures from being too hot, but he could feel spring in the air. The cheery flowers outside the quilt shop danced in the wind.

Maybe artistic ability ran in a family. Asia might not have the decorating or quilt talent Cinda had, but she certainly was an artist.

He went around back and knocked on the door. Was she home? He hadn't thought to try calling or texting even though she now had a phone.

When she opened the door, his stomach did a slow roll. She'd changed out of her jeans and T-shirt for a pair of shorts and sleeveless tank top. She had her hair piled on top of her head in a messy bun with strands trailing around her neck. He wanted nothing more than to drag her into his arms and kiss her like he had that last summer they'd been together. He still remembered the feel of his lips on hers. The scent of her.

The way she fit perfectly in his arms.

A ray of westering sun broke through the trees behind them and caught her. He noted the redness of her eyes. The sunken pallor of her cheeks.

"Hey, you okay?" He stuck his hands in his pockets to keep from flinging the door open and grabbing her. Like she needed some caveman type right now.

"I am." She bit her lower lip. "I guess."

"How did your talk with Cinda go? Want to go for a walk and talk about it?" Inside he was like a toddler with his hands pressed together and the big eyes begging. "There's a pretty good ice cream place about a mile away."

She plopped her hands on her hips. "I am going to have to change my wardrobe for a bigger size if you keep throwing food at me."

He raised his eyebrows. Quirked his mouth.

"Okay. I know I've lost a little, but still, if you have your way, you'll be able to roll me down the street like a giant bowling ball."

"I doubt that will happen." He pulled open the screen door as she slipped on shoes. "But if it does, I promise to avoid the potholes."

She stepped out. Way too close. He needed to back up, but he didn't want to. What…what were they going to do?

"Ready?" She tilted her head back to look up at him. He lost the ability to swallow. Fought to control himself. Stepped back.

"Yeah. This way." He moved aside to let her lead the way to the sidewalk. He took her hand, turning in the direction he wanted to go. "The ice cream shop is this way, or we can go to a tea shop that isn't much farther. Would you prefer a boba tea?"

"You have a boba tea house here? Close enough to walk to?" She pressed her free hand to her chest. "I'm doomed. Get ready for me to roll."

To give her some space to collect herself, he talked to her about Meg's idea. He could see her emotions roiling on the surface. After a few minutes she told him about lunch with Cinda. About the letters her father had written. Her frustration with her mother never telling her anything.

"I want to know the truth, but I have no idea if that will ever happen. With my mother gone and Walter not responsive, I may never find out." Her shoulders slumped.

Was that the gleam of moisture in her eyes?

"You know." He hit the button to change the light for the crosswalk. "I think there might be a way to know without them telling you." The light changed, and they hurried across the street. He led the way into the teahouse.

"Hold that thought." Asia pulled free and reached for a menu. He figured she would demand to know what he meant, but maybe she feared someone overhearing.

They ordered their drinks. The shop was busy and the noisy chatter and the loud banging as the workers made ice cream to fill orders made it impossible to talk.

When the drinks were ready, he grabbed them and followed Asia outside to a small table off by itself.

As soon as they were seated, she leaned forward, her gaze intense. "How can I know? Tell me."

15

"I SHOULD DO WHAT?" Asia's mouth fell open as she stared at Ian. "Get a DNA comparison test done? How am I supposed to do that? Follow Cinda around the shop and pull out a few of her hairs? Wrestle Glenna to the ground and jab a cotton swab in her mouth?"

She rolled her eyes as she took a sip of her almond milk black tea, sucking one of the bobas up the straw to chew on.

"No, you don't have to do that." Ian's dimples deepened. "Although the thought of you wrestling Glenna to the ground has some merit. I could take the video. It might go viral."

She tried to swallow before she choked to death on a boba. "I will not do that, and you won't video anything." She kicked at his foot under the table. "I'm serious here and you're throwing out impossibilities."

"I'm not. This is a very real and simple solution." He sat back, his expression entirely too smug. "I happen to know this will work. Not overnight, but it will work."

"Okay. Explain how, Mr. Know-It-All." Asia twirled her straw in the cup.

"When Walter was living with Glenna and her husband because he couldn't be on his own, Glenna and Cinda sent their DNA to one of those places that advertise letting you know your family history. There have been stories of family members being connected that way. I think they were hoping to find Randall so he could be aware of what was happening with Walter." Ian's dimples disappeared.

Cinda had so wanted her brother to be with them, or even to call. She had talked with Asia many times about the hurt of not knowing what happened to him.

"Did they find anything?" She took another sip, savoring the taste she'd missed so much. She hadn't had an almond boba tea in years.

"They had some interesting lineage results, but nothing about Randall. They would only hear about him if he had also done the testing with that lab, I think. I don't know if they all go into a database or if each lab keeps their own records."

Ian's chair scraped against the concrete as he leaned forward. The traffic on the sidewalk had increased, so he probably didn't want to be overheard. She scooted closer to the table.

"Walter was very angry when he heard what they'd done. He still had some lucid days back then. Well, maybe not days, but parts of days at least."

"Why was he so angry?" An idea niggled in Asia's thoughts, but she wanted to hear Ian's input before she voiced anything.

"I think he was afraid they would find out about you." Ian's face was so close to her she could see the flecks of darker blue around the outer part of his irises. She froze. He'd just put her own thoughts into words. Could this be true? Had Walter been afraid of his daughters finding out they had a sister? That he'd had an affair and cheated on their mother?

Why did he sound one way in his letters to her mother and act another way with his family? Did he want to be part of her life or not? Had he come to his senses and realized the trouble she would bring? If Aunt Mary had found out about her existence, she would have been furious.

Funny, now that she thought about it. Aunt Mary hadn't liked her any more than Glenna had. She'd often been cold to Asia. She tolerated her, but there wasn't any of the warmth she showed to her own children. Had she suspected Asia was really a half sister, not a cousin?

She sat back. How different her life might have been if Walter had only revealed the truth back then. If her being his daughter *was* truth. Oh, this was all so…frustrating!

"A tea for your thoughts." Ian nudged her cup. His blond-brown hair gleamed as the sun caught the gold highlights. Could those blue eyes see everything inside her? All the little hidden lies that would make him turn away. Just like everyone else turned away from her.

"I'd better get back. If you want me to redo those ads, I'll need to get to work. Meg needs to submit them in time to get them in the paper this week. I don't know the deadline." Asia couldn't look at him. She didn't want to see the hurt in his eyes. She scooted her chair away and picked up her drink. He followed suit without a word.

They crossed the street at the corner, getting away from the more crowded walkway in front of the shops. They walked in silence for the next block. Waves of tension battered her. Ian needed her to talk. He wanted to know everything about her, but she had secrets that must be kept.

"So, do you like Meg's idea? It's not too ridiculous?"

The tightness in her chest eased. "I think it's a great idea. But you'll need to get the word out right away, and you'll have a lot of work trying to figure out supplies to bring in for it. Have you ever done anything like this?"

"I've helped out with a couple of events. I remember the logistics and how to figure things. I'm not too worried. I'm just afraid of naysayers and that people won't show up." He shrugged when she glanced up at him, a sheepish grin on his face.

"I can't believe you would even think that. Remember what just happened when that man was so mean to you? You have a ton of friends. They'll be there for you. I'll make some ads that will have them dying to eat your barbecue and dance the night away." She winked at him.

He laughed. "I have no doubt. You can do it."

They chatted more about what groups to invite and his target audience. She agreed to have the ads to Meg within the hour since she already had the mockups done. Changing some wording wouldn't take long.

They parted ways, and Asia slipped back into her apartment. She put her leftover tea in the fridge, then opened the laptop, made changes to the ads and menu, and re-sent the information to Meg and Ian.

She spent a few minutes trying to search online for Joy, her mom's friend, to no avail. She found several women with the same name, but none of them were the Joy she needed to contact. Where could she have gone? How had she met Walter? Could Joy have introduced her mom to Walter?

When she'd lived with Joy after her mother went to prison, Joy used to drive her up the coast to meet Walter. That's when he brought Asia home with him for the summer. No one ever suggested she was any more than a cousin to his kids. When she questioned the family ties, Walter and Joy were both very vague, so she'd stopped asking. How did someone suddenly acquire cousins when there'd been no mention of them before?

She gave up, grabbed her tea again, and settled in her easy chair with a book she'd found at the quilt shop. Maybe reading would settle the nauseating swirl of questions in her head and clarify her thoughts.

After reading the first few pages three times and still having no idea about the story, Asia gave up. She kept picturing Cinda, her forlorn expression, and the sorrow in her eyes.

She'd stared out the windshield at the blustery day. "Asia, I can't imagine my dad cheating on my mom. I keep thinking how hurt she would be if she knew. Do you think she knew?"

Asia had no idea, but even thinking about it made her insides ache. She wanted to curl up in a ball and wait for this storm to blow over. Why hadn't she kept this knowledge to herself? Why had she been so selfish?

The answer was simple. She wanted a family. She might not deserve one, but deep in her heart she had this longing she couldn't ignore. The desire had been there since those long ago summers and only intensified when she'd opened the box and found her birth certificate.

The kintsugi heart lay cool against her skin under her shirt. She still hadn't mentioned the necklace to Ian or Cinda. She touched her fingertips to the hardness of the stone and thought about the broken heart and the veins of gold healing the brokenness. She prayed for that kind of healing for this family. Her family.

A sharp knock rattled her door. Asia set her tea down and crossed to turn the knob. The door shoved open and pushed her backward. Glenna stood there, mouth set in a thin line, anger radiating off of her.

Glenna pushed past her into the apartment and swung around to face her. "I want you to leave town. Today. Your being here is only hurting my family."

Asia leaned back against the closed door. Of course she didn't include Asia in her family. She brought her shoulders forward to ease the ache in her chest. What could she say that Glenna would hear?

Glenna's red nails gleamed like fresh blood in the low light. "I'm not messing around. I'll give you money to leave. Today."

~

WHAT HAD HE BEEN THINKING? Ian rested his elbows on his desk and put his forehead in his palms. He was like a moth to Asia's flame. No matter how determined he was to stay away from her, he couldn't.

"God, what do I do? I can't ask her to leave. I can't leave town. If Walter is her father, she will want to stay here and be close to family. She has no one else. But I can't keep my distance." The hole in his heart became a bottomless pit. Truth was, he had no family either. All his aunts and uncles lived far away and wanted nothing to do with him. They'd made that clear long ago.

He used to walk the streets after dark, staring into houses at families eating together. Watching television together. Playing games or laughing. How wonderful to have a family who loved you for you, even with all your messed up parts.

Speaking of messed up, even as he berated himself for the attraction to Asia, he wanted to toss work aside, cross the parking lot, and knock on Asia's door. He pictured her sparkly eyes, her bright smile that felt special for him, those lips. Mmmmmm. He remembered. He certainly did.

All those stolen nights when the Bryant house quieted and Asia slipped out of Cinda's window. He didn't think Cinda ever suspected. He always made sure Asia returned in plenty of time to get some sleep for the next day. He heard her make excuses for being tired several times, saying she had trouble sleeping because of the sound of the ocean. Or the moon being so bright. Or the beautiful stars.

All true. She just hadn't been in the house when those things kept her awake.

They didn't do anything wrong. They walked to a bluff overlooking the ocean. And talked. For hours on end. They shared their stories. Their fears. Their dreams.

Yes, he'd kissed her, but that was all. He knew the sorrow she dealt with because of her mother's choices. As much as he'd wanted to have a physical relationship, that wasn't best for her. And she meant more to him than anything else. Even his own desires.

Thanks to Asia, he'd gone from a troublemaker being shunted between homes by the county to a model student who respected the law and people. He still kept in touch with his final foster family. He stayed there two years, up to the day he turned eighteen. Even then, they allowed him to stay in an apartment over their garage while he finished high school.

That had all been Asia's doing. She'd risked his anger and got him to open up. She cared when no one else did. She didn't look at him and see his father in the making. She didn't see his mother's weakness. She saw him.

And didn't run away.

He reached for his coffee only to realize the mug had nothing left. He closed his fingers around the cool ceramic, trying not to think about how empty his life had been until Asia showed up. Twice now she'd brought joy to his life. Oh, his faith brought him joy, but Asia brought a different kind.

"God, help me."

He squeezed his eyes shut, but his memories paraded in front of him, each one a dagger to the heart. Memories of his parents. His angry youth. College. Why couldn't they be wiped away? If God wiped away sins, why didn't He erase the memory of them?

A light tap sounded on his door. He said to come in, and Meg stuck her head around the jamb. "Hey, Boss." She came in, closed the door, and took the chair in front of his desk. "I came to tell you I sent in the ads and already heard back from Suzy at the paper. She loves the way the ads are set up. I wouldn't be surprised if she contacts Asia to see about doing ads for other customers.

"I also submitted the order for new menu bags. They got back to me to say they will have the order to us by the end of next week. Dave, at the print place, said they have an opening and can finish them pretty fast."

She folded her hands on her lap and stared at him. Was he supposed to say something? He couldn't seem to get his brain away from his morbid thoughts and onto business.

She shook her head at him. "I wasn't going to sit down at all because we're pretty busy, but I can see you need to talk. So let's hear it. What's bothering you?"

Had she given this same look to her children? Before she lost custody and the right to see them. But that was a different story.

He ached for all she lost.

"I can't." He ground his teeth fighting for control.

"You *won't.*" Meg pursed her lips and frowned at him. "You won't talk because you're afraid. I know that look on a guy. Remember? Two sons? Even if I haven't seen them in a long time." She tipped her head and raised her eyebrows, although a shadow of sadness passed over her face. "So spill. You'll feel much better, and I may have some motherly wisdom to impart, which is much better than a kick in the rear." She winked.

He couldn't help but smile. Meg had always been a force. Since she'd first walked in the doors of I-BBQ, she'd been full of suggestions and help. He'd come to depend on her, and she... maybe she'd come to care about him.

Maybe. Just maybe, he had family after all.

"It's Asia." He cracked his knuckles. Stopped when she frowned at him. Put his hands in his lap.

"I figured." Meg nodded. "You're in love with that girl."

"What? No." Cracked his knuckles again. "I'm attracted to her."

"Whatever." Meg examined her nails, peeked up at him, and smirked. "So, what's wrong with being *attracted* to Asia?"

"I can't." His fingernails dug into his palms. "I can't be with a woman. I have this past."

Meg waved her hand in the air. "I've heard all about your past. It makes for juicy small-town gossip. You weren't at fault for what your dad did. You tried to save your mother."

"You don't know the whole truth. No one does." He swallowed hard. "Asia knows the truth about Dad and Mom, but she's the only one."

"And she still cares about you." Meg gave him a *duh* look.

"Yes, but..." He stared at the picture of Driftwood Cove beach on his wall. He'd taken that shot and had it framed when he first moved back to town. The scene reminded him of Asia and their time together. When they'd had picnics with the Bryants and splashed in the waves.

When they'd been like family.

"She doesn't know what happened in college. It's why I can't be with a woman. I'm not trustworthy." He cleared his throat trying to ease the ache.

"What happened in college?" Meg's low tone soothed even as she questioned.

"There was a girl. We dated. She cheated on me with a friend. I got angry." He pressed his hands to his face unable to think of the shame. "I hit her."

Like father, like son.

"Like your father hit your mother, right?" Meg's question speared through him.

"Yes. I'm just like him." He couldn't even look at Meg.

"I seem to remember you saying something about becoming a Christian in college. Was that before or after this girl?"

He glanced at Meg. She'd leaned forward, waiting for his answer.

"After. I, uh, hit a low spot. A friend convinced me to go to church with him." He shrugged. What did that have to do with any--

"If you are truly a Christian--" Meg waited until he met her gaze. "--doesn't that mean you have a different father? A Father you are to emulate?"

16

On Wednesday morning, tree branches whipped in the wind. When Ian stepped outside, he tipped his head back, enjoying the brush of air against his heated face. He'd been helping with the pies and food prep for the day. Now he was headed to Cinda's shop for another quilt class.

He murmured a favorite chorus as he crossed the lot. He never thought he'd be excited to attend a sewing class. Never. Yet, today, he could almost bounce like Cinda. He couldn't wait to see Asia.

Like Father, like son.

He now had a whole new perspective on the phrase. No, he wasn't on a scale with God, but he worked every day to be more like him. If he failed, and he did, God's incredible forgiveness and grace gave him the ability to try again. To do better and better. He no longer had to view himself in the light of his earthly father, the man who couldn't control his temper or his addictions. Instead, he could bask in knowing how much God loved him and wanted him to be Christlike.

He'd waited to see Asia again, giving time for prayer and meditation. He wanted to be sure he wasn't running ahead of the Lord doing what he wanted instead of what God wanted. Now he had a plan to get closer to Asia. Not to push, but to allow their relationship to develop as it should.

The air swirled the scent of barbecue around as he wove between the parked cars and approached the shop door. Looked like they had a full class today. Cinda would be in top form. She loved teaching.

The chatter of voices drifted out to him before he reached for the doorknob. He winced. Why did women get so excited about different colors or patterns of material?

Cinda chatted with two women who were discussing some medicinal-pink material with butterflies in white on one bolt and gray on the other. Ian tried not to shudder. He really did.

Tansie waved from behind the register. He waved back and headed for the door to the classroom. He recognized several of the ladies making their way in the same direction and spoke to them. Through the open door, he glimpsed the other two men in the class. They were chatting together and didn't act as uncomfortable as they had last week.

He stepped inside and noted the fresh smell and the neatly laid out projects still needing to be finished. Asia pulled the last of them from a cupboard and turned to carry them to the table with the others. She caught his eye and smiled. Not a full I'm-so-glad-to-see-you smile, but at least she wasn't frowning. Had she missed him as much as he'd missed her?

"Need any help?" He stopped beside her breathing in the fresh scent of soap. She'd pulled her hair into an up ponytail, and it swung over her shoulder as she bent to arrange the piles.

“I think this is it. Cinda should be ready to start soon.” She looked up at him, and this time the smile did reach her eyes. He almost forgot the rest of the people in the room and pulled her into his arms.

“Hey, before I forget, some friends and I are going hiking this Saturday. Think your boss would give you the time off to go with us?” He gave her his special puppy-dog look that used to make her laugh. It still worked.

She shook her head at him. “I’ll check with her and see. I don’t know what she plans for Saturday. Last week we cleaned the apartment, and Tansie handled the shop. Maybe she’ll be okay without me.”

“Okay, ladies…and gentlemen.” Cinda clapped her hands as she came in and shut the door. “We’re a little behind, or some of us are.” She glanced at Asia and Ian. He gave her a palms up gesture and his most innocent expression.

“We need to work hard today. Let’s get those tops finished, and then on Friday we’ll put on the back and the binding. You’ll be amazed how easy it is.”

Beside him, Asia gave a soft snort. She clapped her hand to her mouth when Cinda frowned at her. Ian breathed easier at the obvious lessening of tension between the two. Had Asia considered the DNA testing? She might be right about it being a bit underhanded. He wouldn’t push for her to do the test.

Cinda picked up one of the rows of sewn-together squares. Probably done by one of the women who already knew how to quilt. She held the two rows up for them to see. “When you put these together, you have to be careful which way the seams are facing. The seams on one side will face this way and the other side will be opposite.” She demonstrated, urging them to come closer to see what she meant.

"If you don't do this and have both seams facing the same way, this is what happens." She slipped the material in the machine and zipped at lightning speed through the seam before pulling the material out and cutting the thread. She held the pieces up and showed them how the corners didn't line up right.

"You want to have matching points when you are quilting. If your points, the corners, are off, the rest of the quilt will be off, and I will make you get out that unpicker and fix the mistake. Got it?" Most of the class nodded and headed to their machines.

Ian stared at Cinda and the material, his brain trying to comprehend how to do this right.

"Matching points, Ian." Cinda came over and patted his arm. "You can do this. When the material lines up right, your seams line up, and the whole quilt looks beautiful. If they don't match, you'll have something no one will want."

Cinda picked up the seam ripper and started picking at the stitches she'd just put in. "Be sure to raise your hand if you have any questions? Give me some time to get to you." She headed to one of the men who already had his hand in the air.

Asia walked to the same sewing machine that ate her hair last Friday. Her shoulders lifted and dropped.

"You look like someone stole your favorite candy bar." He sat at the machine next to hers.

She wrinkled her nose. "I feel like I've just taken the walk of doom."

"At least you shouldn't be making a hair quilt today." Ian snickered. She smacked his arm with the back of her hand. Cinda cleared her throat, and they both jumped as if the principal caught them doing something wrong in school.

Ian lined up the material the way Cinda demonstrated. Asia did likewise and they both began to sew. When he finished the row, he cut the thread and looked at what he'd done. The corners matched up perfectly. *Yes!* He'd done it.

He glanced over as Asia cut her thread and held up the rows she'd sewn. He bit his lip at the look of consternation on her face. She tipped her head back and closed her eyes. He wanted to laugh, but that would not be wise. The hint of a tear wavered at the corner of her closed eye. Maybe he could switch material with her....

"What's up? Let me see." Cinda took Ian's quilt pieces from his hands and held them up. She studied the seams and smiled. "Nice job. Now you can pin the next row and keep going until you have them all put together. In a few minutes we'll talk about the backing and the batting that goes inside." She squeezed his shoulder and moved past him to Asia.

Ian held his breath.

"Let's see, Asia." Cinda picked up the quilt rows and held them up. Turned them back and forth. Frowned. Studied the wrong sides sewn together. "This is very close. You won't have to do much to set it right." She winked at Asia. "At least you didn't sew your hair into this one."

~

"YOU DOING OKAY?" Cinda handed Asia the box with the quilt squares for the afternoon mystery quilt class. Asia balanced the box in one hand as she put the precut pieces at each of the machines.

"I survived the morning humiliation. How bad can it be this afternoon? I'm not trying to sew." Asia flipped her ponytail back when it swung forward. She'd not only sewn her blocks wrong this morning, but when she finally got the stitching out and started sewing again, the bobbin ran out, then a needle broke. "I have decided the machine hates me. It's really a living being from the Planet of Let's Sew. The alien being recognizes me as a disaster and falls apart when I touch it."

Cinda laughed. The first real laugh Asia had heard from her since the fiasco with the birth certificate and her visit to Walter.

"In that case, Mr. Sewing Machine had better change his ways, because right now he's on our planet, not his." Cinda passed behind her with some extra scissors to put out on the table.

They finished prepping for the class and Cinda studied the room. "I think that's it. We're ready for the horde to descend."

Asia grinned. The horde consisted of fifteen ladies, many of them older. Not the definition she would use for them.

"Cup of tea?" Cinda glanced at her phone. "We've got half an hour before they start arriving. We can sit a few minutes."

Asia sipped a chai tea while Cinda had some coffee with cream. It felt good to sit and relax for a few minutes. Today had been busy. Yesterday had been slow at the shop, but they'd made up for it today. Tansie had been too busy to help with the morning class.

"I hear Glenna stopped to see you on Monday." Cinda studied her over the top of her cup. "Are you all right? Do you want to talk about it?"

Asia almost choked on her tea. She hadn't expected Cinda to bring up Glenna's visit. Didn't realize Cinda even knew. "She's not happy with me being here. She told me to leave town." She tried for nonchalant as she repeated what Glenna said to her and her offer of money to leave, but pain washed through her at the memory. Glenna hadn't raised a hand to her physically, but the emotional backlash had been a staggering slap.

"Actually, she demanded I leave town and never show myself here again." Asia couldn't look at Cinda. If she, who had been a best friend at one time, felt the same as her sister, Asia knew she would have to leave. What use to find your family only to have them hate you?

"Asia, look at me." Cinda's mug clunked as she set it on the table beside her chair. She leaned forward, her hands clasped between her knees. "I do not want you to leave. Is that clear?"

At the kindness in her gaze, Asia's throat tightened. She nodded. Warmth swept over her. She gripped her cup so hard the liquid sloshed over the rim.

"I'm sorry I reacted badly the other day. Finding out your dad—the dad you idolized—may have cheated on your mother is devastating. I wanted to deny it. I wanted to accuse you of fabricating that birth certificate. I wanted to go to the care center and shake my dad until he denied the allegations." Cinda shoved her hair back, pressed her hands over her face, and took a deep breath.

"I don't know what the truth is yet, but I do know you well enough to believe you aren't making this up. You are trying to find out the truth, too." Her voice broke. She bit her lip and clasped her hands together again.

Tears burned. Asia's hand trembled as she set her cup on the floor beside her chair. If she held it any longer, her trembling would result in more of a mess. She wanted to say something. To assure Cinda her dad wouldn't have done anything like this, but the truth was she believed he had. Since seeing him the other night, and his reaction to her, she'd come to believe he once cared for—maybe loved—her mother.

"You know..." Cinda didn't look up. Her voice was soft enough that Asia had to be still to hear her. "I don't want my dad to have done something like this, but once I calmed down, I've been thinking. A lot. I found a few pictures from the summers you visited. I haven't shown them to Glenna yet, but I will." She stood and crossed to the cabinet where she kept her belongings. She pulled out her purse and removed an envelope. She came back to sit in a chair beside Asia's.

"Look at this." She pulled out a picture of the two of them. They must have been fifteen, the last summer Asia had come to visit. They were sitting on the back step of the Bryant house, arms around each other, grinning like they were about to burst out laughing. They both wore their hair the same style. Cinda's had waves while Asia's was straight. Cinda was a little more rounded compared to Asia's stick-thin frame. But their smiles were almost identical. The shape of their faces was very similar. In fact, if she hadn't known who they were, Asia would have sworn these two girls were sisters.

Chills tap-danced up and down her arms. How had they missed this? Had Uncle Walter seen the similarity? Had Aunt Mary? Had anyone else?

Her thoughts stuttered to a halt. What if Glenna had noticed back then? She'd been almost eighteen and getting ready to leave for college when Asia spent her last summer here. Would Glenna have been so caught up in leaving home that she missed the similarity? Or was that what caused her hostility?

"Here come the ladies." Cinda held out her hand for the picture. Asia wanted to keep studying the image, but she had to put on her friendly persona and pretend she hadn't just been shaken to her core. She had to share this with Ian. What would he say?

"We'll talk after class. Okay?" Cinda squeezed her arm and stood. They both grabbed their partially empty cups and carried them to the sink.

The chattering ladies filed in, excited about the new quilt block they would sew today. Some of them were trying to guess the design. Others were sharing the latest tidbits of family life. Mrs. Beasley, an elderly woman, still spry and a delight, took her usual spot and beckoned to Asia.

"Young lady, I am going to need your eyes again today. These peepers of mine just aren't what they used to be." She smoothed her skirt and leaned close to Asia. "I'm even having trouble with my reading. They make the print so tiny."

Her smile faded, a faraway look crossing her face. "To think I used to keep up with all those kids and their reading at school. As the school librarian, I had to know what books were good for each kid to read."

"You kept up with all those books? That's amazing." Asia put her hand on Mrs. Beasley's shoulder. "Have you tried audiobooks? They are quite good if you have the right narrator." She'd learned about audiobooks during her stint in prison. She'd saved up and bought a cheap pair of headphones and would lie on her bed after lights out and listen to a book.

"I've heard of those. I'm not sure where I would get one or what to get." Mrs. Beasley's forehead creases deepened. She tapped a wrinkled finger on the table next to the sewing machine as if keeping time with her thoughts.

"I'm sure you have an account with the local library."

The elderly lady reared back as if she'd been insulted. "Of course I do. I served on the library board for years."

"They have an online catalogue where you can download books to your phone and listen to them through the phone speakers, headphones, or a Bluetooth speaker."

"Asia, you are speaking a foreign language. Besides, I don't know if I could figure out how to do something like that." She patted Asia's knee as Cinda stood at the head of the table and clapped her hands.

Asia leaned closer to whisper in Mrs. Beasley's ear. "Why don't I come to your house and show you how to do it?"

Mrs. Beasley's amber eyes lit up with excitement, as did her face.

17

A WEEK OR SO LATER, Asia pried her fingers from the armrest in Mrs. Beasley's car. Riding with an octogenarian who had vision problems—well, she would be glad to walk back to the shop. Mrs. Beasley only lived a few blocks from Cinda's quilt shop, but she'd nearly sideswiped a couple of parked cars, run a stop sign, and stopped a hair's breadth from her garage door before she realized it wasn't open.

"Here we are." Mrs. Beasley gathered her purse and quilt pieces.

"Let me carry those for you." Asia took the cloth bundle. "You'll need a free hand to unlock the door.

"Phooey." Mrs. B, as she insisted Asia call her, waved her age-spotted hand. "I don't bother with such things. The sheriff does a good job keeping us citizens safe. I've never had anyone in my home that I didn't invite." She swung her leg out the door and turned back to give a saucy smile. "Of course, I've had a few visitors I didn't want there. I made short work of getting them to leave."

She just bet she did. Asia followed her newest friend from the shop up the walkway. Friday afternoon's class had ended, and she didn't have to work tomorrow. She could work on some ads Ian's friends queried her about, and she could help Mrs. B get set up with some audiobooks from the library. She'd already had her make sure that part of her account was set up. They would only have to download the books and put them on her phone. Mrs. B even ordered a Bluetooth speaker and said it arrived this morning.

An eclectic mix of knickknacks decorated every flat space in the living room. Figurines, framed sayings, needlework, and a variety of quilted pillows. The walls were covered with hangings. Cluttered but clean. That was the theme here. The air needed some freshening, but the house appeared tidy.

"You must have been making quilts for a long time. These are beautiful." Asia stared up at the wall hanging with its vivid gemstone colors and black outline and binding. They looked like a walkway through a garden.

"I didn't do much when I was younger. I didn't have children of my own. Mr. Beasley and I were never blessed that way. But we had plenty of neighborhood children who came over for cookies and milk. They played ball in the backyard. Mr. Beasley used to play professional baseball and knew some tricks and tips he passed on. There was even one young man he coached who went on to play professional ball." Mrs. B gave a fond pat to a portrait of Mr. Beasley as she passed through to the kitchen.

"I have my computer in here at the desk in the corner. I do like to play a game of solitaire on occasion but don't do much other than that. I write emails but must have the font giant sized." She laughed as she set her purse on the counter. "Here, let me take that from you. I'll put it in the sewing room if you want to tell that machine to rise and shine."

Asia bit her lip to keep from laughing. Mrs. B had some serious spunk. She was the one Asia had helped the most in the mystery quilt class because she had trouble threading the machine needle. She could see well enough to do most of the quilting, but some of the detail work "tried her patience." Her ongoing humorous monologue helped Asia relax since she didn't have to come up with any conversation starters of her own.

The computer, an older Apple model, was still very serviceable. Mrs. B didn't have a password. Asia typed in the address for the library website, and by the time Mrs. B returned, she had the audiobooks ready for browsing.

"Do you have any idea what you would like to listen to? Do you have a favorite author or book you've wanted to read?" Asia scooted the chair over so Mrs. B could sit next to her and they could both see the screen.

"I know I don't want any of those books with half-naked men on them. Those books are full of indecent talk." Mrs. B sniffed. "Mind you, I agree with married couples having sex. Mr. Beasley and I certainly understood that. But I don't want to read about anyone else doing it. No sir."

Her cheeks burning, Asia sank down in the chair. Oh. My.

Mrs. B patted her hand and laughed. "Let's see what they have in their cozy mystery section. Can you look at those?"

"I can." Asia kept her voice even, thankful for the change in topic. They spent the next hour looking at books, choosing two to download, and Asia showing Mrs. B how to turn on the book and sync it with her Bluetooth speaker.

When the first story began, Mrs. B's mouth fell open. Her papery skin was soft as she squeezed Asia's hand. "This is amazing. I'm going to love having these books to listen to in the evenings when I do my needlework."

"How are you able to do needlework if you have trouble with your eyesight?"

Mrs. B turned off the book and stood up. "Come, let me show you." She led the way into the living room and turned on the lights. Beside a comfortable recliner stood a rounded light with a large magnifying glass. Mrs. B had Asia sit in the chair and look at quilting through the magnifier. The stitches were huge.

"No wonder. This is amazing." Asia followed Mrs. B back to the kitchen. "I'd better get going. I've enjoyed our time. If you need any help with your books or speaker, give me a call."

She programed her number in Mrs. B's phone, said her good-byes, and headed back to the quilt shop. Tingles zinged through her as she thought about lunch. Did she dare go to I-BBQ? Her steps quickened as she thought of Ian's dimpled smile and those penetrating blue eyes.

The parking lot in front of the quilt shop only had two cars, Tansie's and Cinda's. The shop would be closing in a few minutes. Asia stuck her head in the door and asked if either of them wanted to join her at I-BBQ, but they both had plans. She crossed to the restaurant.

Hmmm, a couple of fancier than usual cars were parked outside.

The breeze, redolent with ocean tang, became overpowered by barbecue. Asia's stomach clenched. She probably should save her money, but this aroma invaded her apartment and hung in the air every time she stepped outside. She hadn't eaten here once all week, so this meal was a necessity.

The large sign beside the door announced Ian's upcoming event. Next week. She and Meg had so much fun brainstorming. They'd chattered right over the top of Ian, but he hadn't cared. This event would be amazing. They would set up the outdoor barbecue and have the indoor one going. There would be two bands taking turns performing on a platform in the parking lot. Tables would be set up, along with a dancing area near the bands.

People were already talking about it. The announcement posted in the local newspaper stirred interest. Ian told her this morning he'd seen an uptick in business since the ads posted. His main concern had been that no one would want to attend the event since there wouldn't be any alcohol. But Memorial Day weekend would prove he had more friends than he thought *and* that the town needed venues that were wholesome and fun.

When she stepped inside the restaurant, Meg waved from across the room. She placed a last plate on a table and hurried toward Asia. "Ian is in the back room and wanted you to join him. I'm glad you got his message. And I need your order."

Asia slapped the back pocket of her jeans. She hadn't paid any attention to her phone on her walk back, and she hadn't seen any messages before she left Mrs. B's house. She tugged the cell out and, sure enough, there were a stack of messages she hadn't read.

"The usual for lunch, but give me a minute." She held up her phone to Meg before putting in the code.

I need you to meet me at the restaurant.

Where are you?

There are people here who want to meet you. Come now.

Her heart thudded in her chest. What people? Who would want to meet her?

~

THE MINUTE ASIA stepped through the doorway to the back room, Ian's gaze locked on her. She still had her hair in the high ponytail she wore to quilt class. Her flowy top, a mixture of greens and blues, would highlight her mossy green eyes.

His pulse sang and he stood, even though he'd been in conversation with one of the Chamber members. "Excuse me. I'll be right back." Without waiting for a response, Ian wove around the tables and met Asia part way across the room.

They spoke at the same time.

"I thought you weren't coming."

"What's going on?"

They paused, then laughed. Asia leaned to the side, peering at the occupants still at his table. "Who are they, and why do they want to meet me? I just now saw your messages."

"Thanks for coming." Ian circled his fingers around her arm, rubbing his thumb up under her sleeve. Such soft skin. Her eyes widened.

"These are some of the men from the Chamber. They're business owners and they want to meet the person who designed my latest ads." He really should step away. But he couldn't.

If only they were alone.

"You already got me two jobs with your friends." She tilted her head to look up at him. The lighter flecks of gold in her dark green eyes fascinated him.

"These aren't friends. They're influential businessmen. If you can get accounts with them, you can really build your business."

She stretched up on tiptoe until her breath whispered across his ear. "Does that mean I'll make enough to be free of the quilt class?"

He laughed. "Maybe. But then Cinda would be upset. You *are* the major entertainment."

"And the source of her lectures on what not to do." Asia huffed what might have been distress. Or a laugh.

"Come on. I'll introduce you. Did Meg get your order? She already has ours."

Asia nodded. He felt her hesitancy, so he stepped to the side, placed his palm against her back, and guided her to the table. The men stood to greet her.

They sat down with Asia in the middle. The four businessmen peppered her with questions while Meg delivered their meals and Asia's water. Asia asked Meg to bring a pad of paper and a pencil. As they ate, she took notes. Ian watched as her nerves disappeared and her business side took over. She offered ideas for each of the men, then made on-the-spot mockups of what she'd like to do for each of them.

By the end of lunch, all of the men shook hands with her, exchanging emails and expecting to see something from her by Monday. Asia looked like she could barely breathe. Ian had talked with her earlier in the week about raising her rates and these men hadn't batted an eye over her charges.

After the men left, Meg brought a piece of pie á la mode with a candle in the ice cream. "I know it's not your birthday, but I heard enough to know you landed some hefty accounts. I thought you should celebrate." She handed them two spoons and leaned down to hug Asia, who glowed. She almost looked like the teen he'd once known. Before life had gotten so difficult.

"Still able to go hiking tomorrow?" He spooned up a bite, licking a crumb from his lip.

"I don't know." Asia swirled her spoon in the ice cream. "Maybe I should stay home and work."

Ian's breath hitched. He pressed his lips tight as the cool ice cream slid down his throat. "You love hiking. Why don't you work tonight and see how it goes? I can have you back in time to have all tomorrow afternoon and evening to work." He forked another bite. No whining or begging.

"Good idea. I'll get started and let you know before bedtime." She tugged on the plate of pie. "I'll take this with me. I'll be able to think better." She batted her eyelashes.

"I'm not falling for that." He lowered his eyebrows in a mock glower. "You want the pie, you stay here and fight for it." He held his spoon over the dessert. She clanged hers against his, almost making him lose his grip. They laughed and chatted about class and Mrs. B's audiobooks while they finished the pie.

~

LATER THAT EVENING, his phone dinged. A thrill that spiraled through him. A message from Asia.

Have a good start on all 4. What time is hiking?

Pick you up at 6 am.

There is no 6 am. Dying emoji.

Ha! 7 am and no later. I need my coffee and donut before hiking.

That's better. Not much. But for coffee and a donut, I'll be ready.

He set his phone on the coffee table and checked the score on the baseball game he'd been watching. A grin still stretched across his face as he settled back against the couch cushion while the game played out.

Since his talk with Meg, he'd given a lot of thought to having a Father to emulate. Maybe he had changed. Could he have a relationship and not worry? Would Asia stay even if she didn't connect with Walter?

Oh, to hold her in his arms again. To share sweet kisses. To see if they could continue to develop this closeness. Tomorrow. Would tomorrow ever come?

THE EARLY MORNING sun hid behind a layer of clouds drifting in off the ocean. The day would be warm later, but right now the temperature was perfect. He and Asia laughed and reminisced about previous hikes when they'd had to ride bicycles to get to the trail, walk, then ride back home.

"I should be doing that again." Asia held up the last bite of her donut. She popped it in her mouth, chewed, and sipped her coffee.

"No doubt. If we keep eating pie with ice cream and donuts." Ian patted his stomach.

"That's right." Asia put her coffee cup in the holder. "Next thing you know people will ask if you're expecting."

Ian spat a mouthful of coffee. Asia's laugh rippled through the cab of his truck. He coughed, set his cup down, and pounded his chest. "I can't believe you said that." He turned into the parking area near the trail. "Now I'm going to have to get counseling to get rid of that mental image."

They were still laughing when they climbed from the truck. Two of Ian's friends were joining them, and they were already there. Ian introduced Asia to Ward and Daniel, both police officers in Driftwood Cove.

"Hey, I ran into a couple last night and happened to mention today's hike. They wanted to join us. I hope that's okay." Ward shoved his hands in his pockets.

"No problem." Ian nudged a rock with his foot. Why had he agreed to go with anyone besides Asia?

"Here they come." Ward nodded toward the road. "The guy isn't my favorite person, but you guys are friends with the woman."

Ian and Asia turned to look. Asia took a step back into him, and he felt a shiver run through her. Pulling into the parking area were Cinda and Martin. He groaned. Now what?

They all headed out on the trail. Cinda took Martin's hand as they walked. The first part of the trail was wide enough to be two abreast. Ian stayed back with Asia. She made it clear she didn't want to walk in front of Martin. Ward and Daniel forged ahead but stayed within shouting distance.

At a steep part, Cinda and Martin slowed down. The trail narrowed, and Martin urged Cinda in front of him. He slowed bit by bit until he was only a few steps in front of Asia. Ian glanced at the narrow trail and the drop-off to the ocean. How could he get Asia behind him and away from Cinda's fiancé? The trail was too steep and narrow. The drop-off too great.

Cinda rounded a switchback, Martin on her heels, and lost her footing. Martin backed up a pace and didn't even try to catch her.

"Cinda!" Ian jumped around Asia, holding her so she wouldn't fall.

Cinda shrieked, and Ian dove, skidding on his stomach like a baseball player stealing home, and grabbed her hand.

He glanced back in time to see Martin back Asia up against a tree and a look of absolute horror on her face.

18

He almost let go of Cinda but tightened his grip. "Don't struggle. I've got you." Her eyes were huge, her breath panting.

"Martin!" His sharp command startled the man. Asia shoved at him, and he tottered backwards. Ian growled, gritting his teeth. "Some help here." Ward and Daniel raced toward them from around the curve in the trail.

Martin inched closer. "I was making sure Asia didn't fall too. I knew you had Cinda."

Liar! A pang hit Ian's conscience when he realized he might not have made the same dive in the dirt if Martin had slipped over the edge. Now Martin stood nearby, but not close enough to reach down and help. Probably didn't want to get himself dirty.

"Let me help." Daniel dropped on to the trail beside Ian and reached over the side to grab Cinda's other arm. They counted and pulled together. Cinda scrabbled at the cliff side, and they brought her up.

"You okay?"

Her cheek was scratched, and her clothing was dirty and disheveled. Tears streaked her face.

Daniel slipped his arm around her, and she winced. He angled a look at her. "You need to get checked out. I'll help you back and take you to Urgent Care or call for an ambulance." Daniel glanced at Ian and then at Ward. He ignored Martin.

"I'm okay." Cinda swiped a strand of hair from her face and brushed at the debris on her shirt. Her hands shook, and she wobbled a little as she stood and backed away from the cliff edge.

"Cinda." Asia stood a few feet on the other side of Martin. To come to Cinda, she would have to pass too close to the man.

"Here." Ian stepped back, closer to Martin, and held out his hand to Asia. He focused on Martin and narrowed his gaze. If the man moved a finger in Asia's direction, he'd be sorry.

Martin took the hint and stayed still as Asia took Ian's hand and stepped past him. She hurried to Cinda, put her hands on her shoulders, said something, and then gave her a hug. The two women walked a few feet down the trail to a large boulder and sat down. Heads together, they talked as Cinda wiped moisture from her cheeks.

Ian gave them a few minutes while he chatted with Daniel. Then he went to kneel in front of the girls. "Do you want to go back? Daniel's right, you should see a doctor. You hit that cliff face pretty hard." He glanced from Asia to Cinda.

"No. Let's go on." Cinda's voice wobbled, but she lifted her chin.

Ah. That resolute expression was all too familiar.

"What happened to make you fall?" Ian put one knee on the ground to steady himself. He'd hiked this trail so many times. He'd never heard of anyone falling like that.

"I think I lost my balance." Confusion chased across Cinda's pretty features. "I bumped into Martin and just bounced over the edge. I'm not really sure how."

Had Martin pushed her? Why? He didn't like Martin, but would a guy like that do something so horrible?

"I can't believe you were so clumsy." Martin dropped onto the rock on the other side of Cinda. "I saw how the path narrowed and tried to slip around you so I would be able to help if you needed. I know you saw me. You should have been more careful."

Ian glanced toward the drop-off. His fingers itched to toss Martin over the edge into the ocean below. He might survive. Lots of people did cliff diving and survived the jump. Maybe not right here…

He stifled a growl. Not a good train of thought.

"Pig." Asia's muttered word was too low for anyone else to hear. Cinda was listening to Martin tell her what she should have done and what he would have done. How he would never have let that happen to him.

Ian almost snorted.

A small hand rested on his shoulder. He looked up and met Asia's gaze. He covered her hand with his. Almost pressed a kiss to her palm.

"Let's go on." Cinda, sans bounce, stood up and brushed off a little more detritus from her shorts. "We came here to hike. Let's do it. Maybe afterward you can treat me to a survivor's lunch." She attempted a smile that wobbled before fading.

Cinda's fall put a damper on the hike. Ian kept a close eye on Martin. No way was he getting near Asia again. For her part, Asia stuck to Ian's side as much as possible.

She didn't relax until they got back to the parking lot.

"I can't believe Martin invited himself along today." Asia adjusted her seat belt as Ian closed his door, shutting out the others. Martin helped Cinda into his car as if she'd been mortally injured. The fake gesture made Ian grind his teeth. *Cinda, what are you thinking?*

Ian gripped the steering wheel and put the truck in gear. They were all heading to a local hamburger joint, where Cinda chose to eat her survivor's lunch.

"I feel sorry for his students." Asia shivered and then clasped her hands between her knees. "I wonder…" She shook her head.

"You wonder if he does anything wrong with the girls in his class." Ian caught her startled look from the corner of his eye. "I do too."

"It's a horrible thing to think. I just—" She closed her eyes and rubbed at her face. "I had a teacher like that once. Teachers are supposed to be an example to you, and all the adults respect them. Telling another adult that a teacher touched you or said something inappropriate isn't easy. The student risks being accused of dressing or acting seductively." Her shoulders hunched forward.

Ian stared at the road. A few minutes. Just a few minutes one-on-one with the teacher who did that to her.

"It's also a strike against you when you have a mother like mine." The words were so soft he almost didn't catch them. Yeah, he could see that. People always expected him to be like his father. Why wouldn't they expect Asia to be like her mother?

"I'm so sorry they thought that." He reached over and covered her hand with his. Squeezed.

She turned her hand palm up and returned the squeeze. "Of all the people I've met, you are the one who most understands."

He drove into the diner's parking lot and chose a space between Ward and Martin. Before they climbed out, he touched Asia's hand. "If he tries anything else with you, tell me. I know it's him, not you. I'm here for you."

She nodded. "Please make sure I'm across the table from him but not right across. If he tries to rub his foot on my leg, I may not be responsible for my actions, even if he is Cinda's fiancé."

If he *what?* Had Martin done that?

Asia's door swung open, and Martin stood there, his hand stretched out toward her. Ian almost leapt across the seat to shove him away.

"Let me help you."

That smarmy smile. Ian was going to wipe it from his face. *"I'll* help Asia. You help *your fiancée."*

Martin dropped his hand and stepped back. "I was being courteous." He tilted his chin up and sniffed, as if they were so far beneath him he didn't care about their opinions. He rounded his vehicle and opened Cinda's door without looking back.

Ian replaced Martin at Asia's door. She still hadn't removed her seat belt. He took her hands. "You okay?"

She tightened her grip on his fingers before letting go to undo her seatbelt and swing her legs around. "Thank you. I didn't see him coming."

"Let's get through lunch. We can leave early since you have a lot of work to do this afternoon and I need to get you home. Right?" He tried to make his tone light and his smile warm.

~

THEY FINISHED lunch in record time. Ian didn't relax until he had Asia back in his truck. At the apartment, he followed Asia inside. Everything inside of him wanted to search the small space to make sure she'd be safe.

"Want some tea or coffee?" She lifted the top of her computer, which sat on the small table. An array of papers was spread around. Her notes and jotted ideas.

"Nah. You need to work." He didn't want to leave. At all.

She took a step closer. He caught her waist and pulled her to him. Leaned down. Stared into those mesmerizing eyes.

Don't. You know better.

He didn't care. He was going to kiss her.

Not even the voice of reason could stop him.

~

SHE GASPED as Ian's lips brushed hers. Tingles sizzled through her. She floated closer to him. His arms wrapped tight, and he kissed her again. Longer. Deeper.

Her thoughts stuttered to a halt.

Her only awareness—him. This man who once haunted her dreams and her heart. And was doing so again.

"Asia." He cradled her head against his chest. The thunder of his heart matched her own frantic pulse.

He stroked his hand down her back. "I've missed this. Us." His lips brushed her hair. The warmth of his breath tickled her ear. "When you didn't come back that next summer. When you quit writing." His voice caught. "I was so lost without you."

She felt the same. She'd needed him throughout the years too. So much. Could she stay here? Never let him go?

Prison. Unworthy.

The thoughts pushed into her consciousness. Stabbed through her. Broke her heart.

"Ian." She pushed at his chest with her palms. Everything in her fought against this action. She wanted him. To be his. But even more, she wanted the best for him.

And she wasn't the best.

Not even close.

"What is it?" He released her and stepped back but kept his hands on her shoulders. One tiny pull would have her back in his arms again. Back where she wanted to be.

"Ian, I can't do this." Her throat ached at the hurt in his eyes. "I can't explain." She blinked against the burn. How could she make him understand without telling him the truth? The ugly truth that would make him turn away forever. They'd talked about that all those years ago. How they would be different. They would make better choices. Not like their parents.

He had done all he'd said he would.

She hadn't.

"I want to be friends." She bit her lips. The right words squirmed away. "I can't be more than that."

"Why?" His thumbs rubbed tingling circles on her upper arms. "We have this connection. More than friendship. Don't we?"

The question cut deep. He'd felt her response. *Please don't let this ruin our friendship. Help him understand.*

"I..." She couldn't lie to him. Couldn't. "I have my reasons. I can't explain." She put her hands on his and pulled them off her arms. "Please, trust me on this."

Lines etched the corners of his mouth. He stepped back. Fumbled behind him for the door handle. "I was going to suggest dinner. I'd bring something here." He swallowed hard.

"I have leftovers from last night. I'll be working and will just eat in." Her voice sounded hollow.

He nodded. Swiveled around and strode out the door without a backward glance. She leaned her forehead against the window glass. Sobs clawed up from deep within. Her heart cried out to go after him. To make some excuse. To fix what she'd broken.

But she couldn't.

Not if she loved him.

~

THE AFTERNOON DRAGGED BY. The clatter of her computer keys pushed back intrusive thoughts. She blinked against the burn and adjusted the size of a graphic. Shutting everything out to work had saved her in prison. Would it save her now?

By late afternoon she was close to finished with all four mockups. The ads were good and fit the business needs for each of the four men. Two of the businesses already had logos, but the other two also commissioned her to make logos for them. One of her favorite things to do. Such fun to allow freedom to the creative side of her brain.

A knock on her door made her jump. She glanced up to see Cinda peeking through the glass and waving. Asia closed her computer and stood. Her legs protested the movement as she walked to the door. "Hey. You okay?" She leaned in for a hug. Cinda winced. "I'm so sorry." Asia released her and stepped back for her to come inside.

Cinda touched the dark bruise on her cheek. "I think I'll be sore tomorrow. My face hurts, but I've been using ice. And I think I wrenched my shoulder. Other than that, I'm fine." She laughed.

"Did Martin take you to get checked out? They might want to x-ray the shoulder." During lunch everyone except Martin had thought she should go to Urgent Care. Martin had been very blasé, waving off their concern as if he was some medical expert.

Asia had bit her tongue to keep from accusing him of trying to kill Cinda by pushing her off the cliff. Ian shared her concerns. His actions today showed that. His friends didn't seem to care for Martin any more than the rest of them. Daniel had been especially attentive and concerned. And he was their age. And cute. Why didn't Cinda have someone like him?

"I came by to ask a favor." Cinda sat down in the recliner. She hissed when her back connected to the chair back.

"Did someone look at your back? Maybe you hit against something." Her cousin needed help. "Will you let me look?"

"Let's have some tea first. Do you have any?" Cinda's face had lost color, the red of her lips stark against the pale of her cheeks. Shadows ringed her eyes.

"This apartment is connected to your shop. Of course there's tea. I can get whatever you want. I'll even use your fancy machine." She winked.

"Thanks." Cinda tried to laugh, but the sound was strangled in another hiss of pain.

"I'll make you tea and we'll chat while you drink it. But then I'm looking at your back. Understand?"

Cinda's lips twitched. Aunt Mary's lecture tone echoed in Asia's head. It must have worked because Cinda agreed. Asia hurried into the shop and returned a few minutes later with the tea fixed the way Cinda liked it.

She wanted to drag her cousin from the chair and see what was wrong with her. Or drag her off to Urgent Care and let them look. Instead, she made small talk. Told Cinda about her projects for the Chamber businessmen. Showed her the logos and mockups of the ads.

And listened to accolades about Martin until she wanted to vomit. Still, something was different. Cinda tried too hard to tell Asia how great Martin was. His teaching ability. His knowledge. His doting on her.

Asia almost gagged over that one.

Finally. Finally, Cinda finished her tea and wound down her conversation. She leaned forward to set her cup on the table by the chair and gasped, freezing midmotion.

"That's it." Asia grabbed both cups and carried them to the sink. "Stand up and turn around. I need to see your back."

She steadied Cinda as she eased upright. Asia lifted the shirt. *Be discreet. Don't hurt her.* Asia gasped. *No, no, no.* The left side of Cinda's shoulder had turned dark purple. It was so puffy…

This was more than a broken blood vessel.

"You have to get this looked at. Now." Asia eased the shirt back down. "You have to. I'll go with you."

"Let me text Martin to see if he's done grading papers. He'll go with me." Cinda sent a quick message but received no reply.

"I will drive you. Martin can join us when he's done." Asia grabbed her things. Her driver's license was long expired, but she had to get Cinda looked at.

Ten minutes later they were parked beside Martin's car in the almost empty lot of the high school. Cinda insisted on finding him before she saw a doctor. Asia followed her to a side door.

A janitor answered Cinda's knock. "School's closed."

Cinda adjusted her purse strap on her shoulder. "I'm here to see Martin Hannah. Mr. Hannah. He's a teacher and working today."

"I'm not supposed to let anyone in who doesn't work here." The man scratched at his stubbly jaw.

"Mr. Hannah is my fiancé." Cinda stepped closer. "It's important."

Something in the janitor's gaze changed. Asia wasn't sure what, but he held the door as he moved back to let them through, then beckoned them to follow him.

Their footsteps echoed in the empty hall, an eerie sound in the quiet.

"Down here." Cinda's whisper drifted out like a shout. She approached a closed classroom door. Asia came up beside Cinda, and they tried to peer through the small glass.

Something covered the tiny window. No way to tell if anyone was in there.

Asia stepped back. "Maybe he's in the teacher's lounge." Her phone buzzed. She pulled it from her pocket.

"No. He's here." Cinda turned the knob and opened the door.

Asia looked past Cinda. The room only had a few lights on, but they were more than enough. Enough to show Martin at his desk.

Not grading papers.

He was with a girl. A girl who looked young enough to be his student. Doing....

No!

19

A STRANGLED SHRIEK erupted from Cinda. She went from stiff and in pain to livid in a microsecond.

Asia lifted her phone. Just enough.

Martin and the girl froze. His eyes bugged out, his mouth gaped. He stuttered but said nothing coherent. He let the girl go, and her head cracked on the desktop. They both fumbled to adjust their clothing.

Asia wanted to clap her hand over her eyes. Over Cinda's eyes.

She'd had her suspicions about Martin's character and integrity… but *this?* The reality of Martin's depravity was disturbing beyond words. Why couldn't she scrub the scenes from her brain?

"'Bout time." The janitor—she forgot his name—came to a halt beside the open door, but not where he could see inside.

"You knew?" Asia glared at the man, and he shrugged and shuffled down the empty hall.

"Cinda."

At Martin's smarmy voice, Asia spun back to the scene unfolding before them.

"Sweetheart. This isn't what you think." Martin brushed his hair back and shrugged on his usual air of haughtiness. "I can explain."

"You. Can. Explain?" Cinda's face twisted as she hissed out the words. "I don't *want* you to explain. I can see for myself."

"No. She." Martin made a vague gesture over his shoulder.

"Don't you *dare* say she made you do this." Cinda stalked a couple of steps closer.

Asia reached out. Did Cinda intend to tear Martin limb from limb? A great visual. Cinda didn't need to suffer more than she had. With her free hand, Asia pocketed her phone. She'd delete those revolting pictures. Just as soon as she showed them to the authorities.

Cinda was wringing her hands. Would she accept his explanation? She'd stuck by this reprehensible man all these years. But *this?*

"Here." Cinda yanked the ring from her finger. "We're done." She threw the ring with unerring accuracy and pinged it off Martin's forehead.

Asia laughed. She couldn't help it. The startled look on Martin's face and the way his eyes almost crossed tracking the ring were too funny.

"Let's go." She took Cinda's arm and urged her toward the door.

"Cinda. Let's go for coffee. We can talk." Martin held out one hand in a plea so false even the high school girl rolled her eyes.

"Don't you ever talk to me again." Cinda turned and marched out the door.

Asia grabbed the knob to pull the door shut but leaned in. "Couldn't happen to a better person. Enjoy your stay in jail."

The door clicked shut on Martin's outraged yell. Ha! Prison equaled horror. Some deserved to spend time there. Martin fell in that category. Cinda had to call this in. If not, Asia would.

She needn't have worried. As they strode down the hallway, past lockers and closed doors, Cinda yanked her phone from her pocket and dialed a number. "Chief. I need to report a crime."

Cinda described the scene they'd interrupted, her voice too steady for what she'd just witnessed.

Asia hugged Cinda as she clicked off from the call. For a few minutes they stood there, Cinda's head heavy over Asia's heart. What could she do?

"Cinda--"

Her cousin's hand shot up, and she straightened. Swiped at her cheeks. "Don't say anything. Please." Her voice cracked. "I can't talk right now." She faced away. Asia rested her hand on Cinda's uninjured shoulder. How else could she convey her support?

The police chief and some officers were there in minutes. The school door she and Cinda had exited swung open. Martin and his student stepped outside. Asia pulled out her phone and opened the screen.

Martin stormed over, full of self-righteous indignation. He claimed he'd been helping Destiny study to bring up her grades, nothing more. Destiny confirmed his statements.

The chief came over to Cinda, his expression grim. "If there's no real proof, my hands are tied. I have the two of you as witnesses, but the two of them who say otherwise. I'm sorry." The muscles in his jaw bunched and released as he turned away.

Asia fingered her phone. She had to show the pictures to the chief, but what if he looked into her background? The clang of metal doors, the feel of handcuffs. Tremors shivered through her.

Wait…maybe there was a way. She tapped the pictures, attached them to a text, then leaned close to Cinda. "Check your phone."

Cinda frowned at her.

"Do it." She added urgency to her command.

Cinda pulled out her cell and punched in the code. She opened her messages…and gasped. Her hand flew to her mouth. "Chief."

The man stopped and turned back.

"What about these?" She held out her phone and he took it. Looked through the pictures. Motioned to one of his deputies to come over. Gave the order to take Martin and Destiny into custody.

The chief talked to Cinda and Asia again and sent a deputy to interview the janitor. By the time she and Cinda were able to leave, full dark had descended. Cinda had grown so quiet. Her rounded cheeks were shadowed, her eyes vacant. How could Asia help her?

She jingled the keys as they approached the car. "You still need to go to Urgent Care. Do you want Glenna to meet us there? Or, I could take you and then stay at your house tonight."

"No. I need some time. Alone." Cinda sat sideways in the seat and directed Asia to an Urgent Care. A doctor examined Cinda, took an x-ray, and said there was bruising but no broken bones. He told how to care for the bruising and offered stronger pain killers, which she refused.

I-BBQ had several cars in the lot when Asia got home. Ian. It was almost closing time. Should she go talk to him? Would she be welcome after her earlier rebuff? Maybe she should be commiserating with Cinda. She went back to her work and tried to focus.

Not an easy task at all.

And not just because of Cinda.

A SOFT RAP on her door at nine-thirty startled her awake. She'd drifted off in her chair, her book resting on her lap. She blinked a few times, stretched, and struggled upright as the knock came again.

Ian stared at her through the glass. Her insides did a little flip as she opened the door. Ian. He stood there a minute, his jaw clenching and unclenching.

"Is it true?" He shoved his hands in his pockets. His furrowed eyebrows and tightened fists spoke volumes.

"Come in." She held the door open and stepped back for him to pass. "Would you like something to drink?" He shook his head, pulled out one of her kitchen chairs, and sank into it. She returned to the recliner.

"Is it true? What I heard about Martin?"

"Yes. Cinda and I were there. She called the police." Raw pain chased across his face. Cinda. His heart sister. Did he think he failed as a brother?

"I heard there were pictures." Ian cleared his throat.

"You texted me." Asia touched the phone in her pocket. "I had my phone out reading the text when Cinda opened the door. She was so shocked. Everyone was. But I knew there had to be proof..."

"Thank you." Ian leaned forward to rest his elbows on his knees. "If you hadn't done that, he could have talked his way out of this charge. That's what I heard from the chief when he stopped in for a takeout meal. He seemed to think the pictures came from Cinda though."

"I sent them to her phone." Asia shifted, smoothing her palm down her thigh. His head jerked up, and he stared at her.

She swallowed hard. How to explain? "I had no idea how to send them to the police chief. I..." What could she say? *I'm afraid of the police? I have a history of being arrested?* She couldn't defend her actions without giving away too many secrets.

He kneaded his fingers together. "How's Cinda?"

"I don't know." She explained about the urgent care. "I wanted someone to be with her, but she refused. I think she has to work through this. I didn't know what to do for her." Her voice cracked, so she took a sip from her water cup.

He nodded. Rubbed at his eyes, then stood. "I'll go by her house on my way home. See if she got checked out or if she needs to talk. I'm sure Glenna's heard by now and will be there."

Asia bit back her offer to go with him. Glenna's antagonism added to tonight's events would be too much. Why had Martin done this? She should be praying for him. But she didn't want to. Even if he had something broken inside.

"Ian." She stood as he reached the door. "Ian, I value your friendship. I have very few I can call friends." Asia rubbed the hem of her top between her fingers. What more could she say? Would he even believe her?

"If you and Cinda aren't my friends, then the count is zero." She looked up through a haze of moisture. "I need you. Please."

He stared at her, one hand on the knob. The hand that once touched her with such gentleness. She took a step toward him. Grabbed the chair back like a lifeline. Who was she kidding? She wanted a relationship with him. She wanted the whole thing.

Love. Marriage. Family.

She just didn't deserve him.

"Asia, I treasure your friendship. I always have." He turned his head to stare out at the night. Streetlights lit the pavement in a yellow glow. Moths darted in circles, lifting ever closer to the fatal source that drew them.

Asia's heart reached for Ian. Would he be the light, or would he destroy her?

~

"I CAN'T BELIEVE I'm helping you do this again." Ian took Asia's hand. Night had settled over the landscape of the care center. He could still hear her plea for friendship. His companion growing up. Why hadn't she made other friends? Easy. Her mom had multiple addictions. Asia ended up being the caretaker and moving often. She had no chance to form friendships. Had other kids been warned away from her? Or was it easier for her to be alone?

Either way, she'd needed him.

"I'm hoping there is a different nurse on tonight." Asia squeezed his fingers. "Monday night should be a different staff than the weekend, right?"

"We can hope." Ian slowed to have one more chance to reason with her. "I feel bad for Cinda. She didn't even go to church yesterday. What if she finds out what you're doing?"

Asia gnawed her lower lip. He looked away to clear his thoughts. A piece of trash caught a ride on the wind and whirled in a wild dance across the parking lot. He could almost hear the pound of the surf from here. He'd much rather be on the bluff watching the moonlight on the waves tonight than sneaking into Walter's room.

Again.

"We need to make sure she *doesn't* hear about this." Asia leveled a look at him. She smiled and her whole face lit up. He could watch that transformation over and over and never tire of it.

He reached for the door handle. Low music played over speakers. A different woman greeted them at the desk and had them sign in. At least that was promising. Asia's eyebrows lifted as she glanced at him.

They were late enough that most of the residents were in bed. Maybe they wouldn't be allowed in. Nope. They were allowed back. Many of the residents in Walter's wing were awake all night. Maybe that made the difference.

He let out a slow breath when a nurse buzzed them into the Alzheimer's wing. They exchanged pleasantries and walked hand-in-hand to Walter's room. He stood by the window staring out at the dark sky and the trees directing a symphony of wind.

Asia pulled free and Ian stood beside the door letting her walk toward Walter. She'd talked about different ways to approach him that might help. She wanted to jog his memory. To take Walter into the past. She'd read up on the disease, but Walter appeared too far gone to be reachable. Ian hoped he was wrong.

"Walter. I've come to see you." Asia's voice didn't sound like her. Was she trying to imitate her mother?

"Kim?" Walter turned from the window. His face creased with a smile as he spotted Asia. "You came back. I've been waiting."

"I need to talk to you about your daughter." Asia took a step closer.

Walter tilted his head, confusion clouding his eyes. "My daughter? I don't have a daughter." He shook his head. Pressed his palms against his temples and moaned.

"It's okay, Walter. I'm here." Asia's tone turned soothing. Walter continued to moan, not looking at her. Ian shifted. Glanced at the door. Opened his mouth to ask her to stop. Couldn't. She needed to make her own choices.

"I'm here. Please." Her plea had the opposite effect to soothing him.

His head snapped up. His hands fisted at his side. Walter shuffled forward, his slippers scuffing against the floor, his body rigid.

Asia took a step back.

Ian moved to stand beside her. "I'm not sure this is a good idea." He put his hand on her back, unsure what to do next.

The older man rounded the end of his bed, his focus on Asia, his eyes narrowed and angry. His hands unfisted into claws he stretched toward her.

"Walter. Mr. Bryant." Ian stepped up beside Asia, one hand out in front of him.

The older man stumbled to a stop. He grabbed his head, moaning again, and collapsed on the floor. Just folded up like his bones turned liquid.

"Walter." Ian leapt forward.

"No." Asia skidded on her knees to the man's side. His eyes were closed, his face relaxed.

"He's still breathing. I'll get the nurse." Ian leapt up and raced out the door. He returned in seconds. The nurse who'd let him in outpaced him to the room. Her shoes slapped the floor with firm determination.

In the flurry of activity, Ian and Asia were shuffled out of the room and then beyond the ward. Asia's eyes were so big, her face pale. Did she blame herself for causing Walter to collapse?

"Why don't we go. There's nothing we can do here. We'll call later and see what they say." In the distance, Ian heard the wail of a siren. Had they sent for an ambulance to transport Walter? Something gnawed at his gut. *God, please help Asia. Cinda and Glenna too.*

A few minutes later, Asia trembled at his side as they stood in the parking lot watching the ambulance take Walter away. A car raced into the lot and squealed to a stop. Cinda and Glenna climbed out. Glenna's fury was a thing to behold. She stalked toward Asia. He stepped in front of Asia, and Glenna's hands smacked into his chest. She dodged around him.

"What are you doing here?" Glenna got right in Asia's face.

Asia didn't back down. "I came to see my father." She lifted her chin, all shaking gone. "I have that right."

"You have *no* rights. You know your mother probably faked that birth certificate. Now leave him alone. Leave town." Glenna's hand flexed, but she didn't strike Asia.

Not that he'd have let her do so.

"Glenna, they've taken him to Driftwood Medical Center." Cinda called to Glenna. "Come on." She paused to look at Ian and Asia.

Opened her mouth. Shook her head and climbed back in the car as Glenna did too.

As their car left the parking area, Asia's spunk seemed to leach out of her. Her head fell forward, and her shoulders slumped. Oh, the guilt she must feel.

"Hey. Let's go out to the bluff. Like we used to when life hit too hard. We can listen to the ocean, watch the moonlight on the waves. And this time we can pray." He put his finger under her chin and lifted until he could see her tear-filled eyes. "If you want to talk, I'm a good listener."

She almost leaped into his embrace. Sobs wracked her body as he held her close. The wind whistled around them, tugging her braid and drifting strands of hair across his cheeks. The night closed around them as he rested his cheek on her head. His throat tightened as he prayed for Walter and all his girls.

Peace drifted down over them. Asia's sobs abated. She pushed away, dug a tissue from her pocket, and wiped her nose. "Thanks. I'd like that. Sorry about your shirt." She swiped at the damp spot on his chest.

"You know how much I love salt water." He smiled and took her hand. Guided her to his truck and helped her in.

The drive to the bluff only took a few minutes. They got out and sat close together, their backs to a rock. The waves were frothy and high, crashing ashore like every time might be the last. Out beyond the surf, moonlight glittered and danced, so beautiful his breath caught. He loved it here so much.

Especially with Asia beside him.

She leaned her head against his shoulder. "Do you think he'll be okay?"

He slipped his arm around her and pulled her close. Began to pray aloud and felt the tension drain out of her. She needed the same peace he'd been granted.

At the end of his prayer, they sat in silence, listening to the ocean's song, watching the array of stars overhead. He appreciated the closeness they shared and that neither of them felt the need to fill the quiet with idle chatter.

"Would you take me to the hospital? Is it far?" Asia tilted her head back to look at him. Her countenance spoke of trust. Whatever she asked, he would do. He nodded, stood, and drew her up.

He pulled into the parking area close to the emergency entrance. Lights glowed. An ambulance parked outside the doors. A couple of police cars sat behind the ambulance, their lights flashing.

They went through the automatic doors into a flurry of activity. Medical personnel hurried all different ways. Security and the police were in a huddle to one side.

"Asia." Cinda rushed over to them, her face pale. "Asia, he's gone."

Asia gasped and sagged back against Ian.

20

IAN GRABBED Asia by the elbows as she fell back against him. He held her upright as she trembled in his embrace. Walter would never confirm her as his daughter. She'd lost that chance.

Had she lost all hope of finding a family, too?

"No. No." Cinda slapped her hands to her face, tears overflowing. "Dad's not dead." She reached for Asia's hand. "I'm sorry. He's gone from the hospital. They had him in a bed in emergency. The doctor ordered an MRI. He must have regained consciousness and just walked out." She twisted her hands together. "We don't know where he went."

Walter. Alive. Ian turned toward the entry doors. Had he gone out there? The lights pierced their little space but no farther. The hospital sat on a large tract of land just outside Driftwood Cove. Their land abutted the edge of the Los Padres National Forest. There were acres and acres of uninhabited land there. If Walter wandered into that wilderness... Chills snaked down his back at the thought of the dangers at nighttime. Daytime would be bad enough, but at night he could fall or face dangerous wildlife.

Cinda pulled Asia into a hug. When they broke apart, Asia sniffled. Lifted her chin. "What can I do? Should I go look for him?"

"Don't you think you've done enough?" Glenna's voice scraped Ian's nerves. What was she doing? Where were her priorities that she would attack Asia instead of doing something to find her father?

The older sister leaned close to Asia, lowering her voice. "He wouldn't be out there if not for you."

Asia gaped. Ian drew her close.

"Stop." Cinda yanked her sister back. "You don't know that. The nurse from the center said he's been acting off today. They aren't sure what happened."

"I am. Maybe she snuck out there earlier today, and he's been suffering for it ever since. I know he's been worse since she first saw him." Glenna's jaw jutted forward.

"He's been getting worse for weeks." Cinda's tone softened. She kept her hand on Glenna's arm. Calming the beast. She should give it up. What was with Glenna?

A growl rolled through Ian's gut. He shifted his hands to Asia's shoulders. She looked as if she would shatter at the slightest touch.

"Asia." Cinda inserted herself between Glenna and Asia. "The police are coming up with a search plan. They've called for volunteers. We're waiting to hear what they found on the videos of the entrance. Maybe he's in the hospital wandering the hallways. Security is looking."

Chief Peterson approached and cleared his throat. "We've watched the video of this entrance. Looks like Walter walked out on his own. We have a team of searchers assembling. I'd prefer if you girls would wait here or go home. I can contact you when we find him."

Good that the chief said *when* as opposed to *if*. They would find him, but would it be in time? The days might be warm, but the nights were cool along the coast. What if Walter wandered to the edge of the bluff?

Asia glanced over her shoulder at Ian. Her luminous gaze trapped him. How could he erase the sorrow and worry from her eyes? How?

"Can you use my help?" Ian caught the chief's eye. "I know the hills around here pretty well." He twisted his mouth in a wry smile. The police knew he'd roamed the hills as a boy. First to escape his father's wrath and drunkenness. Then to escape the various homes that took him in after his parents' deaths. An unwelcome child in almost every home. No one wanted a trouble-maker, and that's what he'd been.

Until Asia.

"No denying you'd be a help. Come on." The chief turned to answer another question.

"Me too." Asia lifted her chin when Peterson turned back to scrutinize her. "I know the woods around here some. I can go with Ian and help him search."

No. She should stay with Cinda. But then she would be with Glenna, and that could be toxic. On the other hand, time with Asia. Yes. He nodded at Peterson. "She can come with me. We'll search an area together."

"The team is setting up in the parking lot. I don't know how much we can do at night. Go talk to Jim Thompson. He'll let you know." The chief strode across the lobby toward the returning security officers.

"We'll be back." Ian hugged Cinda. She resembled a forlorn waif.

Cinda grabbed his arm. "Let me come with you. I want to help look for him. I can't sit here doing nothing." A tear wobbled on her eyelash.

"Cinda Loo, you know you twist your ankle on flat ground in the dark. Flashlights don't illuminate that much. Stay here with Glenna and help when we find your dad." He gave her another light hug. She'd be safer here. No more bruises. No twisted ankles. No cliff to tumble over.

She sniffled. Nodded. Reached to give Asia a hug.

"Hey, look." Ian lifted his chin toward the doors. "Here's the pastor coming. Pray with him. We'll find your dad." Ian shook hands with the pastor. Then he guided Asia to the parking lot and their assignment.

The wind whipped at his shirt, his hair stinging against his forehead. The scent of rain hung in the air.

Walter, where are you?

Ten minutes later Ian steered his truck into a pullout a mile from the hospital. He and Asia would work their way back from here, calling for Walter. They had little hope of seeing him in the dark, but maybe he would hear their voices and respond. *Please, God, help us find him. Fast.*

A narrow animal trail led into the hills. Ian led the way, his flashlight beam scanning in the dark. There weren't a lot of trees this close to the coast, but there were a few trails. Of course, there was no guarantee that Walter would stay on a trail. In fact, they'd been told that people with Alzheimer's wandered without rhyme or reason. He had no way of seeing other than the light from the stars. With the wind and clouds moving in, there weren't many of those.

In the distance, beams of other flashlights pierced the dark as teams of searchers combed the hills. Ian stopped on a slight rise before the trail wound through a canyon. He turned a circle, shining the beam of light around them. Asia did the same. Nothing. No sign of movement. No voice calling for help. What now?

"Walter! Can you hear me?" Asia's call whipped away on the wind. No chance anyone would hear if they were more than fifty feet away. Not in this wind.

They trudged on, stopping periodically to shine their lights around and call Walter's name. Only the susurration of the wind and the occasional animal startling from the brush broke the silence.

"We're almost back to the hospital. See the lights of the parking lot? Let's check in." How could they stop now? They hadn't seen one sign of Walter.

"He's got to be here somewhere. We have to find him." Asia grabbed Ian's hand tugging him to a halt. "We can't go back yet. Won't they message you if he's found?"

"They will." Ian peered at the impenetrable darkness. Fat raindrops plopped to earth, a few chilling his skin. "We need to go see where Jim Thompson wants us next. If we go off blindly, that doesn't help the search pattern."

Asia clung to his arm, her grip almost painful. "We can't leave him out in this storm. If he gets wet and cold...." She hiccupped a sob. "Glenna is right. This is my fault."

"Hey, you are not to blame." Ian wrapped his arms around her. How could he shelter her from the storms? She'd been buffeted by both physical and emotional trauma. "The hospital knew he came from the Alzheimer's ward at the center. They should have had someone watching him."

She nodded her head against his chest. The explanation might sound logical, but logic seldom offset feelings.

He took her hand since the trail had widened and led her the rest of the way to the hospital parking lot. One of the other searchers would give him a ride back to his truck. After they received their next search quadrant.

Thompson had his phone out sending messages. The rain picked up, pelting the crew who were rolling up topography maps and stowing them in a van.

"Jim, where to next?" Ian stopped beside the older man. Thompson glanced up from his phone.

"I'm calling the teams back in. The wind is too strong to bring in a helicopter. With the rain starting, I can't put any civilians in danger of being injured. My people will keep searching, but you can start again early tomorrow."

Asia's cry tore at his heart.

~

"You can't leave him out there all night. I don't mind the rain." Asia pushed away from Ian's touch. The chief needed to understand. This is her father. How could she lose him now?

The rain dampened her shirt. She shivered until her teeth chattered. If the wet chilled her, what was it doing to Walter? Would he even know to find shelter? Her head pounded.

"Please, we have to keep looking." She curled her hands together in front of her and prayed Jim would agree.

"I can't be responsible for any untrained searchers being hurt. I'm sorry. I want him found too." The sympathy on the man's face told her he understood as much as he could. He'd seen distraught families too often in his job.

"Can you show me where you've searched?" Ian stepped up beside her, his arm slipping around her back. She leaned into him. Comfort, familiarity, and warmth. How could she push him away? Why couldn't she cling to him? For life.

Not about you, Asia. He can never be yours. Her legs almost gave out at the thought.

"I can show you." Jim looked from one of them to the other, his mouth set in a grim line. "If you go searching on your own, be careful. These hills get treacherous when they're muddy. I don't want one of you getting hurt and spending the night out in the wilderness."

"We'll be careful." Ian squeezed her shoulder and stepped over to the van with Jim. They pulled out maps and leaned inside to study the marked areas. She twisted her fingers together, not sure if she should go inside and let Cinda know she'd failed again or wait here in the rain. Getting dry didn't matter. They would be out in the rain for hours anyway.

Jim gave them a couple of rain jackets to use, then had one of his team drive the two of them to Ian's truck. From there, they drove to the first spot Jim had marked, one closer to the hospital. They trekked and called for the next three hours. When they returned to the truck, Cinda's car was parked behind it.

Asia groaned as she climbed the short slope up to the pullout where they'd parked. Her feet slipped in the mud, and she slid back a few feet. Ian grabbed her hand and tugged. Did Cinda have news? Maybe they'd found Walter, and someone missed notifying Ian. But why hadn't Cinda messaged her?

Cinda's light blinked on as she opened her car door. Exhaustion had written a story on her face. She leaned back in and pulled out two thermoses and carried them over.

"You have to be chilled to the bone." The steady drizzle pattered in the puddles around them. Cinda handed them each a thermos. "Coffee the way you like it."

"Hot." Ian opened the lid and breathed in the aroma like he was making a television commercial. "All I care about is hot." He gave Cinda a tired smile.

"Thank you." Asia pushed the rain jacket hood from her head and shivered when a few raindrops dribbled down her neck.

"Let's sit in the truck. We need this coffee, and you can fill us in on what's happening." Ian hit the key fob, and the lights on his truck blinked as the door unlocked. Cinda retrieved her own thermos and climbed in behind Asia on the passenger side.

"Any news?" Asia's hand shook as she tried to pour coffee in the tiny cup. Cold and exhaustion stole her control. Ian set his thermos down and took hers to help. She smiled at him. His tired attempt at a smile warmed her.

"Nothing. He hasn't been spotted at all." Cinda swiped at her cheek and then busied herself pouring coffee into her own cup. The scent of peppermint filled the truck. The familiar aroma wrapped Asia in a comforting embrace.

"It's well after midnight. You both need to go home and get some sleep. If you aren't rested, we won't be able to find him tomorrow either." Cinda sipped her coffee and sighed.

Asia stared out at the dark. A true and logical statement, but her heart…and her guilt… *Keep looking. Don't give up.*

"Cinda, I'm so sorry." She stared down at her cup. Light reflected in the liquid. "I just wanted to know."

"Hey, I know you did. You do. We'll figure this out. We will." Cinda reached between the seats and held out her closed fist. "Here. I brought this too."

Asia held out her hand, and Cinda dropped a wrapped square of milk chocolate into her palm. She snapped her hand closed and pressed her fist over her heart. Cinda knew all her weaknesses.

That was family.

Ian sipped his coffee and gave an exaggerated sigh. "Thanks. Have you been waiting long?"

"Glenna went home a couple of hours ago. I waited, but there wasn't anyone else searching." She sniffed, the sound more heart-wrenching than ugly crying. Poor Cinda had been hit with so much loss. She had no one to call or talk to now that Martin was out of the picture and sitting in a jail cell. Not that he would have empathized.

Cinda handed Ian a square of chocolate and had one for herself. They unwrapped the candy. Cinda and Ian both chewed theirs up, but Asia bit off a small piece and savored it on her tongue as it melted. Mmmm. She straightened in her seat. Better than coffee.

She peered at her friends over her thermos. "We can drink our coffee and go back out. Ian says there are still a couple of places that would be good to check."

"No." Ian and Cinda spoke together, gave startled looks, and shrugged.

"No." Cinda repeated. "You need to rest. Please. I can't have you out here getting sick or injured." Her voice tightened. "I can't take losing another person. Please."

Ian nodded his agreement. Okay. Cinda made sense. How could Asia inflict more worry on her? After finishing their coffee, Asia carried the extra thermoses back to Cinda's car and gave her a hug before she drove away. She slogged through the damp to Ian's truck. The step up to the cab looked like the slope she climbed earlier. Impossible.

The rain continued, spattering against the windshield as Ian drove. Pictures of Walter out in the storm paraded through her head. She pushed them away. An impossible task. In Walter's state of confusion with the disease, he must be frightened, which for him often displayed in anger. *Please, God, watch over him.* So much to pray about. How could she remember everything? Words escaped her. The hurt ran too deep.

At her apartment, she took a hot shower and fell into bed. Sleep proved elusive. Scenes of the day ran on a never-ending roll. She replayed the visit in the care center with Walter. What could she have done differently? Should she forget her parentage? Some people wouldn't care who fathered them, but she did. So much. That dream of family wavered just out of touch.

The night sky had faded to deep gray when she finally drifted off to sleep. Dreams disturbed her rest. Dreams of Walter, broken and sick, lost in the hills. Dreams of Cinda hurling accusations at her, with Glenna urging her on. Dreams of Ian shaking his head and turning away from her.

She blinked her gritty eyes when something startled her awake. What…? Oh, someone knocking on her door. She forced her weighted limbs to move. "Coming." She croaked out the word, cleared her throat, and tried again. Hurried to throw on clothes and stumbled out to the kitchen.

Ian peered through the door, looking like death warmed over. Even so, he probably looked better than she did. The clock digital numbers mocked her. She groaned. They'd agreed to head to the hospital to help search again at eight in the morning. It was already half past. Ian must have slept in too.

"Come on in." She opened the door and motioned him inside. "I'll be quick. I just need to brush my teeth." She padded toward the bathroom. Wait! Coffee. The timer hadn't been set. Had she gotten it ready to brew?

"Asia."

"Oh, let me make coffee." She changed directions. Rinsed the pot and added some water. Pulled down the canister and the filters. The back of her eyes burned. Ian stood behind her. Her hands shook, rattling the canister.

"Asia."

She dropped the scoop and dark grounds scattered across the counter. She pressed her hands against the edge as her chest tightened. She hunched her shoulders toward her ears. Annoying noises sounded in her head.

Just go away, Ian. I don't want to hear.

21

He watched her fall apart piece by piece and hated that he was the one to cause her pain. No wonder she felt so guilty. The consequences of his decision to take her to the care center kept him awake last night. Now here he was giving Asia this news. He'd volunteered when the chief called, but…

Seeing Cinda's grief and anticipating Asia's dug a crater in his chest. He wiped at the dampness on his shirt from his visit to Cinda. Could he take much more?

"Asia." He held out his hand and took a step closer.

"Don't touch me." Her dark hair swept down to hide her face.

"Why don't you sit down. I'll make the coffee. I'll clean this up." As soon as he had the coffee perking, he wiped up the mess. Cinda would be here soon to talk to Asia, who stood unmoving. Would she shatter at a touch?

"Please, baby. I know you're hurting. But please sit down."

Her movements were wooden as she shuffled to the chair at the table. She sank down and he glimpsed her pale features. Her stricken expression.

"Where did they find him? Were we even close?" She clapped her hand to her mouth as a sob wrenched at her. "We should have kept looking. Why did we listen?"

"Hey." Ian knelt in front of her and took her hands in his. "We weren't even close to where they found him. And he's not dead." He squeezed her fingers when her gaze snapped to his.

"He's alive." The hope in her eyes knifed into his chest. "Barely. He's barely alive. They don't expect him to last long."

She started to stand. Yanked her hands free. "I've got to go. I need to see him."

"Asia." He stood with her, in front of her. "He's unconscious. Not responsive even."

"But maybe." Tears dripped down her face, a steady stream of sorrow pouring out from her. She nodded. Sank back on the chair. "Please tell me."

"He didn't go out in the hills like we thought. He must have wandered the streets of Driftwood Cove without being noticed. Chief Peterson isn't sure how. Maybe the rain. Reduced traffic at late hours. No one knows." Ian knelt down again, took her chilled hands in his, and tried to rub some warmth into them.

"A jogger found him in one of the small parks this morning. She thought he was a drunk or something and called the police to get him before kids came to play. The policeman recognized him from the picture passed around."

"Did he say anything?"

"No, he was unconscious when they found him. They took him to the hospital. The doctor thinks he may have fallen or passed out again." Ian pulled her into his embrace. Her small frame felt fragile in his arms.

"I need to go there. Let me get ready." She pushed back from him. The sorrow he saw in her eyes reflected the same emotion he'd seen on Cinda's face.

His phone dinged. A text from Cinda. "Get ready. I'll take you. Cinda was going to come by but decided to go on to the hospital instead."

She came out a few minutes later, her hair braided, fresh clothes on, and her backpack over her shoulder. She rarely took the pack with her. Why take it now? He frowned as he reached for the doorknob. What was she thinking?

The hospital buzzed with activity. Last night the emergency section had a lot of action from accidents on rain-slicked pavement to a woman climbing from her car getting hit by a falling tree branch. The storm and high winds left a trail of damage still being sorted out.

Cinda and Glenna were seated in the waiting room outside ICU. Glenna surged up when she saw Ian and Asia. Cinda glanced up, put her hand on Glenna's arm, and said something. Glenna sank back down, but her glare at Asia didn't waver. If he stepped between them, he'd be burned.

Fine. Anything for Asia.

I'll stand up for her. Love her.

Lay down my life for her.

"Asia, thank you for coming. I was going to stop by but needed to be here." Cinda enveloped Asia in a hug, then reached around to include Ian. He had no idea how she still managed to put others first after the blows she'd suffered.

Best. Sister. Ever.

Maybe not a sister by blood, but definitely his sister by choice.

"How is he?" Asia swiped at her cheeks.

"He's still unconscious. They're doing some tests and will let us in one at a time when they're done." Cinda glanced at Glenna, who still glared daggers.

Cinda clasped Asia's hands in hers. "I don't think Glenna will let you go in." Sorrow hollowed Cinda's face. "I'm not sure you being in there is best for Dad either. He seems to get upset when you're around, and I'm not sure why. Maybe there is some memory that frustrates him. I just don't know, Asia. I wish I did."

She motioned to some chairs across the room from where Glenna sat. "Let's sit and talk a minute."

Asia chose a seat facing Cinda, with her back to Glenna. Ian eased down beside Asia and put his arm on the back of her chair. Cinda raised her eyebrows, giving him a look as if to say, "Let's talk later," and then focused on Asia.

"I know you have the paper saying my dad is your dad, Asia, but I can't see it. He was always a devoted father and a good husband. He and my mom probably had rough patches, but they didn't really air their problems to us." She swallowed and looked away for a moment. "Do you think he would have brought you to our home like he did if you were his? I can't see him doing that to my mom. Can you?"

Ian had to admit she had a point. From what he'd seen, Walter and Mary Bryant were the opposite of his parents. Their marriage seemed so strong and didn't appear to be a pretense. He couldn't imagine Walter cheating on his wife.

Asia fiddled with the end of her braid but didn't look at Cinda. "I wish I could find Joy and talk with her." She lifted her gaze to Cinda's. "I agree that this doesn't make sense for Uncle Walter to have been with my mother. But I can't deny the connection to your family. And it's his name listed as my father. And then there are those letters… I don't know what to think. I just wanted a family." Her voice cracked. She lowered her face.

Ian cupped her shoulder with his hand and drew her close. Would she accept his intimacy since she specified keeping her distance? His meager offering? No wisdom. No memories. Only himself and his love. Would she accept that?

He studied her sad features. "What did you try before you came here?"

"After I opened the box and saw the birth certificate, I went back to where Joy lived, but she was gone. No one knew where." She shrugged, defeat leaking from every pore.

He took her hands, his face close to hers. "Maybe I can help you find her. I'll talk to Daniel and see what he can find."

The hope in Asia's expression as she gazed up at him stole his thoughts. Her lips parted, but she didn't say anything. His breath caught. Her lips were so close. One kiss.

Right here. Right now.

On the floor beside her he could see the backpack tucked under the chair. She hadn't left it in his truck. Did she mean to leave? If Walter died, would Asia walk out of their lives again? Would she figure she didn't belong and move on, never fitting in anywhere? His heart cried out for her to stay. To choose to make her home here no matter what. To choose a family of people who loved and cared about her.

To choose him.

WHAT HAD they been talking about? Asia's pulse fluttered like butterfly wings against her throat. The promise in Ian's eyes, so similar to years ago, called to her. Could she forget everything she needed to do and go anywhere he wanted her to go? He could be hers.

She could be his.

The PA system called for a doctor. Shoes clicked on the tile floor.

Asia blinked.

Ian's breathing hitched.

What would he do if she closed the distance between them? Touched his lips with hers. Lost herself in the delight of his kiss.

Instead, she stretched her neck. Rolled her shoulders. And turned to Cinda, who sat there smirking at them. Asia's face caught fire. Her mind blanked. What were they talking about?

She glanced over her shoulder to where Glenna still tried to imitate a superhero with a laser gaze to set Asia on fire.

"If you remind me of Joy's last name, I'll message Daniel and get that started." Ian's warm tone spiraled through her. She sank back in the chair. Yes. They were talking about contacting Joy. She wasn't sure why he brought it up. If he and his friend found Joy, she could answer some questions.

Her pack bumped against her ankle. If Walter didn't survive the night, she'd head out today. She'd stayed awake making this decision and getting ready. Preparing her pack had been easy. Preparing her heart hurt.

She loved this town. Loved Cinda and her crazy quilt ladies and her shop. Loved Ian. Her breath caught as she pictured him only moments ago. The look in his eyes. She loved him with everything in her, but she had to go.

"Her name is Joy Shen." She rattled off the last address she'd had for Joy. The one where she'd lived with her as a teen. Except for the glorious summertime when she'd been in Driftwood Cove. "I don't know if she has any other family."

"I hope you find what you need, Asia." Cinda leaned forward in her chair until they were almost touching across the aisle. "Please remember, you are welcome here. I would love to have you stay, even if my dad can't ever tell us anything." She blinked rapidly, pressing her lips together. "I will always consider you family, because you are."

A long curl fell forward over Cinda's shoulder as she ducked her head. Her shoulders trembled. Asia slipped from her chair to kneel on the floor in front of her. Oh, to call this woman sister. Not just a sister of the heart, but a sister by blood.

She lifted up on her knees and put her arms around Cinda, holding her tight. When they pulled apart, Ian handed them both tissues.

"I'm sorry. I'm so emotional lately." Cinda wiped her nose.

"Who can blame you?" Asia patted her leg and sank back on her heels.

Cinda huffed a short laugh. "Funny thing is, I don't feel much sadness about the situation with Martin. At first, the shock and betrayal hurt, but I think that was my pride. I've realized since then that what we had was comfortable and convenient. I don't think I've loved Martin for a long time, if ever."

She kneaded the balled-up tissue in her hand. "I think I'm relieved more than anything to be out of the relationship. That's pretty sad, isn't it?"

"No, it isn't." Asia's fingers curled into a fist at the mention of Martin. She pressed her fingers to the floor to catch her balance. No more narcissistic lectures. No more creepiness.

Ian's hand flattened on her back. He leaned his head back, nostrils flaring, before sitting forward and patting Cinda's knee. Asia bumped his shoulder with hers. Neither of them would hurt Cinda by rejoicing too much over the demise of her relationship. What would happen to Martin? Despite her curiosity, now was not the time or place to ask. Only Walter mattered.

The door to the ICU whooshed open. A male nurse in blue scrubs stepped into the waiting area and stopped. "Is the Bryant family here?"

"We're here." Glenna jumped up and strode forward.

Cinda stood. Asia started to stand, but Cinda put her hand on her shoulder.

She leaned down to speak so only Asia and maybe Ian could hear. "I know you want to come. I do consider you family, but Glenna is having a hard time. Would you wait here? I promise I'll come out and let you know how he is as soon as I can." She bent closer to hug Asia.

The scent of her lemony shampoo brought memories of the first time Cinda discovered the scent and her absolute delight. Asia wanted to give in as she had so many times, but this might be the last chance to see if Walter would recognize her. How could she pass that up just to placate Glenna?

"Cinda, you know I'm family. I have to go in." Asia ended the embrace, rose, and crossed the room to where the nurse waited with Glenna.

"What are you doing?" Ice dripped from Glenna's words.

"I'm family. I'm coming in too." Asia met Glenna's gaze head on. She would *not* look away first. Not this time.

The necklace Walter gave her mother sat heavy against Asia's skin. *Broken hearts made new.* Would Walter recognize the piece of jewelry he'd given as a gift so many years ago? Alzheimer's patients retained older memories the longest. How would he react to the kintsugi heart?

Glenna's face reddened. Her eyes bore deep into Asia, but when Cinda stepped close to put a hand on her older sister's arm, Glenna glanced down and relaxed her posture from rigid to alert.

"Come on." Glenna turned to follow the nurse, and they trailed after her. Cinda glanced back and beckoned to Ian to come with them. Asia's flagging resolve strengthened when he put his hand on her back.

"Is it okay for all of us to come in? Don't you have rules about the number of people who can visit at once?" Glenna sent a pointed glance in Asia's direction.

The nurse motioned to a small room. "Right now the doctor wants to speak to all of you." He ushered them into the room, made sure they had chairs, and said the doctor would be with them in a few minutes.

"I don't like this." Cinda twisted the strap of her purse around her fingers. Worry chased across her face and darkened her eyes. Asia's toes tapped against the floor. Why would they bring them to a separate room? Did they have bad news? The type of bad news that involved a terrible end result for the patient? *Please,*

please, let Walter be okay. Give me another chance to talk with him. She fingered the outline of the necklace through her top.

"Don't borrow trouble." Glenna drummed her fingers against her leg.

"Where's Jeffrey?" Cinda narrowed her eyes as she studied her sister. "Why isn't he here?"

Asia wondered the same thing. What husband let his wife face something like this on her own?

"He's away." Glenna's jaw worked, and her fingers changed to a rapid tempo. "On business. He's moving up in the company, so he has to be away more."

From the set of her shoulders and her reaction to the question, there had to be more to the story. Glenna's marriage must be in deeper trouble than they suspected.

The door whooshed open. A middle-aged woman wearing a white coat came in, introduced herself as Dr. Talbot, and pulled up a chair to face them.

"Your father was brought in this morning with a severe case of hypothermia. The night in the rain and wind were hard on his system. We tried to warm him up but the strain on his heart proved too much. I'm very sorry, but he's gone."

22

"No." Pain flared in Asia's chest. She wrapped her arms across her stomach. Had she misheard? The doctor meant he was still unconscious, right? Walter couldn't be dead. She had to talk to him. To find the truth. Not knowing would leave her adrift.

"I don't understand." Cinda pressed her fingertips to her mouth as if she wanted to say more but needed to hold the words inside.

"There has to be more you can do. Where is he?" Glenna surged to her feet, fists clenched at her sides.

"I'm so sorry." Dr. Talbot's eyes were kind, her expression neutral. How many times had she faced a family's grief and endured their anguish? "By the time he came to us, his body temperature was too low. He suffered irreparable damage. We did our best, but he developed pneumonia."

"Couldn't you have put him in a hot bath? Rub the circulation back? Given him…something?" Glenna paced to the door and back. Asia almost joined her. The same questions raced through her mind. How hard was it to warm up a person who'd gotten too cold?

Dr. Talbot leaned forward. "We did everything medically possible with the limited time available. Giving a person a hot bath or rubbing their limbs as you've suggested can bring on cardiac arrest. We were trying to avoid that. By the time he was found, Mr. Bryant had suffered damage to his internal organs. That is the problem we faced."

The doctor stood, putting her hands in the pockets of her jacket. "Once again, I'm very sorry. If you wait here, we will prepare him and let you in to see him."

Glenna fumbled for the back of her chair and sank to the seat. Asia sympathized with the bereft look on Glenna's face. Cinda dropped her head to her hands and sobbed. Ian's steady presence and his hand gripping hers kept Asia grounded. Grief hollowed his cheeks as tears swam in his eyes.

She opened her mouth. Life was so unfair. Uncle Walter, her possible father, needed to be alive for a little longer. To affirm her deepest hope. Her deepest desire.

Her. His long unrecognized daughter.

The door clicked shut behind the doctor. Asia's eyes burned. She blinked away the tears. Envisioned running from room to room to find Walter. Demanding he wake up. Why hadn't he acknowledged her before? Had her mother put his name on the birth certificate as some horrible joke? If so, why had he agreed to have Asia visit? Why claim her as a niece and a cousin to his children? Why had Aunt Mary gone along with the ruse?

The maelstrom of questions ping-ponged through her head. Ian scooted his chair closer and pulled her against his chest. Her tears refused to be held in check as she rested against the port he offered in her storm. Had God sent him to her for this very purpose? Didn't God use people to offer His comfort? She pictured Him touching her through Ian. Comforting her heart of grief and hurt. Whatever happened from here on out, God loved her. His provision was enough.

Faith. She must have faith.

When the nurse in the blue scrubs returned to lead them to the room where they'd put Walter, Asia hung back. Ian stayed with her as Glenna and Cinda followed the nurse down the hallway. Neither sister looked back at them.

"You don't want to go?" Ian's voice rumbled in his chest, and she realized she'd rested her head against him again.

Asia straightened. "No. This is for them." Her sisters turned into a room toward the end of the short hallway. "I don't know what to do."

"I'm sure Cinda won't mind you joining them." Ian kept his arm around her.

She didn't have the strength to move away from him. "I know. But Glenna would. I can't make this more difficult for her." She met Ian's gaze.

His blue eyes held steady on her.

What would she do without him? "Please take me back to the apartment." Surprise flashed across his handsome features. Had he expected her to grab her backpack and head out, never to be seen again? Well, she *had* planned to do that, but now… Prayer first before any decision.

The drive to the apartment seemed surreal. Traffic had picked up while they were at the hospital. People hurried to work or to shop. Life continued on as if hers hadn't taken an unexpected and shattering turn.

"Would you like some breakfast first?" Ian motioned to a restaurant.

"No thanks. I'm not really hungry." Her empty stomach twisted.

"You need to eat, Asia. You didn't get much last night since we were out searching so late." Ian passed the restaurant. "How about at least a cup of coffee? I can do drive-through."

"Okay." Her smile faltered into more of a grimace.

He pulled into the drive-through at the coffee shop, started to ask something—probably what she wanted—squeezed her arm and put in an order. He not only ordered coffee, but croissants and muffins, all her favorites.

At the apartment, he climbed out with the bag of goodies and came around the truck to open her door. She still hadn't sipped her coffee, but he'd downed at least half of his. And a croissant and muffin. She rubbed at her prickly arm. Ian's needs hadn't crossed her mind. Only her needs.

Again.

Ian held her coffee as she unlocked her door and then handed her both the cup and the bag as he helped her inside. He didn't follow her in. "I'll be at the restaurant if you need me. Don't hesitate to call or come over."

He started to turn away but swung around again. "Do you still have your marketing meeting today? Weren't you showing the mockups at lunchtime?" He glanced at his watch.

"Oh." She leaned against the doorjamb. Closed her eyes. How could she even think about the ads? How could she make a presentation that would sell her work when she couldn't muster two coherent thoughts?

"Tell you what." Ian's lips brushed her forehead, and her eyes flew open. He smiled down at her, his heart in his eyes. "I'll talk to them and see if I can get you a reprieve. With a death in the family, they're probably okay with a postponement."

"Thank you." After Ian left, she sipped coffee and nibbled the muffin. When he called to say the men were all sorry for her loss and would meet with her later in the week, she cleaned up and slipped out to walk to Mrs. Beasley's house. The older woman was almost always at home.

Mrs. B inspired such confidence. She not only welcomed Asia into her home, but she listened as Asia poured out her whole story, even the parts that she hadn't shared with Cinda or Ian.

Asia relaxed into the overstuffed chair facing Mrs. B's rocker. The older woman cradled her cup of tea and took a sip, her brow furrowed in thought. Asia picked up her cooled tea. The taste of citrus and cinnamon, lightly sweetened, buoyed her.

"I've known Ian and the Bryant children for years. I even remember when you were here visiting and used to come in the library." Mrs. B set her cup down beside her and resumed her gentle rocking. "I used to pray for all of you just like I prayed for every child who crossed my path." Her wrinkled face creased in a soft smile.

"You must trust God, dear. When you withhold who you are, you are carrying the load and not allowing Him to work."

IAN SAT next to Asia in the pew behind Cinda and Glenna. Oh, to be anywhere but here. Funerals always reminded him of the two from his youth. His mother's, lightly attended. His father's, unattended. Except for Ian.

The church gradually filled with murmuring people dressed in somber colors, all awaiting the start of Walter's service. The cloying fragrance of flowers made his head pound, while the sadness of the Bryant sisters made his heart ache.

Walter had been a well-known and loved community figure. He'd served on the town council for several years, been the mayor, plus owned a thriving business that he sold for enough to have a great retirement. After that he did a lot of community work with the underprivileged and helped others in all walks of life.

No wonder people filled the sanctuary.

The week passed slower than a sloth at rest. Loneliness etched Asia's face every time Ian saw her. Glenna wasn't ready to accept her, and Cinda had been too depressed to fight for her to join them. Instead, Asia spent her time helping Tansie at the quilt shop —classes had been cancelled for the week—and building her marketing and design business. She tried so hard, but her efforts were not up to her full potential. Ian frowned. Had something other than Walter's death and her sisters' lack of acceptance distracted her? If so, what?

She'd mentioned yesterday she needed to talk to him about something. He'd been busy at the restaurant at the time and then forgotten by closing. The thought nagged at him. What did she want to say? Did she plan to leave again, as he suspected? A pit opened in his stomach, and he bent forward to ease the ache.

The pianist finished a beautiful rendition of "Amazing Grace," and the pastor walked up to the podium. Cinda kept her head bent. She wept through the pastor's comments and the memories shared by several of Walter's longtime friends. Asia trembled beside him. He folded her tight fist in both his hands, and she gradually relaxed.

Asia didn't shed a tear during the church service, but afterward on the way to the cemetery she sobbed into a tissue, trying to be quiet in the confines of the truck. He draped his arm on the seat back to rub her shoulder. By the time he'd parked in line with the other vehicles and came around to open her door, she had dried her tears. Only the redness of her eyes told of her breakdown.

The graveside service was blessedly short. Asia didn't sit with the family. Several of the ladies from the quilt shop spoke to her as she and Ian walked back toward his truck.

"Do you want to go back to the church for the dinner? The church ladies have prepared food for family and friends." Ian pulled out when the vehicle in front of him eased on to the road.

"No. I'll go back to my apartment." Asia stared out at the headstones as they wended around the curving drive to the gates leading out to the road. "I'm sorry you couldn't find Randall. Cinda and Glenna needed him today."

"I know they did. It's like he disappeared from the face of the earth." Ian cleared his throat. How much should he say to Asia? "Daniel helped me search. With the internet and tracking, it's nearly impossible for someone to hide."

"Did you find anything?" Asia straightened in her seat, her gaze steady on him.

"Nothing." Ian turned on to the main road. "Daniel thinks...he wonders..." The words jumbled in his throat.

"Wonders what?" Asia's hand pressed against her chest as if she already suspected what he might say.

"He wonders if there was foul play involved. He's looking at the original disappearance and what the police recorded." His fingers tightened on the steering wheel. "Asia, his family may never know what happened to him. It's as if he fell off the face of the earth."

She slumped back against the seat. Turned to stare out the window and swiped away a tear.

"There is some good news." He waited for her to calm. "Daniel has a lead on Joy Shen."

"Joy." The name was a whisper from Asia. She closed her eyes for a moment. "Thank you. Maybe when he finds her, you can let me know how to get in touch."

"I will." Ian turned into the mall and parked in front of A Time to Sew. Memorial Day and the big event at the restaurant would be here soon. Maybe he could find Joy and have her here by then. Asia needed her now more than ever.

"Do you think you could come in and talk for a few minutes?" Asia twisted her fingers together but didn't look at him. What had her so nervous? What could she possibly have to say that worried her so?

He glanced at his watch. His crew expected him at the restaurant. And Cinda needed his support at the church. But Asia rarely asked for anything. Would she go to the luncheon with him if he listened and set her mind at ease?

"Sure." He ignored the demands pressing on him. Asia flung her door open and climbed out before he could get around the vehicle. He followed her up the sidewalk.

She fumbled her keys, then dropped them. When she snatched them up and dropped them again, he rubbed her back and bent down to retrieve the keys and unlock her door.

"You okay?"

Her stiff nod spoke volumes. A vivid picture of her grabbing her pack and leaving town flitted through his thoughts. Could he survive losing her again? He almost groaned aloud.

As he closed the door behind him, his phone buzzed. Ian almost let the call go to voicemail. Asia first, right? But, as a business owner, he had the responsibility to answer.

Meg. She wouldn't call unless something important needed his attention. He sent an apologetic glance to Asia and clicked to answer. "Meg, what's up?"

"Ian. Get here now! Fire!"

He heard sirens in the distance. He froze.

"What?" He pulled his cell away and gaped at it.

Asia's eyes widened. She'd heard too. She leaped around him to swing the door open and they ran. They rounded the quilt shop to see smoke spiraling from the back of I-BBQ. His pulse thudded.

People poured out the front door. He couldn't get through there without endangering someone or impeding their progress out of the burning building. He changed course and raced for the back door. *Please, please, don't let this be bad. Don't let anyone be hurt.*

As he rounded the back, Meg and one of the cooks stumbled out, coughing and gasping for air. Meg grabbed his arm before he could charge inside.

"It's out." She coughed again. "The fire. It's just thick smoke now."

"Is everyone out?" Ian took a step toward the door. Meg tightened her grip. Asia grabbed his other arm. The whine of sirens made talking next to impossible. Smoke poured out the screened door and burned his throat.

"It's empty. We made sure." Meg released his arm and bent over, still gasping. The cook went around the corner toward the front.

"Let's move away." Ian urged both women to move away from the smoke.

The sirens cut off, and his knees almost buckled. The loud noise, while necessary, only added to the horror.

"I need to go out there and talk to the fire chief and the police. Come on, Meg. You need to get checked out." He led his head waitress to the melee in the parking lot, making sure Asia followed.

They approached a waiting ambulance crew, who were checking for smoke inhalation. Ian strode toward the fire chief. How could this happen? His cook, Brent Wilson, was already there talking with the chief.

"Ian, I'm sorry. My men just went inside to confirm the fire is out." Chief Anderson's grim expression echoed Ian's feelings. "We'll check for the cause as soon as the smoke clears. I'm sorry this happened. Any ideas?"

Ian glanced at Brian. "None. We have the grills and equipment cleaned regularly. In fact, they were due in last week, weren't they, Brian?"

His cook nodded. "The guy came when I was off last week. I came in this morning and realized the vent hadn't been cleaned properly, but by that time we were in full swing for lunch and really busy. I'm sorry." Brian frowned and glanced at the building. Smoke still filtered out but not thick like before.

"We've had trouble with the new guy. The one we had before did a better job. I don't like people who aren't thorough, and this guy wasn't the last time either. You were away, so I cleaned the vent myself after hours, and then forgot to say anything. I didn't realize they would send the same guy. I sent them a message. I should have said something to you too and regret that I didn't." Brian's jaw tensed as he met Ian's gaze. As if he expected to be fired on the spot.

Ian gritted his teeth. Imagined being at the bluff, where the surf would drown out any sound, and yelling until his lungs ran out of air. Yes, he should have been aware, but Brian had followed protocol in notifying the company.

"We'll get you cleared as soon as we can, but for now you're shut down." Chief Anderson nodded and strode off to meet some of his men.

23

Ian clicked off the call and put his cell on the table in Asia's apartment. He leaned his head back against the chair and closed his eyes. Think! The swirl of need-to-do items spun through his mind in a nauseating array.

"Any progress?" Asia spoke from where she sat in the recliner holding the laptop. She'd been designing another set of ads for one of the businessmen who liked her work so much he wanted more.

"The restaurant cleaning service fired the worker. Turns out ours isn't the only complaint, but it is the most serious. They will still honor their guarantee. Now that the fire chief determined the cleaning is at fault, they will stand by their work." Ian cleared his throat. If only he could clear the fog from his head as well.

"At least that's something. Any projection for opening again?" Asia set her computer on the side table and rose in a graceful unfolding of limbs that made his mouth go dry. He wondered if working here was a mistake. He needed to be close to I-BBQ while the cleaning crew came in to do another deep clean after the renovation crew finished. Focus. He dragged his attention back to the figures on his computer. Working with Asia in the room had been so distracting he'd gotten behind.

He, Meg, and Asia were still planning their outdoor event for Memorial Day. The past few days had been a flurry of last minute details. Setting up tables and cooking areas. Simplifying the menu. The menu would be limited: two types of sandwich, barbecue meats, chips, and pie. Not even pie á la mode. Asia insisted he still offer a peanut butter and jelly for kids because it wouldn't be hard to make and would require no extra cooking. Meg agreed. Ian did too.

Meg and Asia assured him the music would be such a draw that no one would care about the menu. They would be happy to grab a sandwich and listen or dance. He'd ordered extra tables and chairs, which would be set up early on Saturday. At least with the restaurant closed, he could store the extra tables and benches in the back room to pull out and set up Saturday afternoon.

"Tea? Coffee? Water?" Asia took the pitcher of water from the refrigerator and filled her cup.

"No, thanks. I'd take coffee but my stomach would go into full rebellion." He put his head in his hands and massaged the back of his head. A low throb resonated across his shoulders and into his scalp.

"Here, have these. A sure cure." Asia set something on the table in front of him. He opened his eyes to see the half glass of milk and the package of chocolate cookies he loved to dunk. He picked up a cookie and breathed in the scent. Dunked it in the milk and sucked the softened chocolate into his mouth. The headache faded a bit.

"Let me see if this helps." Asia stood behind him. Her small fingers massaged the tight muscles of his upper back and shoulders. She worked her way up his neck and back down. He melted into a puddle right there. Had anything ever felt so good?

When was the last time someone had touched him like this? Did Asia miss a loving touch as much as he did?

He caught her hand, pulling her around and down on his lap. ""Thank you. You always know the right thing to do." He cupped her chin and tilted her head up. She pushed her hair back from her face but didn't pull away.

He lowered his head slowly, giving her time to object. When her breath hitched and her lips parted, he closed the distance. He lost himself in the kiss. Floated in a sea of sensation. This. He missed this. He missed her. He'd longed for her with every breath.

She had to stay.

Ian buried his fingers in her hair, the silken strands a waterfall down his forearm. He trailed kisses across her cheek and down the softness of her throat. Her pulse skittered beneath his lips. She released a quick gasp of breath. A soft moan that resonated through him.

Stop. Before you can't.

"Asia." He buried his face in her neck and tugged her closer to him. "I've missed you so much." She lifted his chin, gave him a light kiss, and snuggled against his chest. Perfect.

They sat there, heartbeats steadying in tandem. Thoughts of work faded. He hadn't held a woman since.... Oh, yes.

"I can't do this. I'm afraid." Asia's murmured words barely registered.

Afraid? Of him? Had Meg said something about what he did in college? He didn't recall telling anyone else. Or, maybe she remembered the stories of his dad and mom.

Like father, like son.

He straightened and held her away until he could see her face. Tears pooled in her eyes.

"Why are you afraid?" He brushed her hair back from her cheek. "What scares you?" His heart clenched as he waited for her answer. *Please, don't let it be me.*

She shook her head and stared out the window. Should he ask again or wait? Waiting wasn't what he wanted to do. What if she told him her fears, and he didn't have an answer that would relieve her and bring her back to his arms.

Her hair fell forward across her face as she chewed at her lower lip. He had the wild urge to pull her close and kiss that lower lip. Kiss her until all her doubts faded.

"I'm sorry."

At his words, she glanced up, her silky strands falling back, revealing her distraught gaze. He prayed for the right words and held up his hand to stop her from saying anything.

"I know what people say. I know how my parents died and that people believe I'm just like my father. But I have to tell you what Meg said...and what I did years ago." His throat closed, trapping his words inside. He swallowed hard against the pain, then took a couple of deep breaths.

He told her about the girl in college. About his anger and how he hit her. "I could see my dad standing over my mom, his face twisted with rage, his hand raised." Ian's eyes burned and he couldn't look at Asia. He couldn't bear to see the condemnation that he deserved in her eyes.

"I haven't dated since then. I didn't want to. The thought of being like my dad and hurting a woman was terrifying." He looked out the window. Why did honesty hurt so much? Did she want him out of her apartment forever? Out of her life?

"What did Meg say to you?" Asia's soft voice called him back from the horrible memories. He met her gaze. There was no condemnation. Nothing but...empathy? Caring?

Love?

Did he dare hope she cared enough to overlook his past? Accept him for who he was, not who his parents were?

"You know my father's last words to me."

"Like father, like son."

He nodded. "Meg reminded me that I'm a Christian now, with a different Father. She said that changes the whole meaning of *Like Father, like son.* She's right. Everyone has a choice to make. I can be like the father who raised me, or I can be like my heavenly Father, or try my best to be like Him. It's why I have no time for people who break the law, who deliberately choose to do wrong. I won't be that person."

~

SHE HAD TO TELL HIM. Had to. But the words stuck in her throat and refused to come out. He would hate her. Reject her for the choices she'd made. She pictured the horror on his face when he realized *she'd* broken the law.

He'd never understand why she'd done something illegal.

His phone beeped. He glanced down. "Meg. She says there is a delivery van and I need to come help." He pulled her close for another sweet kiss that made her toes curl. She breathed in his scent. Memorized the feel of him. Pushed down the certainty of the forthcoming train wreck when he learned the truth about her.

"Be back soon." Ian's dimples deepened as he traced his fingers down the side of her face before leaving. She closed the door after him, dulling the sounds of traffic. Leaning her forehead against the doorframe, she squeezed her eyes shut.

Lord, what do I do? If I tell him, he'll hate me. If I don't tell him and he finds out some other way, he'll hate me more. If that's possible. I'm in a no-win situation.

She stumbled to the recliner and sank down. Her coffee sat on the table, probably too cold to drink by now. She had no energy to warm the drink or to even get up. Her leaden insides weighed her down.

Eyes closed, she waited. Listened. Hoped God would speak. God would work this out to her benefit, wouldn't He? Didn't the Bible say something about Him working things out for her good? That had to mean she and Ian would be together, because the thought of them being apart was more than she could bear.

Trust Him.

The words whispered through her soul. The woman who came to the prison, who led her to Christ, said that to her all the time.

Trust Him with every part of your life.

Could she do that? She hadn't so far. Maybe with small things. But with something this important, trusting and having faith that God would work everything out…

How could that be possible?

Yet still the words whispered inside her heart. Her mind. Her soul.

Trust Him.

Tears trickled down Asia's cheeks.

Trust Me.

Her eyes widened. *Lord...?*

Trust Me.

She pictured the cross and herself kneeling there, her hands stretched out, palms up and empty. Giving all to Him. Her whole life His to do with as He saw fit.

Not my decision, but Yours, Lord.

Peace dribbled through her.

Surrounded her bruised heart.

Soothed her harried thoughts.

Gave her a place of refuge none would ever see. She *could* depend on Him. No matter what, He would see her through. Even when she told Ian the truth.

She wasn't sure how long she prayed, but when she opened her eyes, Ian still wasn't back. She stepped into the quilt shop to see if Cinda or Tansie needed her. Tomorrow the classes would start again, so today might be a little slower. Surprise at the amount of activity caught her off guard. Several women bustled around the room or sat at sewing machines, the whir of the machines adding to the hum of conversations. What was going on?

Cinda fast walked into the classroom from the sales floor. "Asia, I'm glad you're here. Can you help out for a little while?" Her arms were full of pieces of cloth in various colors.

"What's happening?" Asia hurried to take some of the pile. "Are you having a special class?"

"We have a project." Cinda bounced a little. Something had her excited. Asia was glad to see her on the mend.

"What are you making?" She studied the women who were sewing. Most of them came to the advanced class or the mystery block class. A few she had seen in the shop, but they didn't attend any classes.

"We all love Ian and his restaurant. We thought we would make some quilted items to sell when he has his event this weekend. All the proceeds will go to help cover the cost of restoring the I-BBQ. I know his insurance doesn't cover everything. And there's the lost revenue."

Asia plopped the material on an empty table. "This is amazing. A great idea. What do you need me to do?"

For the next couple of hours, Asia cut pieces of material, ran to the shop to get thread or other notions that were needed, and cleaned up scraps that littered the tables and floor. She listened to the good-natured chatter of the women and realized how much she loved being here.

Since Walter's funeral was over, she had no hope of finding the truth about him being her father. Nothing kept her here. Glenna still hated her. Cinda went from being sad to putting on a false happiness.

Asia shook her head. If she stayed, she'd be a reminder of everything that had happened with Walter. How selfish would that be?

But she loved Driftwood Cove.

"Here." Cinda handed her a box and a roll of tissue paper. "Maybe you can put the placemats in here with a layer of tissue between each set. They come in sets of four. I'll get another box for the wall hangings Mrs. Beasley and her friends are making."

"How are you going to display these?" Asia picked up one of the placemats, white material with whimsical cats.

"We can put the placemats and other small things on a table, but I'm not sure how to display the wall hangings." Cinda gnawed at her lip.

"Why don't you open up the classroom? You can hang the wall hangings around so people can see what they look like. Plus, it will be dark outside, and the cute patterns won't show up in the dark." Asia turned a circle to note the blank walls that would easily hold all the quilted pieces.

Cinda lifted on her toes and clasped her hands under her chin. "Perfect idea. I'll have one table outside, and they can direct people to come in here to look. One of us can be out there and a couple in here to help customers." She pressed her fingertips to her mouth and turned around as if she could already picture how the walls would look.

Asia continued to pack the handmade items, her heart lighter. She'd never lived in a place where people were so quick to help one another. So many had come to help search for Walter. Now these ladies were giving of their time and talent to help Ian.

She hadn't realized that in her desire for a family, she also had a desire for extended family, or community. Would she never be satisfied? The dream she wanted seemed so distant. Maybe God intended for her to be alone. Maybe His plan meant she had only Him for family.

If so, she would have to accept Him as enough. And He would be.

They were cleaning up at the end of the day when Cinda's phone chimed. "Ian says they've been working on the outdoor grill, testing it out. He wants us to come over for dinner. The meat will be done when we get there."

She wiggled her eyebrows at Asia, whose stomach growled. "I'd say that's an affirmative from you." Cinda laughed. Asia threw an empty spool at her, but Cinda ducked.

Cinda locked the door behind them. Asia stared up at the evening sky, the cloudless expanse turning a deeper blue. A light breeze brought the fragrance of ocean, and she drew in the scent as if starved for air.

They went to the back of I-BBQ where the back door stood open. Brian waved from the large outdoor grill, the aroma making Asia's stomach clench.

An underlying scent of smoke still permeated the building, but not enough to keep people away. Asia suspected that once they finished cleaning and began to barbecue in here again, that smell would vanish.

A couple of the businessmen she'd been working with and a police officer were talking with Ian. They glanced up as she and Cinda entered the room. Meg looked up from the table where she was placing utensils and waved to them. Ian motioned them over, his face grim.

Asia's heart pounded as the officer turned and met her gaze. It was Daniel. In his uniform. On duty. Her knees trembled, and she nearly stumbled.

"Asia Jessup?" Daniel separated from the other men and strode toward her. "We need to talk."

24

SHE GLANCED TOWARD THE DOOR. *Run.* She hadn't done anything wrong. Nothing. Yet the horrible images of being arrested surged forward. Arms jerked behind her back. Handcuffs clicked in place. People staring and pointing. Rough hands hauling her to the police car. The miasma of scents as she huddled in the seat, leading to the horror of being booked at the station. The trial. The sentencing.

Prison.

Her stomach heaved. She held her breath to keep the contents of her stomach from spewing on Daniel. He didn't look menacing. In fact, his expression conveyed some kindness. But the uniform. The uniform.

Shivers traced through her. Ian. The uncertainty on his face. The hurt in his eyes. Oh, why hadn't she told him herself?

"Ms. Jessup, would you step outside with me where we can speak in private?" Daniel motioned to the door. She hesitated. The frowning businessmen clued her into the fact they already knew what the police had found.

Her past.

All of it.

"What's going on?" Cinda's brow furrowed as she glanced around at everyone. "Asia? What is this?"

There wasn't any help for it. She'd missed her chance to talk to Ian or anyone else about her mistake. Why had she waited so long? Telling them upfront would have been so much better, but she hadn't put the pain of what she'd done into words.

Now she faced the truth. And it might be best done with everyone listening at once.

"It's okay." Asia blinked hard to keep tears at bay. Tears she hadn't realized were forming. "You can say what you need to in here."

Daniel glanced at Cinda and over his shoulder. He frowned. Nodded. "I've become aware of your arrest record and that you were incarcerated."

"I served my time and am free to go where I want." Asia squared her shoulders. Sort of. Cinda gasped. Oh, to crawl under a table and hide.

"I realize that." Daniel's squared-off stance made her think he expected her to run. "I want to know your purpose in being here and to make sure you don't do anything to jeopardize the people of Driftwood Cove."

He didn't say his friends in Driftwood Cove, but Asia could read that in his expression. Did he suspect she was doing ads and marketing as some sort of scam? Had he even read her file? How could she defend her honor when all the cards were stacked against her? Who even knew the truth?

I do. Trust Me.

The words whispered through her, giving her strength and peace that left her in awe.

"I don't intend to harm anyone here." She met Daniel's gaze head on and didn't look away. "I am trying to find my way after making a...mistake." This time she did look away. *Liar.* That was no mistake. What she'd done had been on purpose, but not for the reason everyone had believed.

"I've discussed your record with these men. They say you've been honest in your dealings with them. I made them aware of your history with drugs, and they will do what they believe is right." Daniel hesitated, his mouth thinning. "These are my friends. I'll be keeping an eye on you. I can't make you leave town, but if you do anything out of line, I'll be there." He nodded at Ian, the businessmen, and Cinda, then left.

Asia's chest rose and fell as she waited. Breathe. She still had a lot of questions to answer. Or maybe accusations.

"Drugs? Prison?" Cinda's face mirrored the horror in her words. "What happened to you? Why didn't you tell us?"

Before she could say anything, the two businessmen stopped beside her to let her know they wouldn't need her services anymore. Ian approached, his eyes darkened to stormy blue.

"I trusted you." His jaw clenched as he spoke. "I can't believe you did something like this and then didn't have the decency to tell us. Not only that, but I put my name behind you. A name I am trying to build, trying to rid myself of my father's image. Now you come here and..." He looked away. "You're as bad as he was."

The slap of his words nearly took her to the floor. How could he think that? Had she hurt her child over and over? Had she beaten a spouse to death? Her throat tightened. She couldn't breathe. Couldn't swallow. The edges of her vision darkened.

Cinda said something, but Asia couldn't hear past the ringing in her head.

She whirled to run but collapsed to the floor.

As though underwater, she heard Cinda and Ian. Wake up. She struggled up from the haze. To no avail.

"Call 9-1-1." Cinda's voice, edged with panic.

"I think she just passed out. I caught her so she didn't hit her head. Give her a minute." Ian's practical answer to Cinda's worry.

"Here's a damp towel." Meg said something else Asia didn't catch. Something cool ran over her face, down her arms. Tiny needles of pain prickled across her skin.

Daylight crept into her vision, chasing away the grayed-out edges. She blinked. Saw Cinda and Ian kneeling next to her. Noted the concern in their eyes. Understood when they realized she was awake again and concern faded to...distrust? Anger? Betrayal?

Probably all three and more.

"I'm okay." Asia shook her head. Cleared the fog and winced as nausea rippled through her. Her head swirled like she'd been turning circles until she collapsed. Calm. Be calm. I need to leave. Both Cinda and Ian wanted to be rid of her.

Yesterday.

"Give yourself a minute." Ian's hand on her back steadied her as she sat up. He moved away, and the loss of his touch sent an ache through her so profound the universe might have shifted. Just when she'd hoped... *My fault. I should have told him.*

"Asia talk to me." Cinda sat cross-legged on the floor facing her. "What is this business about you and drugs and prison. Why didn't you tell us?"

Asia stared at her. How could she make Cinda understand the way her life spiraled out of control?

"I was in Mexico with my mom and her boyfriend." Asia closed her eyes, seeing that horrible day. The crowds. Her mother's too-pale face. The boyfriend's leer. She shuddered.

"The bag I carried had drugs in it. I was stopped at the border and arrested." She clamped her teeth together. No need to defend what she'd done. Some things must remain secret. Some things only she knew.

"I served two years and had some time on parole in a halfway house. When that ended, I came here."

As if those few sentences could tell of years of pain and suffering. The years even before prison. They didn't need to hear about anything else. Since she'd come here, she'd done nothing but help them and try to show who she was by her actions. Would they be able to see? Or would they judge her by one error in her past?

"Why? You had a choice. Why did you choose drugs? You..." Ian's tone was like frost in the summer air. "Leave. Cinda doesn't need this. You. Were you going to sell drugs from her shop or something?" He shoved to his feet. "I don't know what happened to you, Asia, but you aren't the girl who spent her summers here."

Okay. They were judging by the past.

Asia's heart became an aching wound. Why had she thought life would be any different now? All her life had been like this. A moment of happiness followed by months or years of despair. How could she expect Ian or Cinda to be different from anyone else in her life?

Different from her mother?

Ian held out his hand to help her to her feet. She ignored him and pushed up on her own. The kintsugi necklace swung free, and she left it in the open. She couldn't even look at Cinda.

"I'll get my backpack and leave the key in the shop with Tansie. Unless you'd rather go with me to make sure I don't take any of your valuables." Bitterness bled into her voice.

"I told you." Glenna's triumphant words hit Asia and nearly knocked her back down. "I told you she was bad to the core. You wouldn't believe me and now look what you found out."

Glenna sashayed across the room until she stood in front of Asia. Her face twisted in a smirk. Asia couldn't even find the strength to stand up to her. What could she say anyway?

Eyes narrowed, Glenna leaned close. "I always told Cinda you were bad news. The truth always comes to light." Her eyes strayed to the necklace--

And widened.

~

THE CHATTER of the Friday night crowd in the parking lot and the rhythm of the band's bass did nothing to lighten Ian's mood. Oh, he greeted people with a smile and spent a few minutes with those who called out to him, chatting about their day and this excellent event. The tables were filled and the barbecue cooks busy trying to keep up.

No one seemed to mind the strong breeze. The wind chased away the remainder of the day's heat and cooled the sweaty dancers. Children played in a roped-off area or danced with their parents. Asia and Meg's idea of child-friendly food had been a spectacular hit, and he planned to keep it on the menu. In fact, Meg showed him the child's menu Asia designed as a surprise. It was printed on a smaller bag and would come with a cookie and a small container for leftovers.

Asia.

The hole in his chest opened wider. He pasted on a smile for the customers waving at him. *You aren't the girl who spent her summers here.* How could he have said that to Asia? Words spoken in haste through hurt and anger. Because of her betrayal. Now he wasn't so sure.

He and Cinda had talked several times since Asia's disappearance. Flighty Cinda sharing memories of who Asia had been when she was here. How they'd never seen any evidence of her doing drugs or anything else wrong. How she'd been there with a helping hand and good, creative ideas. If she had taken drugs all those years ago, she was clean now. Cinda wouldn't believe Asia had been on drugs. Ian wasn't as sure.

"Your expression could put a damper on this party if you're not careful." Cinda squeezed his arm, her big eyes dark with concern. "Have you heard from her?"

Chase away this gloom. He tried but failed. He shook his head, unable to speak past the lump in his throat. She'd been gone a couple of days. The reality proved much worse than his imagined loss.

He'd driven up the highways out of town to see if she'd walked or hitchhiked away. He'd gone to the bus station. Nothing there. He'd called her phone, only to have Cinda tell him Asia left the cell in her apartment. No options left. Except prayer.

Lots of prayer.

A gust of wind spiraled smoke from the grill across the parking lot. The scent of barbecue turned acrid instead of salivating. He pictured the look on Asia's face the first time she tasted his food. Her sparkling eyes when they shared that first piece of pie á la mode. The sheen of light on her hair as she bent over a piece of paper to make a mock-up of an ad.

"Hey." Cinda reached up and brushed at his cheek. Tears? Not here. Not now. He turned away and wiped away the moisture, sniffed a couple of times, and turned back.

"We'll find her." Cinda's blue eyes held both concern and determination. "I know we will. I've been praying. Something will happen. You'll see."

The band finished a song, and the dancers paused to applaud. Ian's mood lightened. Being part of this event to encourage families to be together and have fun was rewarding. Almost like being part of a family that laughed together or went to fun events. His mom and dad never laughed or had fun with him. Tension ran too high in their house.

"I hope you all are enjoying yourselves tonight, because my band and I are having a blast." The lead singer's words elicited cheers and clapping. Kids jumped up and down, their faces shining in the glow of the lights.

"I'd like to take a short break and have the person responsible for this event come up and speak to you about his plans. I think this is something you'll want to listen to and be a part of. We'll be back in a few minutes. Put your hands together for Ian Kittredge and I-BBQ." The singer motioned to Ian as the other band members put down their instruments and left by the back stairs.

Friends and customers slapped his back as he made his way through the crowd and climbed up to the stage. *Please, God, give me something to say here. A way to encourage these people. I'm so empty.* He took the microphone, and the lead singer exited off the back.

"Good evening." Ian smiled as the crowd erupted once again. "Thank you for coming out tonight. This wasn't just my vision. I've had several friends who came alongside me and encouraged me to give our community a safe place for families to spend an evening together having fun." He paused for more clapping and cheering, then explained the vision he, Meg, and Asia had come up with. The family-friendly nights at the restaurant. The alcohol-free atmosphere. The games and camaraderie.

"We've had a setback." His throat tightened, and he looked toward the restaurant. Maybe people would think he meant his business, not the loss of the woman he loved. Loved. His knees trembled.

"I plan to have I-BBQ open and ready for business in the next week. We have a new kids' menu, and on Friday nights we'll have live music featuring local artists." Loud applause. People stood up to clap. The cheers were louder than the music had been. Meg beamed at him from the back. Why couldn't Asia be here to see this? To see her part of this dream come to fruition. To feel the excitement of the crowd.

To give him a chance to ask her forgiveness.

He said a few more things, then turned the microphone back to the band and made his way through the crowd. Meg beckoned to him as he finished. People closed in around him, impeding his progress. They deserved their moment. For the most part, they were parents excited about the prospect of what he'd proposed. Some shared ideas, others just wanted to thank him.

By the time he reached the back, Meg and Cinda were talking with an older woman he didn't recognize. The music blasted, and he leaned close to hear the introduction from Meg.

"Ian, this is Joy Shen. She says you contacted her. She wants to see Asia." Meg's voice had a hesitant quality. They hadn't talked much since his outburst. Cinda gave him a sympathetic look and nodded toward the restaurant.

"Joy, I'm so glad you're here. Let's go inside so we can talk without yelling. Okay?" He led her around the side of I-BBQ, glancing back to make sure Meg and Cinda followed. The inside of the restaurant was almost restored. Only a faint odor of smoke still hung in the air. Ian gestured to a table and Joy sank down as if glad to be off her feet.

"I'm sorry I didn't let you know when I'd be here for sure. I was so excited at the prospect of seeing Asia, I just drove like a crazy woman." Joy's smile warmed him.

"Would you like something to eat or drink?" Ian waited for Cinda and Meg to sit down, then took the chair across from Joy. "We have some barbecue or pie, if you'd like dessert."

Her eyes lit up at the mention of pie. Meg offered to bring the slice of pie and the glass of water Joy asked for and was soon back at the table with them.

"Joy told us she's been traveling in her camper, enjoying the company of friends. That's why we had trouble finding her." Cinda caught Meg up on the conversation. "She wants to make sure Asia is settling in okay."

Ian took a deep breath. He told her all that happened since Asia came to town, Walter's death, Asia's desire to find her family, her growing business, and finally the harsh words he'd spoken after learning about her prison time.

"I wish I could take back what I said. We were all shocked, but I never should have said what I did. She hasn't exhibited the qualities of a drug user even once since she's been here, so we think she's clean now." Ian noted Cinda and Meg nodding beside him.

Joy pushed her empty plate away and patted her mouth with a napkin. Pointed at him with the business end of the fork she'd wiped clean. "You don't know anything, son, if you think that girl has ever taken drugs."

25

The computer screen blurred. Asia swiped the moisture from her eyes. Once again she had nothing. No one. No home. No job. The chasm inside her threatened to pull her down into a darkness so deep she'd never find her way out.

God, if You're listening, give me one sign of hope. Anything.

"I brought you a cup of hot tea." Mrs. Beasley set a dainty china cup on the table beside Asia. Delicate blue and purple flowers wound around the side of the cup and a gold line rimmed the edge. Asia blinked against more tears, keeping her head lowered so this precious woman who had taken her in wouldn't realize Asia's emotions were so close to the surface.

Thank You for the reminder, Lord.

"Thank you, Mrs. B." Her voice caught. Asia cleared her throat and picked up the cup to take a sip of the steaming brew.

"How is that computer working?" Mrs. B carried her own cup to a nearby recliner and sat down. "I know it's a dinosaur compared to what you were using, but I hope it helps."

Asia took another sip. The warmth of the tea spread through her. "Your computer is a little slow but it's a good one. I think you are teaching me patience." She forced a wobbly smile.

"How was your quilt class today?" Maybe Asia's question would get Mrs. B's focus off of her. The sweet woman could talk for hours about sewing and the quilts she made. She always had something interesting to say, although Asia had trouble focusing. It was awful to lose Cinda, but…

Ian.

He invaded her dreams at night and her thoughts during the day. His smile. His laugh. His eyes when he cracked a joke. Every memory dug a deeper trench in her heart. A hole that might never be filled.

"Asia, I need to say something to you." Mrs. B's tone brought Asia out of her reverie. The older woman cradled her teacup in her hands. Hands that might be wrinkled and have age spots, but still crafted incredible art from material and thread.

"At class today, Cinda asked everyone if they'd seen you. She is very concerned about you." Mrs. B took a sip from her cup. "I had to be a little misleading and bite my tongue to keep from saying much. You know I'm not good at hiding anything." She frowned. "This felt like lying. I don't like lying."

"I'm sorry." Asia's throat tightened. Once again she was hurting a friend. She'd only come here because Mrs. B had seen her walking away from her apartment and stopped her to talk. When she noted Asia's distress, she brought her home, and they talked for hours. This time Asia told her the whole truth about her background. Mrs. B offered compassion and a place to stay for a few days. Now…

She should leave. Be on her own once again. "If you'd like, I'll pack up and leave right now." She set her cup on the saucer beside her before her tight grip broke the fragile china. "I didn't mean to cause problems."

"You'll do no such thing." Mrs. B's saucer sang as she set her cup down too hard. "You've been running away too long. That's what you learned from your mother, I suppose? Now is the time to stand up, swallow your pride or fear, and give your friends a chance to show what they're made of. I know Ian Kittredge and Cinda Bryant. They both want to make amends. Don't you dare run away from that."

Her words rang through Asia. Did Ian and Cinda want to give her another chance? She recalled Ian's harsh words. He probably believed her to be a drug addict as well as a drug pusher.

"I don't think there's any way Ian will be able to get over me reminding him of his dad." She dug her fingers into the cloth of the chair. "How could he ever find forgiveness or a way to move past that? It's impossible."

"That's true." Mrs. B took another quiet sip as Asia's stomach tumbled toward the floor. Even the older woman understood she didn't stand a chance with Ian.

"For fallible humans. We always mess things up and let our emotions get in the way. But Asia..." Mrs. B paused so long Asia looked up...into an understanding gaze.

"My sweet husband and I had to learn a lot about forgiveness and letting go of the past. What is impossible for us humans is not impossible for God. With Him all things are possible. Try praying."

"I have." She blurted out the words. Bit her lip. Took a deep breath. "I've been praying nonstop. But He hasn't answered. I think I'm not important enough or something."

"That is not true." Mrs. B leaned forward, her gaze so intense that Asia couldn't look away. "Maybe His answer is *out there,* not sitting in this house hiding from what He wants to give you. Go. Give your friends and family a chance. Give God a chance to work."

The truth of her words settled in Asia's heart. Something dark and heavy took wing and lifted from her. Her chest didn't ache. She could breathe. What had changed? Was this an answer to her prayers? It had to be, because it was…

Hope.

God answered her prayer in more than one way. Now it was her turn to act.

"Come. Let's have something to eat. Maybe you can take a walk this evening and see what God has in store." Mrs. B pushed up out of her chair and carried her empty teacup to the kitchen. Asia picked up hers and followed. What did God intend to do with the mess she'd made of her life? There wasn't much hope, but a glimmer was more than she'd had earlier today.

She didn't contribute much during their meal of leftover lentil soup and half a grilled cheese sandwich. They shared an apple, with Mrs. B touting the blessings of dentists and being able to eat the crisp fruit at her age because she still had all her teeth. Asia grinned. Mrs. B found a bright side to everything in life. Not a bad outlook to have.

"I'll do the dishes." Asia gathered the bowls and carried them to the sink.

"You'll do no such thing." Mrs. B carried the plates over and gently moved Asia aside. "There's still plenty of light. Why don't you go for a walk? I hear there's a special event at the park beside I-BBQ. There might be something fun to do there."

"I…" Asia fumbled for an excuse. How could she face the people of this town when they knew what she'd done? "I don't think I can go."

"And why not?" Mrs. B rested her palms on the edge of the sink as the hot water ran. "Surely you aren't too cowardly to face a few naysayers, are you? Asia, anyone who is a true friend won't care about your past. They will accept you for who you are now, and you are a fine person." Her voice softened. "Give them a chance."

Her footsteps dragged as she went to her room to change into something more presentable than a pair of leggings with holes and a ragged T-shirt. She didn't have much, but going out in these clothes wasn't an option.

"I'll be back in an hour." She called to Mrs. B. She could walk the streets of the town for an hour and be back well before Mrs. B's bedtime. Armed with a plan, she opened the door and slipped out to Mrs. B's parting words telling her to not hurry back because she would leave the door unlocked.

No matter how hard she tried to direct her feet away from I-BBQ, Asia ended up across the street, standing under the same tree where she'd stood that very first day. Lights lit the interior of Cinda's quilt shop. The scent of barbecue filled the air. More traffic than usual sped past on the street, many of them turning into the park.

A sign at the park entrance was too far to read from here. She walked a few steps closer down the sidewalk to peer across and read what it said. An arts and crafts fair. Her heart skipped a beat.

How fun to browse the vendors stalls and see what they had to offer. Not that she could buy anything, but she loved to look.

She glanced back toward I-BBQ. Ian stepped outside. Their gazes met and both of them froze.

~

For the past week, Ian had spent hours talking with Joy, taking her places Asia enjoyed when she spent summers here and that they'd been to since she'd come back. The underlying hope had been to find Asia, but that hope dwindled, leaving only a bare trickle.

Joy planned to pack up her camper and leave in two days. She promised to keep in touch in case he heard from Asia, but they both knew that wouldn't happen. This time Asia had disappeared for good. Neither one of them had a way to track her down. She was gone the same way that Randall, Cinda's brother, had disappeared.

How did you find someone who didn't want to be found?

Walking through this fog of grief and self-flagellation proved exhausting. Cinda and Meg looked as drawn as he felt. The more Joy shared with them, the more they realized how they had wronged Asia. She'd never shared the true horror she'd gone through with her mother. Her best years had been when her mother was in prison and she'd lived with Joy part-time and in Driftwood Cove part-time. Even then, she hadn't felt comfortable telling him or Cinda what she had endured.

His phone buzzed in his pocket, and he pulled it out. Cinda's name flashed on the screen. He clicked to answer and stepped into his office. "Hey, what's up?" The little uptick in his heart rate still spoke of the glimmer of hope hiding deep within.

"I'm looking for some poor sucker willing to walk through the arts and crafts fair with me." Her voice didn't contain the same enthusiasm as usual. She'd been hit so hard this past week. It had proved almost too much for Cinda's usually indomitable spirit.

He opened his mouth to decline. Why would he even want to walk around at an arts and crafts festival? Yes, in normal circumstances he would be there. His cooker was there, and they were selling barbecue sandwiches and chips, maybe drumming up future business. But he didn't have the heart to put on a happy face and talk to people. Not today.

Still, the sadness in Cinda's tone pricked his heart. How could he turn her down? "Sure, I'll go for a while. Are you looking for something in particular?"

"No. I just." She sighed, the gust of air carrying a plethora of emotion. "I need to get out and do something to take my mind off…things."

A valid reason. They didn't have to talk with people. They could drift from booth to booth and see what happened. "When do you want to go? The restaurant's pretty dead since they have all the food trucks at the fair."

"I'll be out in a couple of minutes then. I just have to make sure Tansie is all set to lock up. See you soon." She clicked off.

Ian locked his office, checked with his employees to let them know where he would be if they needed him, and stepped outside. The sun dipped toward the horizon. A breeze danced through his hair. He could smell the barbecue and hear the chatter of the crowds at the park.

Something tugged at him. He glanced toward the street. A couple of cars drove past, slowing to turn into the park. And…

There she was.

Asia.

Standing near a gingko tree. Her hair, swept up in a ponytail, blew across her neck. She didn't move but stared back at him. She reminded him of a wild animal poised to run if he made a move toward her, but he couldn't stay here. He had to go to her. The magnetic pull dragged his feet forward and, just like that, the moment changed.

Asia's hand swept her hair from her face. She turned and hurried down the street.

"Ian. Where are you going?"

Cinda closed the door to her shop. He pointed toward Asia's retreating back. He mouthed her name, but actual words wouldn't come. Cinda waved him on. She'd be praying for him to catch Asia and make amends. To bring her back to Cinda. To become the family and friends they needed to be.

He began to run.

Flat-out.

A car honked as he raced across the street. He waved but didn't look. His gaze was riveted on Asia. He would *not* lose sight of her again.

She glanced back and saw him bearing down on her. Was that fear that flashed across her face? She turned to meet him. He slowed as he approached. Fought the urge to rush up to her and grab her in a hug and never let go.

Chest heaving, he stopped. Drank in the sight of her. Ignored the way his heart battered his ribs. *God, I love her. Help me not to mess this up. Please.*

"I'm sorry."

"I'm sorry."

They spoke at the same time. She snorted. Glanced down.

He took a step closer.

"You have nothing to be sorry for, Asia." He stuffed his hands in his jeans pockets so he wouldn't reach for her. If he made the wrong move, she might leave forever.

"I was insufferable. A complete idiot. Thank you for making me take a hard look at myself. For making me see the truth." His chest ached. He blinked hard against the burning in his eyes.

"I wanted to tell you." Her dark hair danced across her cheek, and she brushed it away. "I meant to." The pleading in her eyes begged him for understanding. Tore his heart to shreds as he thought of all his unkind words about people who had gotten in trouble or made poor choices. He'd been digging a deep hole, and now he needed to fill in the cesspool that had filled it.

"Can we go somewhere and talk?" Should he drop to his knees in front of her and beg for another chance? Her hesitation lasted an eternity.

"I…I have things to tell you." She bit her lower lip. He couldn't tear his gaze away.

"We can talk in the restaurant." He motioned over his shoulder with his chin. "Seems like everyone is at the park, so we don't have any business. Or we could go to Cinda's and include her." He glanced back to see Cinda standing outside her shop watching them.

Asia still hesitated. What to say to convince her he still cared? Still loved her. Without frightening her away.

"I can call Joy, your mom's friend, and have her come over." He held his breath watching the play of emotions on her face.

"Joy is here?" She tilted her head to the side.

"She showed up last Friday night when we had the family event. I found some contact information for her. She's been traveling around in her little camper and staying at different campgrounds. She doesn't check her email very often, so it took her a while to see my note." He pulled one hand out of his pocket and held it out to her.

She stared at his outstretched hand. In the park across the street music began to play. A country song about love lost and won again.

Please, God. Please.

Asia slipped her slender fingers into his palm. He closed his hand around hers. Drew her to him and wrapped her in an embrace. Breathed deep, taking in the scent that was all Asia. Felt the brush of her silky hair on his arm.

He didn't care who saw them. He wanted to stand in this place with this woman in his arms and never let her go. She trembled against him and wrapped her arms around his waist. His heart swelled.

"I was so afraid I lost you for good." He struggled to speak past the emotions. "Please don't leave me." He kissed her forehead as he rubbed his hand up and down her back. "I need you. I love you more than I can say."

She leaned back to gaze up at him. The mossy green of her eyes swam with tears. "I have so much baggage. I know you're trying to get out from under your past, and I don't want mine to drag you back down. I can't be good for you."

"You are perfect for me. Just as you are." He cupped her cheek and gave her a light kiss. "I'm not worried about what anyone else thinks."

She stared up at him, her gaze troubled.

What hadn't she told him?

26

The noise from the park, muted through the closed windows of the quilt shop, still carried too much energy. Ian checked his phone to see Meg's message and slipped it back in his pocket. Asia needed a break from talking. She'd explained some about her incarceration and where she'd been staying since she left the apartment. Mrs. B deserved a medal for taking such good care of this woman he loved. Deserved to be shown some love by him and Asia.

Together.

His phone buzzed again. "Meg says things have slowed a bit. People have eaten and are either shopping or listening to the music. She's going to bring us sandwiches, chips, and what she calls the best ice cream in the history of the world. She's on her way." He kept his tone light to counteract the despondency coming in waves off both Cinda and Asia. Food would relax them, even though Asia insisted she'd already eaten. How could he and Cinda eat in front of her?

"What ice cream?" Cinda gave a half smile. "And you thought I wasn't listening. You said the magic words."

Asia brightened a bit. Her slim fingers wrapped around the heart-shaped necklace he'd seen only once before, on the terrible day she'd left. Had she worn it before? "I noticed your necklace the other day. Where did it come from?"

Her expression morphed into one of guilt. She tightened her fist around the heart, looked toward the door, closed her eyes, and visibly relaxed. Why had he asked?

"You don't have to tell me if you don't want, Asia. I thought it was important to you, and I'm just curious." He sat still instead of jumping up to pace the floor. Cinda glanced toward him and shrugged. She must not know what the necklace was either.

"It's okay." Asia opened her eyes and breathed deeply. "No more secrets." She reached back to unclasp the necklace and handed it to Cinda, who was closer to her.

"I found this in the letters to my mom. I think your dad—our dad—gave it to her. Does it mean anything to you?"

Cinda gave a small gasp and ran her thumb over the black and white stone.

A loud knock on the front door made Ian jump. "That's probably Meg. I'll be right back." *Don't say anything while I'm gone.* He pushed the juvenile thought away.

Meg handed him a big bag from I-BBQ's stand and a smaller one that must hold the ice cream.

"I put some sodas in with the ice cream. Don't you dare let that ice cream melt. That would be a major sin, because it's the best." She backed up a step. "I've got to get back. Tell Asia I'm glad she's okay." Her smile warmed him a little. Meg would pray for them. *Thank You.* Good friends who prayed were priceless.

When he came back to the quilting room where Cinda and Asia were, he put the ice cream in the freezer first. He handed out the sodas and meals before he sat down.

After they prayed, Cinda said, "We waited for you to come back. We both agreed you would want to hear everything." She glanced at Asia, who nodded.

Cinda looked at Ian. "My dad gave my mom a necklace very similar to this one years ago. It was one of her favorite pieces of jewelry and meant much to her. I didn't think about it at the time, but she said something about the piece representing a healing in their marriage." Cinda swallowed hard, pausing for a moment. "I think this was the time when he broke off his relationship with your mom, Asia. We may never know for sure, but that's my thought."

Asia picked up a chip and broke off a minuscule piece. She didn't put it in her mouth but rubbed the crumb between her fingers. "I'm so sorry this happened, Cinda. I didn't mean for any of you to get hurt."

"Asia. Look at me." Cinda set her food aside and leaned forward, her elbows on her knees. When Asia looked at her, she smiled. A wobbly smile, but a smile nevertheless. Asia relaxed.

"Asia, we have no control over what our parents did. I am hurt that my father cheated on my mother..." She held up her hand, palm out, as Asia started to say something. "But I have no regrets about having you as a sister. None."

She rubbed her hand across her mouth and released a shaky breath. "I actually understand a little better how my mom might have felt. I had no inkling that Martin was involved with anyone else, especially not a student."

Cinda's jaw clenched as she looked down at her tight-knit fingers. "I remember my mom being so angry all the time the last summer you were here. Every little thing set her off. When I think about it, I guess she found out you were Dad's daughter and struggled to come to terms with all that meant. I can't say I wish I'd known back then. My teenage self would never have been able to handle the drama."

Asia's mouth opened, then snapped shut. Had she meant to say she was sorry once again and realized the futility? The tension in the room was taut as thread when they sewed.

"You know what?" He put his uneaten sandwich back in the wrapping and dropped it in the bag. The chips went on top. Both women were watching him with puzzled expressions. "I believe we started with the wrong course. Meg said the ice cream is the best she's ever eaten, and she considers herself an expert."

He pushed up from his chair and strode to the refrigerator. "I say we start with ice cream." He pulled out the bag and held it aloft. Both women smiled, the delight on their faces such a natural expression that butterflies took flight in his chest.

"Let's see what we have." He sat down, opened the bag, and peered inside.

"I don't know if we should trust you to choose who gets what." Cinda raised up and craned her neck as if trying to see into the bag.

"Hey, you wound me." Ian slapped his hand to his chest and pasted on an innocent expression.

"She knows you." Asia smirked. Cinda snorted a laugh.

"Well, it turns out you are besmirching my character for nothing. The containers are all the same size and the same flavors." He pulled them out one at a time, passing out spoons and ice cream to each of them, reserving the last for himself. "Now, we need to test this so we can give Meg our very informed opinion. Is this the best ice cream ever?"

They all peeled off the lids. Inside was a small scoop of what looked like French vanilla, one that might have chocolate in it, and one that was purple. "Purple ice cream?" Ian looked up to see Asia and Cinda both watching him, a bit of purple on their spoons.

"Okay, I'm waiting to see if you survive that before I try it. Any idea what flavor that would be?" He poked at the frozen purple dessert.

Asia laughed. His pulse did a dance. Such a beautiful sound.

Asia wiggled her spoon. "This is Ube. It's made from purple sweet potatoes." She slipped the ice cream in her mouth and closed her eyes.

"Sweet potatoes? Seriously? Who makes ice cream from sweet potatoes? Aren't they orange?" He sniffed the purple mound.

"Stop being such a wimp and try it." Cinda popped hers in her mouth. Her whole body seemed to deflate a bit as she smiled and closed her eyes.

"You only live once." Ian muttered. Both women chuckled. He licked a tiny bite off the spoon. Tilted his head to the side and absorbed the unusual flavor. Earthy but sweet. He took a bigger bite. Asia and Cinda grinned at him. He shrugged.

"Oh, yum. The vanilla has sage and something else. Can you figure it out, Asia?" Cinda popped another bite in her mouth.

"I think it has a hint of caramel. That is so good." Ian's chest tightened at the way Asia closed her eyes as she savored the taste. They needed to get back to matters at hand, but this time was too precious.

They had just finished their ice cream and Cinda had gathered the cups when someone rapped on the front door.

~

Joy.

Asia leapt from the chair and rushed to hug the woman who had provided a home for her when she needed one and who had been there for her mother and her when times were hard. The hug touched a place deep inside. Left her grounded and safe in a way she hadn't been with Ian and Cinda. Maybe someday, but not yet.

"Baby girl, it's good to see you. I worried when we parted ways." Joy cupped her cheek and her dark eyes shined.

"Please, come sit down, Ms. Shen." Cinda pushed another chair close to Asia's. "Are you hungry? We were just eating, and I'm sure there's enough."

"No. I've already eaten." Joy lowered herself into the chair and reached over to pat Asia's arm as if she couldn't believe they'd finally reconnected. "Is everything okay with you now? I hope you don't mind I set these people straight about those charges against you." She frowned at Ian and Cinda.

Asia's face warmed. "What did you tell them?" She picked up her still-chilled soda can and held it against her heated face.

"I told them what your mama told me." Joy's gaze didn't waver from Asia's. "She told me you took her bag at the border and sent her on across ahead of you. She said you saw her worthless boyfriend put the drugs in the bag, but it was too late to get them out. Instead, you pretended like the bag was yours. You ended up going to jail." Joy frowned. "Did you know your mom had cancer? Or suspect it?"

The memory of that day washed over her anew. Asia recalled every moment, like a horror movie running through her head that couldn't be shut off. The shouts. The snarling dog straining at his leash. The boyfriend grinning. Her mother's horrified expression.

She shook off the memories and opened her eyes again to see Joy still studying her. "I knew from the tests the doctor did. He talked to me and told me cancer was what they suspected." She cleared her throat. "I couldn't let my mom spend her last days in prison. I just couldn't."

Ian's face darkened. Her legs twitched with the desire to leap up and run away. She forced herself to meet his gaze. "I know you're angry about what I did, but it was a decision made in a moment's time. I would do it again for my mom, even though I hated prison. Hated that whole time." She choked on a sob.

Ian stepped to her chair and dropped to his knees. She froze, but when she looked into his eyes, she saw only compassion...and love.

"Asia, I am not angry with you. I am angry that someone would put drugs in a sick woman's bag just to try to get them across the border. What kind of person does that? I'm angry that he didn't step up and confess so you didn't have to go to prison." He wrapped his fingers around her chilled ones. "And I'm angry that I judged you without knowing the truth, even though I knew your character. I knew deep down you wouldn't have done what you were accused of. Please, forgive me."

"I guess I need your forgiveness too."

Asia glanced to the front door, tensing for battle.

Glenna.

When did *she* come in? She hadn't knocked. But then, she had her own key.

Her cousin's—sister's—sharp cheekbones stood out in relief tonight. Dark circles under her eyes hadn't been covered with her usual makeup. Had Glenna ever looked this despondent? As if all the joy—not that she ever showed much—had been sucked out of her?

Wait… *What* had Glenna said? Why would she be asking for forgiveness?

An idea reared its ugly head. Cinda just said her mother must have known about Asia…

Of course. *That* was why Glenna hated her all these years.

"You heard them talking." Asia saw resignation flitter in Glenna's eyes. "You heard your dad tell your mom about me, right? I wondered what changed that summer. You'd never been overly friendly, but that summer you became hateful."

"Sit down, Glenna." Cinda rose and pulled a chair next to hers. "Tell us what you heard and why you didn't tell me."

Glenna sank into the chair, setting her bag on the floor beside her. She nodded at Cinda's offer to fix her favorite tea. Bit at her lower lip, and finally met Asia's gaze again.

"I was in the pantry when Dad came home that night. Mom had come down to the kitchen, and I didn't want to be caught pilfering a snack that late at night." She glanced at Cinda as she carried the cup of tea to her. "You know how Mom felt about midnight snacks."

"Strictly forbidden."

Glenna nodded. "I hid there, hoping they would go to bed and I could sneak back upstairs. Instead, Mom opened with an accusation." She accepted the steaming cup of tea from Cinda. The hot liquid sloshed as she took a sip, and she set the cup down.

"They kept their voices down. If I'd been in my room, I never would have heard them, but the pantry was right there." She swiped at a tear. "Mom accused Dad of having an affair with Asia's mom, Kim. Turns out she hired someone to dig up the dirt on Dad. He admitted Asia is his daughter. The rest was…awful."

She huffed a sound like she was trying to laugh but couldn't. "Hearing your parents fight and throw hate at each other is almost worse when they are whispering the hate rather than shouting. I was seventeen, and I loved my parents, but that night put Dad in a different light for me. Mom too." She swiped at her cheeks.

"I didn't notice you treating them differently." Cinda reached over to squeeze Glenna's arm. "Why didn't you talk to me? I know I was young and flighty, but I hope I would have listened."

"I couldn't." Glenna took a tissue from the box Cinda held out to her. "Somehow, in my teenage mind, I thought if I blamed Asia, I could keep seeing my parents in the same light I always had. So I hated Asia and treated her as if all this was her fault."

When she met Asia's gaze, her eyes were filled with so much pain and regret, Asia flinched. Ian had settled on the floor beside Asia, his palm cupping the calf of her leg. His touch grounded her, so she didn't bolt for the door.

Outside the music ramped up again. The band must have been on break. The air conditioner kicked on, and cool air brushed at the sweat on Asia's brow.

"I'm sorry, Asia." Glenna cleared her throat. "Since you came back, I've been going through a difficult time. I guess it was still easier to hate you than to face the truth. When I saw your necklace the other day, it hit me how much my dad must have loved your mom. I'd heard rumors of her behavior after you were born. I think maybe my dad broke off their relationship and she never recovered."

The truth of that stole Asia's breath. Had her mom been heartsick and lashed out in her own way? By allowing herself to be used by one man after another? Trying to find another Walter Bryant?

"I believe you are right." Joy patted Asia's arm and nodded at Glenna. "I remember that time. Broke Kim's heart. Broke all of her." She squeezed Asia's shoulder. "I need to get back to my camper. These old bones need some sleep. I'll see you tomorrow." Asia walked Joy to the door, hugged her, and returned to the room.

They talked for another two hours. While they hashed over the past, the event in the park closed, and Meg stopped by to give Ian a report.

"I have to get back to Mrs. B's." Asia took her uneaten sandwich and chips to the refrigerator. Her limbs weighed more than she could lift.

"We'll talk more." Cinda drew her in for a hug. "Please feel free to move back to the apartment and work at the shop. I miss you."

"I've got to go, too." Glenna gave her a quick hug and hurried away.

"Let me drive you to Mrs. B's." Ian clasped her hand in his. She loved the feel of her hand in his. Loved the look in his eyes.

He pulled to the curb in front of Mrs. B's house, with a porch light on and a dim glow showing Mrs. B left on a light for her.

"Asia." He turned to her, his eyes dark pools, the stubble on his cheeks giving him a dashing look that she liked. "Please tell me you forgive me for being so thick-headed. I love you so much."

Warmth spread through her. Her whole being came alive. How she loved this man. "Oh, Ian, I decided to leave, but I couldn't. At Mrs. B's you were all I could think about. Because I love you too. No matter what. You always have my heart."

He pulled her close and kissed her. His heart thudded in a rhythm that matched her own. She sank into the kiss, drowning in the sensation.

27

EPILOGUE

Three Months Later

THE SUN DIPPED to kiss the ocean, painting the evening sky in brilliant colors. Asia leaned back on the towel, the beach sand scrunching under her palms as the last rays warmed her before the cool of evening. Laughter rang in the air. The happiness from everyone playing in the incoming waves today echoed the joy in her memory.

She opened her eyes and smiled at Ian as he raced up the beach toward her, chased by Meg's preteen son, Aaron. His teenage brother, Austin, played in the surf under the watchful eye of his mother. They were all surprised when Meg received custody rights from her husband who had taken an overseas job and couldn't take his sons. The boys were amazing, although Austin struggled with the change.

Eyes sparkling, Ian dropped onto the towel beside her. His chest heaved, and he held up his hand to stop Aaron. "Time out. This is a safety zone." Ian grinned as the boy groaned.

"Come on." Aaron leaned over, his hands on his knees as he sucked in air.

"You two have been running up and down the beach so much that *I'm* exhausted." Asia sat up and rubbed the back of her neck. "I think I have a kink in my neck from the back and forth." She tipped her head toward Ian and winked. He grinned, and she swayed toward him before remembering their audience.

Ian enjoyed spending time with Meg's boys, which Asia loved. They'd found out recently that Meg's husband, who had full custody due to a difficult time in Meg's life—her words—had decided to take a job with a lot of overseas travel. He'd given Meg part-time custody, which she'd been ecstatic to have. Now she was trying to reconnect with her boys, but they were in dire need of a father figure. Ian had stepped in, and Asia loved the time they spent with Meg and her boys.

Today's evening picnic made her want to dance. Cinda and Glenna were here, but Glenna's husband was on another out of town business trip. Mrs. B had stopped by but didn't want to stay because the evening ocean air didn't agree with her. Tansie planned to come as soon as she closed the quilt shop. And Ian's hiking buddies, Ward and Daniel, were joining them when they got off work.

"I asked the pastor to come, but I don't think he can." Ian leaned close and dripped water on her. "We have a lot to thank him for."

"We do." Asia pressed her cheek to his shoulder. "Counseling with him has been beyond what I hoped. Dealing with the past, growing my faith, not to mention the perks for our relationship." Her face warmed at the intensity in his expression.

"Family." Ian pressed a kiss to her brow.

"Eeewwww!" Aaron threw himself backward to the ground in mock disgust. Preteen boys! Asia and Ian laughed. Then Ian kissed her, and they listened to Aaron's sounds of disgust again.

Family. Ian pegged it. Her contentment was reflected in Ian's eyes. For the first time since she'd lived with Joy, Asia had a place where she belonged.

She still helped with the quilt shop and had moved back in the small apartment. Her design business had grown and kept her busy. Most of her customers had come back and brought others with them. She had enough saved to get an actual apartment, but she enjoyed living at the quilt shop and being close to the restaurant. She'd come to crave the smell of barbecue as much as she craved time with the I-BBQ owner.

Oh, how she craved him. Sometimes she worked at a table in his restaurant, and he would stop by when he could. They talked for hours. Laughed together. Hiked with his friends. Even Daniel had become a friend. Ate dinner with Cinda and Glenna. Took Mrs. B out when the woman agreed to go.

They helped Cinda understand how to make better choices in men, even though she swore she would never date again.

And they finished their quilt class. Cinda begged Asia to redo her quilt and match the points so the quilt wasn't off kilter, but she refused. She loved having the reminder that when her life wasn't synced right with God, or with the man she loved, everything would be thrown off. She wanted her *life* to have those matching points, so the quilt hung on her wall, a beautiful reminder.

"Look." Ian pointed offshore. She and Aaron looked out to see a pod of dolphins swimming through the ocean, their sleek bodies disappearing and reappearing.

"Can we show her now?" Aaron widened his eyes at Ian.

"Show me what?" Asia looked from one to the other and noted the conspiratorial glance that passed between them.

"We have something special to show you." At Ian's nod, Aaron grabbed her wrist and tugged. "Come on. There's a tide pool down there with some anemones you'll love. Ian said you would."

"I don't know." Asia resisted his pull. "I'm not sure anemones are enough to make me walk very far."

"There are starfish too. Big ones and little ones. Come on." Aaron dug his heels in the sand and pulled. Ian chuckled beside her as if he knew what she planned. She made a face at him and jumped to her feet, giving so much slack to Aaron's grip that he landed on his bottom in the sand. She and Ian chuckled. Aaron laughed too.

"Okay, show me this world of wonders." Asia strolled hand-in-hand with Ian. The others on the beach asked where they were headed. When Ian mentioned the tide pool, Austin raced to join his brother. Meg and the others tagged behind them.

One of the dolphins lifted on to its tail, seeming to skim across the water against the backdrop of the twilight sky. The sun slid out of sight and the sky faded to shades of gray.

"We'd better hurry up so we can start a fire." Asia shivered as cooler evening air caressed her skin.

"Here we are." Aaron danced beside a cluster of rocks. Austin smacked the back of his brother's head.

"We waited too long." Aaron frowned as he leaned over to peer into the darkened pools. "Now what do we do?"

"Modern technology to the rescue." Ian pulled out his phone from his waterproof pocket and clicked on the flashlight. "You can hold this Aaron, but don't drop it in the water. Understand?" He held the cell out of reach until Aaron seemed to grasp the importance of not ruining the phone.

The boys dropped to their knees in studied concentration as they stared into the first pool. Asia couldn't tear her gaze from them. Seeing something like this through a child's eyes gave her such a thrill. These boys had never seen the ocean until they came to spend time with their mother a month ago. This was their second trip and maybe their first tide pool.

The anemones waved with the motion of the water. Austin reached in to touch the pebbly exterior of a starfish but didn't try to pick it up. Aaron acted like he wanted to, but he didn't have the temerity of his older brother.

"There's another pool over here." Aaron moved past the first set of rocks to another basin lined with rocks and sporting more anemones and starfish. "What's this, Mr. Ian?" Aaron reached into the water and pulled something out. Asia couldn't see what it was and leaned closer as Ian took the object from the boy.

"This, boys, is buried treasure washed ashore from a pirate ship." Ian's voice held a hint of mirth. A wave of love ran through Asia again. Of course, this man would make this an adventure the boys would remember.

"Pirate treasure." Aaron's eyes widened. He glanced out toward the darkened ocean as if expecting to see a ship full of pirates flying toward them to reclaim their lost treasure.

"Let's see." Ian turned toward her. "Aaron, hold that light over here."

Aaron scooted past his brother and shined the light on Ian's hand. He'd closed his fist around the treasure and the suspense of what he'd found hung in the air around them. Even the seagulls overhead had quieted.

Ian rested on his knees in front of Asia and opened his hand. She leaned closer. A small box nestled in his palm. He eased open the lid. Inside a sparkling ring gleamed in the light from the phone. Asia gasped.

"Asia." Ian paused. She looked up to find his gaze steady on her, not on the ring. "Asia, you are the one God designed for me. You complete me. Will you marry me?"

Words fled. Her mouth fell open. He'd planned this. He hadn't found pirate booty. He'd planned to propose.

Her heart thumped against her ribs. She pressed her hands to her chest to slow the beat.

"Well?" Ian's warm gaze drew her back to reality. "Will you marry me?"

"Yes." She shook as he stood, pulled the ring free of the box, and fit it on her finger. "Yes. Yes. *Yes.*" She threw her arms around his neck. Everyone behind them was clapping and cheering. They'd all known.

Ian's kiss reached inside her, washing away the last of her uncertainty about him loving her.

Later, they sat together, listening as everyone took turns telling stories and eating cookies. Daniel settled down beside Cinda and, from his expression, Asia wondered if he was interested in her. Time would tell.

Asia glanced up at Ian and smiled. These people brought him such pleasure. She understood exactly how he felt. He must have felt her eyes on him because he looked down and kissed her on the nose.

"I know what you're thinking." He murmured the words for her alone. "You're thinking how blessed we are to have family like this."

She snuggled her head against his shoulder. A family. Her dream, and his...

Was finally a reality.

AUTHOR'S NOTE

From the moment I first pictured Asia standing across the street from that quilt shop, I knew I had to tell her story. She carried so much emotional baggage and such longing, but I didn't know why. Going on that journey to find where she'd come from and why she was here at this place, in this moment, was such a roller-coaster ride. I do hope you enjoyed reading Asia's story as much I enjoyed writing about her.

Exploring the theme of family and how our families impact our past and out future proved both exhilarating and painful. I remember hearing a man say he couldn't help being the way he was because of his father's influence. That man was a Christian. My first thought was that he has a new Father and he is to be like Christ. Like God.

This is why both Ian and Asia struggled with the concept of having a parent they were compared to in an unflattering light. Ian couldn't change what his father did, he could only make his own choices and be a different person. To be like Father, like son. Asia, too, had people assume she would be her mother's daughter, but she wasn't. Her choice was to live a different life, despite pressure to be as immoral as her mother.

Our choices make us who we are. How we choose to live. How we choose to forgive. How we choose to love. And Who we choose to love and follow.

One of my favorite verses is Joshua 24:15—*And if it seems evil to you to serve the LORD, choose for yourselves this day whom you will serve, whether the gods which your fathers served that were on the other side of the River, or the gods of the Amorites, in whose land you dwell. But as for me and my house, we will serve the Lord.*

Choosing to follow God, to try daily to be like Jesus Christ, is the theme of my life. I often fail just as Ian and Asia made poor choices. Yet, God is so forgiving. He sets the example for us to learn to love and forgive one another.

Remember, you can't change your past. You can't change your family. You can't change those traumatic events that left their mark on you. But, you can forge ahead and make the choice to become a better person. I pray that you seek Jesus Christ and walk in His footsteps to become like Him.

Thank you so much for going with me on this journey. I love to hear from my readers. Please visit me at www.nancyjfarrier.com and leave me a message.

DISCUSSION QUESTIONS

1) Asia became her mother's caregiver at a fairly young age. She had the responsibility of getting her mother home or watching out for her. Why do you think Asia had this responsibility? How did this impact her life? Did her role change her view of her mother?

2) Ian grew up hearing "like father, like son" after his father murdered his mother. With Asia's help, he chose to live a different life. How did Asia help him escape "like father, like son"? Why did Asia reach out to Ian when no one else did? Where do you think Ian would have been without Asia's encouragement?

3) Asia's had a glimpse of family when she spent summers with her "cousins" in Driftwood Cove. She longs to have family again and approaches the Bryant's at great risk with her newly discovered information. What is she risking when she claims Walter as her father? Why is she reluctant to do so? How does Cinda respond to the news? How does Glenna respond?

4) Ian and Asia put aside their discomfort of sewing to take a quilt class from Cinda. Why did they do this? What did they learn from

trying a new skill? What did their willingness to try show about their love of family? Of friends?

5) Cinda and Glenna were very protective of their father because of his disease. Why do you think they didn't want Asia to see him? Would Walter's reaction have been better if one of them accompanied Asia to visit him? How were Cinda and Glenna different in their desire to keep Asia from Walter?

6) Ian's barbecue permeates Matching Points. The smell. The taste. The comfort food. Why does Ian enjoy fixing food for others? What did Ian learn when the councilman spoke out against him? How did Meg and Asia help him to reach out to more in the community?

7) Both Ian and Asia love going to the beach. The tide pools or dolphins are so fun. But they also love watching the moonlight on the waves. Why do you think they found solace there? Do you think the memories of their time at the beach at teenagers helped connect them again? How? How does a place help them have a deeper connection?

8) Ian was hurt not only by the truth of Asia's past but by the fact that she withheld the truth from him. Why do you think she withheld the truth for so long? When should she have told him about her past? Would Ian have been prepared to forgive if she'd told him the whole truth right away? Why is forgiveness so important?

9) Ian and Asia worked together to plan a community event that would benefit families. Why do you think they went to such lengths to help the community? What did their pasts have to do with their desire to reach others? Why was Ian so intent on having a safe environment for families?

10) Asia helped Mrs. Beasley get set up to listen to audiobooks. Taking the time to assist the elderly woman with something she didn't know how to do helped to forge a friendship. What does

this show about Asia's character? How did her reaching out to help Mrs. B help Asia later? What was Mrs. B's role in Asia's life and choices?

11) Ian and Asia learned to make matching points in their quilt class. This helped their quilts to have the seams lined up so everything fit together. Where else did Asia find matching points were helpful? In her relationship with Ian? With Cinda? With God? How does having a life matched to God's purpose help her with other relationships?

12) When Walter wanders away from the hospital, Ian and Asia join the search. They return to find the search team calling in the members because of rain. Ian understands the futility, but Asia wants to continue searching. Why do you think he's willing to search when the odds of finding Walter are almost nil? What does this say about Ian as a person? About his love for Asia?

13) Asia's main purpose in returning to Driftwood Cove is to find her family. Walter is the key to knowing the truth. But, his Alzheimer's makes it impossible to delve into his memories. Asia must come to terms with this, but it's hard. What struggles do you think she faces as she loses hope of getting answers from Walter? What lessons does she learn? Instead of finding her value in being Walter's daughter, where does she find her value? How did this change her life?

ACKNOWLEDGMENTS

Writing a book can be a lonely process, but publishing one takes a team. I am so thankful for my team. They come beside me to encourage and guide, to make this story much better than I can do alone.

To my editors, Karen Ball and Louise M. Gouge. Thank you for your changes that shaped my words and thoughts. You are both amazing.

To my team of early readers, Anne Anderson, Alyssa Farrier, Marie Harris, Junie Hostetler, Ardra Tsuei, and Karen VanHorn. Thank you for catching the little typos and mistakes and for your encouragement.

To my cover designer, Ken Raney. Thank you for the hard work you put in and for this incredibly beautiful cover.

To my husband, Robert John Farrier. Thank you for putting up with such a weird wife. One who talks to people who aren't there, or who zones out in the middle of a conversation when inspiration strikes.

Thank you to my readers. You encourage me, and I am so thankful for all of you.

Most of all, thank you to my Lord and Savior, Jesus. Without Him I am nothing. In Him I am all I need to be.

ABOUT THE AUTHOR

Nancy J. Farrier is a multi-published, award winning author of historical and contemporary Christian fiction. She writes Southwest fiction with real life issues. She lives in Southern Arizona in the Sonoran Desert with her husband, cats, and dog. Nancy loves reading, hiking, bicycling, needlework, and spending time with her family.

Find Nancy at nancyjfarrier.com

Thank you for reading Matching Points. Please consider leaving a review.

ALSO BY NANCY J. FARRIER

Driftwood Cove Series

Matching Points

Land of Promise Series

Bandolero

The Ranchero's Gift

The Ranchero's Love

Other Titles

The Cowboy's Bride

The Immigrant Brides

Made in the USA
Coppell, TX
17 October 2022

84809420R00174